Angel's Gate - Excerpt

Nate moved through his work in auto-pilot, expertly inserting new wood slats and sanding rough spots. His hands knew the work, freeing his mind to think about other things. Things like Emelie. The woman who was now always pervading his thoughts. He couldn't stop reliving the kiss of a few nights ago.

Go slow. Take it easy. You might be rushing into the wrong thing.

"Ready to break for lunch?" Frank asked, wiping the sweat from his brow as he stood from the floor.

"What? Oh, yeah. Sure. I'll be right out." Nate took a rag and wiped the wood clean of the fine layer of sawdust, then inspected his work. Not too bad. Stain and varnish, and this job would be done. Getting to his feet, he leaned back and stretched; he'd been sitting too long. Overhead was his next task: a light fixture that was in danger of falling from the ceiling. It wasn't his normal forte, doing electrical, but this was a simple task that wouldn't require any wiring work. At least he didn't think so.

Curiosity piqued, Nate retrieved a ladder from the side of the room and set it up beneath the ailing light, then climbed up to get a closer look. The fixture had definitely seen better days and nearly fell into his hands when he touched it. He wondered when the lighting had been updated last. Without too much coaxing, the cylindrical predecessor to the "can" light came loose and freed an accrual of dust and bugs which fell to the floor in various pieces. Nate figured he might as well clean out all of the muck and stuck his rag up into the opening to brush away more cobwebs and dirt. He was surprised when his fingers snagged something small but more substantial than the dust bunnies that had already fallen out. A small bag with a drawstring top dropped to the floor with a decided "clink."

Nate descended the ladder and picked up the velvet bag, originally dark red but now gray with dust. It was about the size of his palm and heavy.

"Hmm." Carefully grasping the edges of the bag with his fingertips, Nate pulled it open and turned the bag upside down into his hand. Five gold coins, each about the size of a silver dollar, slipped onto his palm. Nate's mouth opened at the sight, but before he could register the magnitude of his discovery, Frank appeared in the doorway.

"Hey, you comin'?"

"Yeah. Sure." Nate casually slipped the bag, and the coins, into the pocket of his jeans and went to retrieve his lunch.

"What was that?" Frank asked.

"What was what?"

"What were you just looking at? In your hand?"

"Oh, nothing. Just checking my coinage. Gotta do laundry tonight."

Frank stared at Nate for a moment before nodding. "Right," he said. "I hear ya. Hate doing it myself."

The two sat outside together to eat their brown bag lunches. The weather was sunny and cool, the salt spray tickling Nate's face from time to time. He ate slowly, trying to remain calm and relaxed while inside, his mind raced. What kind of coins had he discovered? Were they real gold, and if so, how old might they be? How long had they rested in between the floors of Angel's Gate Lighthouse? He couldn't wait to get home and look at them with Emelie.

Cape Seduction:

"Romance, a lighthouse, suspense, a California setting, a double story, the golden years of Hollywood, and ghosts...this book has everything. The author does a fantastic job of keeping the suspense going and both stories mutually interesting. The ending is satisfying for both romance and mystery readers.

"I love the way the author has researched her topic and brings in lots of references to old movies and lighthouses. It is clear that she knows her subject and has a talent for weaving it into a very interesting story. Anne Carter's first lighthouse mystery, Point Surrender was great so I was really looking forward to Cape Seduction and I was not disappointed!"

Angel's Gate:

"This is the third in the series, and while they each revolve around different lighthouses, they have overlapping characters. Her books are insanely easy to read, and always have an element of mystery, romance, history and a touch of supernatural. I believe that this installment may be her best.

"This story pulls together quite a few characters from past books, plus a couple of new ones...a young Hopi Indian man and an absolutely adorable young South American woman... I appreciated this truly pure, uncomplicated love story between these two new characters. No drama, no cheating, no games, no lying, just two people who are loyal to each other and their friends. Like a breath of fresh air. I also love that the author has incorporated so much cultural diversity here.

"This book is an excellent, historical mystery. One that I read in record time, one where I felt GOOD when I finished it."

Angel's Gate

By

Anne Carter

Beacon Street Books

Contemporary Romance Suspense

ANGEL'S GATE

by Anne Carter

A Beacon Point Romance – Book Three

Copyright © 2014 by Pamela Ripling
Cover © by Pamela Ripling

Print ISBN 978-0692214978

Published In the United States of America

June, 2014

Beacon Street Books
Santa Clarita, CA 91355-2026
http://www.beaconstreetbooks.com

Dedication

*To the reader who came back to the booth
twice asking for this book: please come back!*

*To Tina, Susan, Debi, Jenny and Sandy
For all your help and encouragement.*

*And to my lovely daughter, Mikayla,
who always listens,
always shares,
and always says, "It's fine."
I love you.*

Prologue

February, 2012 - San Pedro, California

"Was anyone hurt?"

"Naw. It was just a couple of drunk kids taking the Periwinkle out for a joy ride. She was more than they could handle in their inebriated state." L.A.P.D. Harbor Division Detective Rick Cordell tossed down a slim folder onto his partner's desk. "The boat's got some damage to the hull. Hopefully, they'll get the damned thing towed out of there before she sinks. Coast Guard's already on it."

"Power boat?" Chuck Beeman picked up the folder and opened it.

"Yeah. That pretty Jeanneau 36 operated by Targa Tours. One of the thieves' dads owns the company. Kid stole it sometime after midnight."

"What'd they hit, anyway? A buoy?"

"Breakwater. You know, where the lighthouse is."

"They hit Angel's Gate? Shit."

Rick chuckled. "Ain't the first time. Won't be the last. Back in the thirties, a Navy ship smacked it during the night. Can you imagine bein' the keeper out there when that happened? Crazy."

"Anybody in the lighthouse last night? I mean, it's normally empty, right?"

"Yup. No reason for anyone being there, the automation takes care of everything. They're still working on that big renovation project. Good thing, too. That lighthouse has

1

looked like hell for years."

Chuck stood, stretched and yawned. "I'm headin' out. I might take a run out there to eyeball this little disaster. Wanna come?"

Divers worked to rig a temporary patch on the hull of the ailing Periwinkle. Chuck watched from the Harbor Patrol boat several yards away, a rapidly cooling mug of joe cupped in his gloved hands. "You couldn't pay me to get into that water," he muttered. Beside him, Rick lifted a pair of binoculars.

"Me neither. I'm freezin' just standing out here. And I'd be afraid of getting crushed between that speeder and the rocks. Every time there's a swell, those divers need to move quick."

"The damage isn't as bad as I thought. Still, expensive boat, expensive repair..."

"Don't forget about the bail for his kid." Rick started to lower the lenses when he paused. Voices coming from the divers were raised as one of them held an object up to a fellow Guardsman onboard the Coast Guard vessel. "What the hell?"

"What? What's he got?"

Frowning, Rick tried to focus the binoculars. "Can't tell, it's brown, sorta roundish... crap. The guy's in the way. Whatever it is, it's got those Coasties all stirred up. Probably just an abalone or something."

Rick picked up his plate from the coffee table and stood, his eyes intent on the television screen. Jethro Leroy Gibbs aimed his gun at the smarmy, beady-eyed marine killer and tilted his head. Rushing up to his side, Special Agent Tony DiNozzo also leveled his weapon. "It's all over, Trinidad."

Rick blew out a breath and turned toward the kitchenette, where he put the plate into the sink and ran some water over it. "You should know better than to screw with NCIS, Trini." He started to return to the couch when his cell came to life. "Yeah. Cordell."

"Hey man, I just thought you might like to know about that thing this morning," Chuck said, his agitated voice an octave higher than normal.

"What thing?"

"You know, that the Coastie diver brought up? You won't believe this. It was a *human skull*."

Chapter 1

June, 2012 - Los Angeles, California

Nate stood amidst a group of teary-eyed strangers, mourning a man he didn't know. Watching from behind scratched dark glasses, he perused the people surrounding the gravesite, only remotely listening to the words being offered by the minister. Words about a life so foreign to Nate he nearly smiled at the irony.

He bowed his head, his hands lightly clasped before him. He'd already spotted the one he'd really come to see. A man whose own sunglasses failed to hide the grief in his eyes, whose jaw worked as he fought to restrain his emotions. A woman sat beside him, clutching his arm, occasionally turning to check on three children and one teen sitting on her other side.

Nate trained his eyes upon them for a while, wondering about their lives, so different from his own. There was affluence there. While he couldn't name or even know the labels, Nate recognized that the clothing they wore was tailored from fancy materials. Looking down, he brushed a tiny leaf from the borrowed suit coat that hung loosely upon his narrow frame.

Several of the mourners were elderly men. A couple in wheelchairs, some with attendants. Nate grimaced at the sight of a frail man with a tube emerging from his throat, possibly some kind of breathing apparatus. The man wore a military uniform.

Perhaps the men were relatives of the deceased. Nate looked back to the younger man, seated in the front row with his family, whose shoulders now shook gently as his wife tried to comfort him. Nate's own throat tightened at the sight. He sucked in his upper lip and bit it lightly, wondering if the trip to L.A. had been a mistake.

At the point where the pall bearers began to lower the ivory, flower-strewn coffin into the ground, Nate slowly backed away and turned to go.

"Too bad Sean couldn't make it." Maddie slipped out of her heels and into a pair of flats.

"My brother is clearly too important to attend his own father's funeral," Jack muttered, hanging up his suit coat. "But why should today be any different?"

"I'm sure he'll be here soon. It was sudden, Jack. Sean's in the middle of that big mess. He is the dean of the university..."

"Yeah. Whatever. It's just that whenever Mom and Dad need him, he's in the middle of something. It's always me." Jack sat down on the bed and hung his head. "Never mind. Just feeling sorry for myself."

"You're entitled. By the way, there was a message on your phone from the board and care. Your mom's doing better. The doctor said not to worry about her, nothing will change for now."

"That's at least a relief."

Maddie nodded. "Hey, did you see that guy today?" she asked while helping Claire to untangle her discarded sweater. "Standing in the back?"

"There were a lot of people there, Mad. Who are you talking about?" Jack loosened his tie, slipped it off. "Dad had lots of friends I didn't know."

"He was young. Black hair, sunglasses, black suit..."

"And that describes a lot of the guys there." Jack tried to keep the annoyance he felt from his voice.

"But *young*. Maybe... twenty-five, twenty-seven. He had a scar on his forehead, over his left eyebrow. He walked away during the interment."

Jack shrugged. "Who knows? Maybe he worked for the company."

"Just seemed odd, that's all. I don't think he spoke to anyone else. Like he was a complete stranger."

"We're all strangers."

Maddie went to her husband and embraced him. "You gonna be all right?"

"I will be. After a pint of Guinness."

The reception dragged on into the early evening, with several of Angus McKenzie's war buddies offering perpetual toasts to their fallen comrade. Jack allowed himself to accept the whole affair, not caring much about anything after his third or fourth ale. Maddie, he knew, would be the responsible party today, riding herd on their three children and keeping tabs on the wandering teen, Todd. He hadn't known his step-grandfather, but Todd politely participated to the extent that any seventeen-year-old could while suffering text-withdrawal. Duncan, Davey and Claire had all bounced upon Gus's knee in their short lifetimes, but Jack wondered if the younger two had a handle on death and the fact that their grandfather was truly, permanently, gone, a concept he had trouble with himself.

Case McKenna handed him a cup of coffee. "You okay?"

Jack looked at his best friend and almost broke down, again. Case had been by his side since the phone call, the one saying Jack had better get to L.A. fast if he wanted to catch his father's dying moments. Now, Case grasped Jack's shoulder, the question lingering in his blue eyes. "You want me to shut this thing down?"

"Thanks, man. No, we need to let these guys hang around just a little bit longer. I'm okay." Jack took a sip of the coffee and ran a hand quickly across his eyes. "It's just something you can't quite prepare for."

Case nodded and gave Jack a gentle slap on the back. "I'm here. Right over there with Amy and Matt. Let me know if you need me to do anything."

Jack allowed a brief smile as Case walked away.

A man whose face reflected the ravages of a hard life waddled unsteadily up to Jack and put his beer down a little too hard.

"Your dad was one of a kind," he asserted, reddened eyes wide. "He should'ena been taken."

Jack nodded wearily.

"He was a fine sholjer. We's in Normandy together. Never let his men down. An' a gentleman ta boot."

"A fine soldier he was. Thanks. Thanks. I appreciate it. I know Dad would be happy you came today."

"An' you don't think I woulda missed it, do you?" The man lurched forward in emphasis. "Miss Gus's goin' away party? Not on your life, kid."

Jack hardly felt like a kid. At forty-three, he more often felt the older of the two when caring for his father during the weeks preceding his death. One look at the brood waiting to leave the wake aged him even more.

"No, Floyd. I didn't think you'd miss it. You were a true friend to Dad."

Floyd nodded in aggressive agreement. "You got that right. True. To the end." Lifting his mug, Floyd straightened and spun around. "To Gus!"

"To Gus!" went the boisterous call around the room as mugs, steins and champagne glasses were raised again. Jack caught Maddie's expression and stood himself.

"I want to thank you all for coming," he ventured. "Truly. It's been a wonderful tribute."

Nate closed his suitcase. The zipper pulled easily; there wasn't much inside, for his stay in Los Angeles was brief.

He'd return to Arizona today, having failed his mission, no closer to settling his mind—and his past—than when he'd left Flagstaff three days before.

He dropped the small case to the floor, jerked the telescoping handle out in irritation. Why had he been unable to approach the man called Jack, the one with the sun-gold hair? What was he afraid of? The guy's pain couldn't be any greater than his own.

In the small motel office, he placed three dollars on the counter.

"You've already paid, Mr. Sinquah. And tipping isn't necessary."

"I broke a water glass," Nate explained, looking to the counter briefly before flashing an embarrassed grin. "I cleaned up the pieces."

The clerk shook his head. "Cost of doing business, son. I appreciate your honesty." He pushed the bills back toward Nate.

"I, uh, also took the shampoo and stuff."

"And why does that make you any different?"

"They're for the kids. Back home."

"Of course. Have a safe trip, Mr. Sinquah."

Nate picked up the cash and carefully folded it. He was nothing if not honest. He knew the value of a simple glass tumbler, the luxury of shampoo and body lotion. Nodding in gratitude, Nate grasped his suitcase handle and turned. "Thank you. The room was nice."

"Why, thank you. Do you need me to call you a cab or something?"

"Nope. The bus station's only, what, a mile and a half? I'll make it."

The events of the previous day foremost in his mind, Nate didn't rush. His bus to Phoenix wouldn't leave for an hour, and he preferred the brisk morning walk to sitting in a dim and aging terminal. There'd be plenty of time to sit.

As he thought about Jack McKenzie and his family, he tried to keep the jealousy at bay. Envy was a liability, not an asset. It solved nothing. And Jack surely wasn't a bad man. Look at the outpouring of love at the funeral! His many friends were a testament to his character.

Yet Nate couldn't help the lingering desire to be a part of that world.

Johnny was waiting for him at the bus station in Phoenix.

"I don't know why the hell you don't fly, man." His lifelong best friend clapped him on the shoulder and pulled a set of keys from his pocket. "It can't be that much cheaper."

Nate grinned. "If man was meant to fly, he'd—"

"Have wings. Yeah. I heard that once. Your grandfather. More Hopi bullshit."

"Okay. It's eighty bucks round trip. Nice new bus. I slept."

Johnny chuckled. "Your granddad imparted more than just a fear of flying. You got that honesty gene, brother."

Nate shrugged, lifted his suitcase into the back of Johnny's 1979 Ford Bronco. "It's not such a bad thing."

"Honesty can get you into trouble. Especially with the ladies."

The two men got into the truck and immediately put down the windows. Nate retrieved a leather lace from his pocket and pulled back his straight, ebony hair, tying it into a short queue. "I don't have to worry much about the ladies. When you gonna get the A/C fixed on this junk heap?"

"What, you hot? Get used to that cool California air in just two days?"

Nate smiled, shook his head. "It was hot there, too. But not like this." He swiped at a loose lock. "Phoenix has the market cornered on hot weather. How is it at home?"

"Beautiful. As usual. And why is it you don't have to

10

worry about the ladies? When's the last time you got laid? Or even went out, for that matter? You know Fawn Michaels would take you back in a heartbeat."

Nate wet his lips, looked out the side window as Johnny sped up on the I-10 on-ramp. "She's a serious girl. I already broke her heart once. It's not worth it."

"Don't be such a bleeding heart. Sentimental fool."

"Yeah. So."

"So. You're almost twenty-five. You can't go limping through life without a woman, bro. I'd be a train wreck without Mari."

"Yeah, you would be. Lemme know if you find another like her. Then maybe I'll consider."

The two hour drive to Flagstaff gave Nate a chance to bring Johnny up-to-date on his trip. Johnny filled Nate in on the happenings at home, and soon they were parking at the Summerwind Apartment Complex.

July, 2012 - Grogan's Head, California

"Would it really be so bad to move back to L.A.?"

Maddie lifted her red pen off of a student's essay and stared at Jack. "You're really serious."

"Aw, I dunno. I just—just felt like I missed everything. There's stuff going on, y'know?"

"Mmm. Stuff. Like drive-by shootings. Earthquakes. Triple digit heat. Road rage. That kinda stuff?"

"Well..."

"Traffic, smog, property taxes..."

"Culture. Art. Creativity. I have a lot of friends there. I miss the business. Hell, I couldn't even name one of the nominated pictures this year. Pathetic."

His wife resumed her task. Quiet ensued, until she again paused and put down her pen. "If it's that important to you, you should go."

"*I* should go? Not *we* should go?"

"You should go, for a while, see if it's really what you want. Rent a place, sniff around, see if you can find work."

Jack stood from the table and went to Maddie, placed his hands on her shoulders. "Forget it. I couldn't go without you."

"Take Todd. He's dying to get away from here. If you go now, maybe he can pick up a couple of classes at the community college next month." Maddie stood and placed her hands on Jack's cheeks. "If it works out, you know I'll pack up the kids and be down there in a heartbeat. I just want you to make sure this is what you truly want before I uproot them."

Jack considered, stared into her eyes. "I'll think about it."

"You can come back every other weekend or so. Try it for a few months, anyway. We'll be okay; we have Case and Amy close by. And we'll come down there for a visit or two."

"You are one in a million." Jack embraced her, held her close, breathed in the scent of her hair. "Maybe it could work, for a brief time."

"We'll make it work."

"I like it when we make things work," Jack whispered, nuzzling her ear. "Kids asleep?"

"Mm-hmm." Maddie closed her eyes and slipped her arms around Jack, and he chuckled.

"Am I sensing an invitation, here?" After six years of marriage, Jack still saw Maddie as his sexy, blushing bride, and he never tired of showing her just how much he cared.

Minutes later, she emerged from the master bathroom in a dark green, lace teddy and crawled onto him, sliding her fingertips up his bare chest and leaning forward until her breasts pressed against his. Jack sighed audibly. "Remember when you used to make me turn the lights off?" he asked, caressing her back and then cupping her behind.

"Remember when you tried to seduce me in your apartment that rainy night? You made me close my eyes."

"I wasn't trying to seduce you. Just testing your trust."

"Well, now that we know I trust you, we can get on with the seduction." Maddie kissed Jack's neck and let her hot breath encompass his ear, causing him to shiver.

"No complaints here, babe. I'm all for seduction." Jack never thought their lovemaking could get any better, and yet it did. Every time. Maddie had a way of holding back on him, just a little, doling out her passion in small bits until at last she unleashed it all. It was some kind of magic, he was sure.

Afterward, they snuggled while their bodies cooled and their hearts slowed to normal. Jack finger-combed Maddie's hair away from her face. "What do you say we get Amy and Case to watch the kids one day soon, and we go up to the ice rink in Medford? I can pretend you don't know how to skate and you can entice me all over again."

Maddie traced his lips with her finger. "As long as I don't have to skate with Sam Bony."

Chapter 2

August, 2012 - Flagstaff, Arizona

Nate lay awake in his small studio apartment, weary from the tedious trip to the old mesa where he'd reluctantly left his grandmother. It wasn't like he wouldn't be back, but his grandmother's health warranted concern. Their last visit had been clouded by her confusion, but she became lucid and matriarchal just before he'd gone, impressing upon him her "theory" or tutavo about his future.

"You have a purpose, Nah-tah-n'l," she whispered hoarsely, selecting a few English words amid her comfortable Hopi expressions. Nate knew only a smattering of Hopi, but he understood that Sobo was speaking about honor, and about her daughter—his late mother. She charged him with carrying forth his mother's clan's purpose.

"Whatever *that* is," he muttered now, his eyes open in the dark as he fingered the string of turquoise she'd struggled to slip over his head just before he took his leave. But he'd been brought up to believe in fate; what would happen was pre-ordained, and he would be guided toward that end. He only needed to follow the path as it was revealed to him.

That path led to Los Angeles.

Once the City of the Angels slipped into his mind, Nate knew sleep wouldn't come. A groan escaped as he tumbled out of bed, went to the window and peered out at the inky night.

What should I do? What can I do? The letters lay spread out on the desk across the room. Letters spanning three decades, words of love and longing from a white man in a big city to a young Hopi girl in Winslow, Arizona.

Did it matter why? They were both dead; no one had mentioned their relationship while they lived, and no one seemed the worse for it now. Yet Sobo's whispered words haunted him. It was that damned purpose she'd dropped on him. Did this purpose have to do with the letters? With his own lineage? There, in the dark of one of his loneliest nights, Nate couldn't shake the feeling that something bad had happened. Something that affected his future—his whole life. Because if this man had been sending love letters to Nate's mother for over thirty years, had they also met physically? Could the writer be someone more than just a stranger?

Nate walked to his desk and switched on the table lamp. He pushed the letters all together into one stack and stuffed them into the lap drawer, holding his hands against the drawer front as if it might pop open and throw the sheets back out. Standing very still, Nate closed his eyes and tried to grasp the clearest thought he could muster. That thought was the same one challenging him for months—since the week following his mother's death, and one day in particular when he'd found the letters. He needed to find the man who wrote them and ask the question.

Unfortunately, Nate had procrastinated too long. Gus McKenzie was dead.

Jack stared through the wide, arched window at the sea of lights comprising Hollywood. Behind him, Todd lugged boxes between the attached garage and the kitchen adjacent to the living room.

"Dude. Are you gonna stand there staring at the city all night?"

Jack shook his head. "I always loved this place. I could never understand why Matt didn't finish the remodel. Now, I'm living here myself. Too weird." He turned, accepted a box from his step-son. "Sorry."

"I hope you got a good deal," Todd called over his shoulder as he returned to the garage.

"Seriously good. Farralone's got more dough than he knows what to do with. He doesn't want to rent it out, but he doesn't want it to sit empty, either."

"Where does he live when he's not up north?"

"Beverly Hills. His granddad left him a virtual palace."

"Sweet. Hey, can we set up the Wii in here?"

Jack offered a lop-sided smile. For *his* seventeenth birthday, his dad gave him six months—to get out and support himself. "Yeah. After everything's unpacked and put away."

Todd rolled his eyes, picked up another box and headed for the stairs that led to the bedrooms on the lower level.

Hours later, Todd's question brought a smile to Jack's lips as he sat on the couch watching the twinkling city below. Maybe he *would* stare at the city all night. Back in Grogan's Head, he'd actually grown a little tired of seeing the waves below the deck of their house, of always chasing the cold away with heavy coats and blankets and weather stripping. When he complained, Maddie was quick to admonish. "It's easier and cheaper to get warm when it's cold than it is to cool off when it's hot."

"Not necessarily. Depends on where you live. Some places heat is expensive."

"Well, then... it's more *romantic* to warm up together," she'd say, snuggling up close to share his warmth after the lights went out.

Jack chuckled softly, thinking about his wife up in Northern-Nor-Cal with her fleece pajamas and hot herb tea on the nightstand. From behind him, the opening theme from *The Tonight Show* wafted faintly up the open stairway. It reminded him of film; of Hollywood, and the business. He squeezed his hands into fists and then released his fingers, turning his open palms toward his face. The hands were itching to design, to build, to bring to fruition the settings, the worlds surrounding the stories and give them life.

Tomorrow he would start looking for work.

"Jack! Well I'll be damned. When did you blow into town?" The broad man with the bushy gray moustache clasped Jack's hand as they met in the vestibule at Denny's. "What's it been, a couple of years?"

"More than a couple, Miles. But I couldn't stay away."

"You mean you're here for good? Back in the business?"

"Looking around, yeah. I miss the spotlights."

Miles's smile waned. "You, uh, still with Maddie?"

"Of course. Mad's just keeping the home fires burning up in Coldsville while I check things out down here. We might move back, I don't know. But, yeah, I'm seeking gainful employment, as they say. Know of anything?"

The coffee shop was crowded, but Miles brightened. "Let's get a table. I was just on my way out, but I could use another cup."

They sat down in the booth Miles had just vacated and ordered coffee. "This place always did have the best java," Jack said. "On this block."

"You still addicted?"

"Even more so in the frozen tundra of NorCal. But tell me what you've been up to. Are you working?"

"Just finished another one of them Bourne flicks. I literally lost weight moving that steady cam around so fast. Man! I might be gettin' too old for this stuff. Next job will be a Mr. Rogers biopic."

Jack chuckled. "Now you're making me feel old; I've got at least five years on you."

"But set design isn't as strenuous as camera work, dude. So what have you been doing up north? I heard you were working with fish or something."

"This will sound crazy, but you know me; I've done

everything from forestry to sky-diving. For the last few years, I've worked at the Olsen Institute of Oceanography. My cousin runs the place—he's a marine veterinarian—and I've been learning how to reacquaint patched up sea animals with their natural environment. A "rescue and release' deal."

"Crazy? I'm amazed! What the hell? Do you enjoy that sort of thing?"

Jack looked away, imagining the seals, otters and water fowl he'd recently assisted. "It's rewarding," he mused. "It's also tough. Sometimes you get really invested in an animal, and then it doesn't make it. Takes me days, maybe weeks to recover. But I've enjoyed it, yeah." Jack paused for a sip of coffee. "When my dad died last month, I came down here for the funeral. I realized how much I missed L.A. and all the creativity. It's a whole other world, you know?"

"I'm sorry to hear about your father."

"He was 88. Lived a good long life. His heart just stopped while he slept."

"Best way to go. But I hear you about L.A. I couldn't live anywhere else. Say, my next gig is a music video for a singer. I think they might be looking for sets. Interested in something like that?"

"Absolutely! Good way to get back into the game. I'll give you my cell number. I'm staying in Hollywood."

Miles grinned. "Glad to have you back around, Jackie. You've been missed."

"I met the rock star today. Nice guy, actually," Jack said, his cell phone wedged precariously between his shoulder and his ear as he loosely folded t-shirts on his bed. "Todd says he's been around a while, but I'd never heard of him. He's older, in his late thirties maybe."

"What's his name? Maybe I know him," Maddie suggested.

"Robert Evans. No, wait. Robin. But goes by Rob. His

music is some alternative, some a little countryish but not twangy. Good stuff. Any guy who brings his wife and kids along is okay by me."

"Is she nice, too?"

"Her name is Kate. Yeah, nice girl. She's a makeup artist. Anyway, I got the gig, we're going to be shooting a music vid around some famous L.A. sights. And—get this— I'm production designer. How about that?"

Maddie sighed. "I'm happy for you, babe. Does this mean it's time to start packing?"

Chapter 3

September, 2012

Nate stared out of the bus window as the Blythe, California, Greyhound station came into view. Was it the right thing to do, go back to Los Angeles?

Of course it is. I have no choice. It won't leave me alone until I do.

The going-away party had been tough. Especially the kids. *"Why are you leaving, Mr. Sinquah? When will you come back? Who will teach us our soccer lessons?"*

So deep into his thoughts, Nate didn't notice the girl standing in the aisle until she spoke, apparently for the second time.

"I'm sorry, I asked if this seat was taken."

"Oh! No, no, it's not. It's empty. I mean, no one is sitting here. Yet. It's, uh, free." Nate moved closer to the window, despite the fact that the seats were individual.

The girl sat down and sighed. "Thanks."

"Sure." Nate forced himself to look straight ahead. It would be rude to stare, but from what he'd glimpsed, the girl sitting next to him was unbelievably beautiful. Long tresses of dark, chestnut brown hair hung in gentle waves around her bare shoulders, framing a heart-shaped face like he'd never seen before. Warm brown eyes with attractively curve brows. Fair, flawless skin.

"So where did you get on?"

Nate started. "Uh, me?"

His companion pretended to look around. "*Uh*, yeah. You."

"Oh. Um, Phoenix. I mean, I live in Winslow, but I got a

ride to Flagstaff, then Phoenix, you know, it's not that far, but the bus... the bus doesn't connect... at the right time." *Crap. I sound like a blithering idiot!* "What about you?"

The girl lifted her perfect eyebrows as her eyes searched his face. "I just got on in Blythe. You know that, right?"

Nate pursed his lips. "Yeah, right. I meant, do you live there? Or, are you going someplace else? I mean, home, like, do you live in L.A.?"

"You're cute. I'm Emelie." She stuck out her hand, and Nate stared at it for a moment before taking it in his.

"Nate. For Nathaniel. Nice to meet you."

"Same. I live in Santa Monica. And I would be home by now if I was not being punished. Dad thinks I need to be humbled. Hence, the bus ticket."

Nate looked at his hands, clasped in his lap. "I'm sorry. That's too bad. What did you do?"

"A little personal, isn't it?"

"Oh, sorry, I thought—you know, you offered the part about being punished, so..."

Emelie laughed. "I left school without telling him. I never wanted to go there in the first place. It's worthless information for a world I do not live in."

"What world do you live in?" Nate asked softly, wondering how anyone could turn down a college education, something he could only dream about.

"Certainly not the one that turns out corrupt politicians, greedy corporate moguls and white collar criminals. So we had a fight, and he cut me off. Just like that. It's okay, though. I will be fine."

The frivolity in her voice dimmed toward the end of her short tirade. She's not fine, Nate thought. She's scared and sad.

"Besides," Emelie continued. "I have other talents. I can earn good money with what I have. Personal services."

Nate felt himself blush. "You—you don't need to resort

to that, you know. You could do lots of other things."

"Resort to what? Oh! Not that!" Emelie laughed again, and Nate's face grew even warmer. "I'm... special. I have a special talent. I'll tell you if you promise not to laugh."

"I won't laugh."

Emelie grew serious and stared past him out the window, so long that he was tempted to wave his hand in front of her face.

"I am psychic."

"Psychic? Like, you can read minds or something?"

"It's hard to explain. I... get visions in my head. I hear things. Things that happened in the past. I get feelings from, you know, others. It comes and goes."

Nate's eyes widened. "Why would I laugh at something like that? Back home, on the mesa, you would be..."

"Would be what? What mesa? Wait—are you an Indian?"

"Hopi."

Now it was Emelie's turn for astonishment. "You don't look like an Indian."

"Well..." Nate searched for the right words. Outside the bus, the cactus rushed by. "Let's just say that someone in my heritage might have been white. I'm a...a throwback?"

Emelie reached over and took a strand of his hair between her fingers. "You certainly got that Tonto mane."

Nate licked his lips. References to the Lone Ranger's Indian sidekick had long grown stale.

"The cheekbones work, and the dark eyes, too. But your skin's too fair and those dimples just don't say 'How!' to me."

"'How'? Are you kidding me?" Nate smirked and looked toward the front of the bus, shaking his head. "Right now, I could say that your brown hair doesn't match your *blonde* personality."

Emelie's quick intake of air reflected her outrage.

Crossing her arms, she turned her head the other way. Nate continued to smile.

In Indio, they got off the bus for a cold drink. Nate went into the restroom and washed his hands and face, then neatened his hair with a comb. He stared hard at himself in the mirror and tried to chase the worry from his mind. Los Angeles was a metropolis. He was an under-educated *Native American* with common skills. He didn't know the first thing about finding work in L.A., or where he would stay when he got off the Greyhound. His last job was in a reservation elementary school, but he had no teaching credential. He could build furniture, but didn't have so much as a photograph of the beautiful pieces he'd designed.

Taco Town. All-Green Landscaping. Sunny Acres Rest Home. Johnny's suggestions brought a smile. Yet Nate had left one important trait out of his self-assessment: he was a survivor. He would find something.

Back on the bus, he half expected the-girl-who-didn't-use-many-contractions to find another seat, but she sat down beside him just before they rolled. After a few moments of silence, she giggled. "I did bleach my hair once. Platinum blonde. I thought Daddy would have a heart attack."

Nate turned to look into her face. "Your hair is far too beautiful to mess with. No wonder he disowned you."

Emelie colored and smiled with a glimpse of shyness.

Encouraged, Nate ventured a question. "What were you doing in Blythe, anyway? Doesn't seem like a very fun place."

"Havasu. I was up at the lake with a friend. I got a ride down to Blythe to catch the bus. I had to trade my watch for bus fare. But it's okay, I did not need it. I almost never looked at it. And besides. I have my phone. That is, until Daddy remembers to cancel it."

"Living without a cell phone isn't so bad," Nate murmured. "I gave mine up... oh, wait. I never had one."

Emelie appraised him. "I like that. I think you're a pretty smart guy, Mr. Nathaniel Hopi."

This time, instead of taking offense, Nate smiled. Inside his shirt, against his chest, he felt the warmth of the turquoise beads on the leather string.

Los Angeles, Nate soon learned, was good at lightening his wallet. The fifteen hundred or so dollars he'd scraped together wouldn't last long, despite the fact that he'd spent five nights at a youth hostel. He didn't mind bunking with four others or sharing the community bathroom; but at almost $40.00 a night, he needed to find work soon and more permanent lodging.

Today, he cashed in a five dollar bill for quarters and staked out the phone booth near the hostel. The phone number Emelie had written on his arm was faded but legible—he'd tried not to scrub there in the shower—but apparently Daddy had caught up with his daughter's expectation and canceled her cellular phone service. Loneliness settled over Nate as he hung up the phone and leaned back against the wall. While she wasn't really a friend, Emelie was the only person he knew outside of his small Arizona sphere. And she had, after all, told him to call her.

Nate jingled the remaining coins in his pocket. Emelie had a job, a part time job, at some kind of studio. She taught yoga, she said, and Nate had rolled his eyes. *Yoga. Wow. Must be nice.* He turned back toward the telephone and found an outdated, dog-eared phonebook tucked into the shelf beneath. He quickly turned to the Yellow Pages listings for "Yoga."

Was it in Hollywood? Beverly Hills? *Wait. She said she lived in Santa Monica.* Scanning the listings, he was stunned to see the number of yoga studios in the Santa Monica area. There weren't enough quarters to call them all.

He picked three. The first was closed, the second out of business. The third knew no one by the name of Emelie. Nate looked back at the list, closed his eyes and jabbed his finger onto the page. Although his fingertip pointed at *Bethany's YogaTime,* Nate's eyes were drawn to another name on the page: *Mystic Moves.* Fishing two more quarters from his pocket, he dropped them into the slot and dialed.

"Emelie? Yeah, she works here. Not here right now. She teaches on Mondays, Tuesdays and Thursdays in the morning."

"Great. Where are you lo—"

Before Nate could complete his question, the receptionist hung up the phone. He had nothing to write on or with, so after a guilty look around, he gently removed the page from the phone book, carefully folded and stashed it in his hip pocket. Surely someone at the hostel could give him directions.

Chapter 4

Late September, 2012

Jack rolled up the sketches he'd just shared with Tim Cole, art director for Rob Evans. Tim was nodding, so Jack was encouraged.

"It's a go. Great ideas, Jack. The L.A.-theme is cool because Rob has a lot of fans here. Let me know when you round out the list."

"Will do. I'm gonna grab some lunch. Join me?"

"Nope. I'm off to the next. Talk to you Tuesday."

A half hour later, Todd picked through the French fries on Jack's near empty plate, looking for the crispy dregs. "What's 'the list' about?"

"The list of locales where we'll be shooting. I only had a few suggestions when I pitched the idea, and Tim wants something like six or seven."

"Didn't that guy Bublé already do that?"

"Yeah but no. This is different. Bublé is a guy walking through studio settings, like he was James Dean sitting in a Porsche Spyder that looked like Dean's. We're not doing that kind of stuff. We're going to actual locales. You'll see."

"Like the beach?"

"Maybe. I'm thinking uncommon but recognizable So Cal sights. Something like... inside Dodger Stadium. On the Arroyo Seco bridge. Or, like, on the deck of a ship in L.A. Harbor."

"An aircraft carrier!"

"Sure, why not? If we don't have to build sets, we can spend money on bribing people."

Todd's raised eyebrows prompted Jack's grin.

"Yeah, palms are greased. No question."

Nate lay back on his narrow bed and stared at the bottom of the upper bunk. Although he shared the room with three other guys, his roommates had all gone out for the day. Two were working, the other seeking employment like himself.

Los Angeles was a great place. Always lots going on, everywhere you looked. L.A. was also a great place to leave your cash. Nate reached into his back pocket and pulled out his wallet, grimacing at how thin it felt. He didn't feel like counting it, again, but he'd only spent about four dollars since the last count yesterday morning. That left right around seven hundred fifty.

The room was eating up the money. Wouldn't be so bad if he had any income, but he'd had to buy some new clothes for the interviews, pay bus fare, cash out coins for the payphone and cover his one allotted meal per day. He let the wallet drop from his fingers and sighed. If his roommate, a smart guy with a bachelor's degree in economics, couldn't get work, then how could Nate expect to get anything?

Someone in the breakfast room told him to become a sign twirler. While always polite, Nate had scoffed inwardly. Dress up like a cow or a chicken and stand on a busy street corner all day? It wasn't exactly the kind of work to write home about. He wondered what Emelie would say.

Emelie. Why couldn't he stop thinking about her? They'd talked briefly on the phone a few days ago, and they'd promised to get together for a meal. But she couldn't call him, and he felt awkward calling her at work when he had no good news to share. When he got a job... if he got a job... he would get a taxi ride and take her out to dinner.

Nate looked at his watch. It reminded him of Emelie hocking hers for bus fare. He would never get rid of his; it was a graduation gift from his late mother. A simple man's Timex, but it kept excellent time. Right now it was telling him it was time to get into the shower. He stood up, stretched, and pulled a small toiletry bag from his locker before heading down the hall to the shared bathroom.

In the hall, he passed his unemployed roommate just returning from outside and gave him a cursory nod. The young man returned a smile before continuing on to the room. Nate wondered if his bunkmate had found a job. Maybe he'd ask, after the shower.

The white tile was cold, at first, but the hot water felt good on Nate's back. He leaned into the steaming spray with his eyes closed. The bunk, while decent, wasn't the same as his bed back home, and he felt the resulting stiffness every morning.

That's another thing I'll get. A good mattress.

Today was harbor day. He'd gotten a lead on some construction jobs in El Segundo, and Nate figured he at least had some experience with buildings. After all, he'd helped with the remodel of the school last year and had taught himself basic carpentry during high school. He was strong and able bodied. Surely he could lug lumber and throw a hammer.

As he dressed, he made a mental note to get more quarters for the laundry. A few dollars should do it. He rummaged through his locker for his wallet, only to come up short. Toiletries, dirty clothes and his alternate, dry, towel. Nate closed his eyes and tried to remember when he'd last seen his wallet.

On the bed. Quickly he patted down the bedclothes, sighing in relief when he felt the small billfold under the blanket. He started to slip it into his back pocket when he remembered the laundry change, so instead opened the wallet. Inside, a lone twenty dollar bill lay askew.

What? Where was his cash? Could it have fallen out in the bed? Nate tore back the blanket, then the sheet, finding nothing. The floor was empty as well. Incredulous, he looked back into the bill section of his wallet and withdrew the twenty. Behind it, a crumpled scrap of torn paper had been hastily stashed.

Nate's face flushed in anger and he sat down on his bunk. The note was written in pencil. "Sorry, dude, I need this more than you do." The words swam before his eyes. "Good luck." Nate had been robbed.

The hostel management insisted he make a police report, although Nate was not naïve enough to believe anything would come of it. He'd left over seven hundred dollars cash money on his bed, accessible to anyone. The roommate, now known to him by the probable alias *Steven Shay*, had checked out while Nate showered. Now, not only did he have only twenty bucks to his name, the hostel knew it, too. He'd paid for the week in advance, and three nights remained. But after that? They asked him if he could borrow from anyone. Emelie was his only contact in L.A., and she was probably not in the best financial circumstances herself. Still, he would call her. It was that or become homeless on the street.

She was even prettier than Nate remembered. Emelie held the door open for him and he stepped into her small apartment on 20th Street.

"Finally!" Emelie stepped back, her hands clasped at her waist. "I thought we would never make this happen! I hope you're hungry."

Hungry didn't begin to describe how Nate felt. The smells coming from her tiny kitchenette were already causing him to salivate big time. "What are you cooking?"

"Lasagna! I hope you like it. It's ground turkey, sorry, I just don't eat much beef anymore."

"It could be made of seaweed for all I care."

"Come. Look, I splurged. Wine! It's only two-buck Chuck, but what the hell, right?"

Nate smiled. He wondered how long before he fainted

right in front of her. Wine would only make it worse. No food for 48 hours did stuff like that.

"Right. What kind of wine is it?" he asked, watching as she uncorked the bottle and tilted it over the first wine glass.

"It's red. That's as much as I need to know about wine. You probably know wine, huh? You use it on the reservation? For rituals and stuff?"

"Yeah. Sure. Mostly for the sacrificing of virgins. We pour it all over them."

Emelie paused in mid pour, looked up to assess his seriousness and saw the dimpled grin. "As long as they are boy virgins," she asserted, handing him a glass. She picked up her own. "Here is to Greyhound."

"To Greyhound," Nate repeated, keeping his eyes fixed on hers while he sipped. He was more of a beer guy, but the wine wasn't bad. At least, he didn't think so.

They sat down on her couch. "So. What is the good word? Any call backs?"

"Well, not yet. This one guy down at the pier might have something." *Probably not soon enough, though.* "How about you? Things okay down at the yoga place?"

"I have to increase my hours. Ever since my father shut me down, I'm in the hole. I will not be able to afford this place much longer. I might have to move in with you," Emelie joked. "You are still at the hostel?"

Nate took another sip, shook his head. "Nope." He watched as Emelie's eyes darted around while she spoke. It reminded him of some of his young students. "You have a...slight thing when you talk. Where are you from?"

"Sorry. I am... *I'm* working on that. *I'm* from here, but my father is from Chile. I spent some of my childhood there. My mother is Italian. I know, I know—don't ask. It baffles me, too. But they have this sort of...formal way of speaking, and it rubs off on me. Now, where are you staying, then? Did you get a place?"

"Not exactly." Nate tilted his head slightly, enjoying the first warm buzz brought on by the wine. "Currently looking. I hear the Union Mission has a cot I might borrow."

Emelie's expression went from mellow to horrified. "The *mission*? Are you kidding me? Nate, Christ, what happened?"

Nate drank down the rest of his wine. "I got ripped off. Some guy lifted all my cash a few days ago. So."

"So? *So?* Nathaniel Hopi, you can't just go to the mission. You can...you can stay here, until you find a job." Emelie, too, gulped down the wine and placed her glass on the coffee table. "Christ," she repeated. "Did he get your credit cards, too? Oh, man, you should have called me!" Leaning closer to Nate's face, Emelie squinted in appraisal. "When was the last time you ate?"

Nate shrugged. "I dunno. I'm okay. But I can't lie, I'm pretty anxious to dig into that pasta, ma'am."

Over dinner, they laughed about the perils of being penniless.

"I wondered why you walked in with your backpack," Emelie offered, cutting off another slice of garlic bread for her guest.

Nate nodded. "Sorry about that. Everything I own is now strapped against my back. And to answer your earlier question, I don't have credit cards, which I guess now is a good thing because he'd probably be using them."

"No cell phone, no credit cards, no iPad—you really are a relic, you know that?"

"The manager at the hostel gave me another twenty when I left. Sometimes a kindness like that offsets the pain of all the badness in the world."

Her eyes solemn, Emelie stared at Nate across the table. "I'm glad you said that. I'm glad you came here. I'm glad we're friends. And I promise, I will do everything I can to help you find a job and get yourself settled."

"And just how much wine did you drink?"

"No. I'm serious." Emelie reached across the table and grasped Nate's hand. "You're one of the good people in the world."

"Well, then, so are you."

Emelie's couch was no worse than the hostel bunk bed, and with his stomach finally full, Nate dropped quickly off to sleep once she had covered him with a blanket. He'd worry about tomorrow...tomorrow.

"HO PEE! Wake up! I have to go to work. I left some coffee on, and my laptop's on the kitchen table. You can use it to look for jobs. I'll be back around two to check on you, beings I CAN'T CALL you..." Emelie rushed across the room, picking up her tote bag and keys.

Nate sat up, rubbed his eyes. "Okay."

"Facebook is logged in. Check around with some of my friends. Post about your skills."

"Yeah, sure. Facebook. Post. Right."

From the door, Emelie looked back. "Make yourself some breakfast. Don't be shy."

Nate smiled, and Emelie hurried back toward the couch. "If you go anywhere, leave a note, 'kay?"

"Yes, Mom."

Emelie smiled and patted Nate on the head. "See you."

After she'd gone, Nate wandered over to the kitchen bar. He rarely drank coffee, but in light of Emelie's kindness, he thought he'd try a cup. The brew was strong but not too bitter. In the fridge, he found some milk to tame it down and then turned to the open laptop.

"Facebook, huh?" Nate sat, scratched at his chest and perused the screen.

What's up, Emelie? The question was posed in a rectangular box near the top of the screen.

"I am hot. I am smart. I have a cute guy sleeping on

my..." Nate stopped typing and laughed before backspacing out his message. After a few moments of thought, he resumed. *"Hi. My name is Nate and I'm a friend of Emelie's. I am looking for work in Los Angeles. I am..."* Nate paused, looked around the room before turning back to the computer. *"Good with my hands. I am a skilled carpenter. Please leave Emelie a message if you know of anything I might apply for. Thanks."*

Chapter 5

Emelie straightened her stance and lifted her chin.

"I understand," she stated confidently, smiling briefly. "I'm really sorry."

Angela Murphy, owner of Mystic Moves, dabbed at her wet cheek. "We tried, right? We really tried. But I just can't keep on borrowing money to keep the place open. Rent's too high, parking is crap, and there's two other studios within a block. I might be able to get on at Bethany's, but if I do it will be only a few hours a week. I'm going to apply at Macy's."

"You'll be okay, Ang. We all will."

Emelie turned and headed for the ladies restroom. Closing the door behind her, she leaned back against it and switched on the exhaust fan. Her quick intake of air preceded a shudder that washed over her entire body and she felt the burn in her eyes.

I cannot lose my job. Not now. What am I going to do?

Try as she might, Emelie couldn't stop the tears. The more she cried, the angrier she became; she detested self-pity and rarely let herself succumb to it. Swallowing hard, she whipped off a length of toilet paper and dried her eyes, further chagrined by the black stains of eye makeup on the tissue. She stifled a primal groan and went to the sink to wash her face.

I won't let this beat me. Screw the job. Screw the economy. Screw Daddy's self-righteous moralistic bullshit!

In five minutes she had reapplied her makeup and emerged from the restroom. She went to Angela, who sat hunched over a clacking calculator. Emelie wrapped an affectionate arm around her boss's shoulders.

"We can sell the equipment. I'll help you get it on CraigsList. Okay? If you wanna take off for a while, maybe go over to Macy's, I can stay with the shop for a couple of hours."

Angela looked up, her eyes rimmed with sorrow. "Emmie, you're the best. We don't have any reason to stay open the rest of the afternoon, no classes, and it's not like we'll get any walk-in business. You go on home, babe. And thanks for the offer about helping me sell the stuff. Maybe tomorrow?"

"You got it. Okay. You sure you're all right?"

"Go."

Emelie drove home in auto-pilot, mentally calculating what funds she had left and what she would need to get by until she found something else. Her father's words came wafting up from somewhere inside, a place where she'd stashed them that awful day in Havasu.

"You'll see what it's like not to have things. You need to get that there is no free lunch, Emelie, that you cannot just keep sliding through life without something to fall back on. I don't mind—didn't mind—helping you get there, but when you turn your back on education, well, that's just dumb."

Dumb, huh? "Not all education comes from school, Pop. I can do this." *Just watch me.*

She'd nearly forgotten about her house guest and she stopped in the doorway when she spied him standing at her kitchen bar.

"How's it going?" Emelie asked, dropping her bag on to the couch, which, she noticed, had been neatly tidied up.

"This Facebook thing just might catch on," Nate said.

"Oh yeah? Any job leads?"

"Well...not exactly, but two offers of marriage, one request for a full-body massage, and two guys who want to meet for drinks."

Emelie smiled. "You must have posted your photo. Did

you use my webcam? Welcome to social media."

"The library at First Morning has a Facebook page, so I sorta know my way around. Oh, and you got a couple of private messages. I didn't click."

"What's First Morning? Is there any coffee left?"

"Yes on the coffee, and First Morning Elementary is the reservation school where I used to work."

"Are you a teacher?" Emelie dumped out a cup of cold coffee and rinsed it before filling it back up. "I thought you were a carpenter."

Nate sauntered to the window and looked out. "My best friend's wife is a teacher there. She's having a rough pregnancy, so I sorta stepped in. They put me on payroll as a classified, like as a clerk or a custodian or something, since I can't be shown as a teacher. No big deal. The kids are great, I teach them P.E., local history, and we work on their reading. It's second grade." He paused, then turned to face Emelie. "I also wrote a grant request and started up a foundation to administer it when it was awarded."

"Wow. Who knew?" Emelie smiled and went to the laptop. "You're a lot smarter than you look, Cochise."

"It wasn't that difficult. Just a few people to keep track of the money. The kids really need the funds for books and materials."

"You amaze me. Now, let's see." She took a moment to read through her messages. "Okay, here's something. My friend Jerry says he knows where you can get some day work. In construction. He says it's in San Pedro. He wants to know if you're interested, and if you want to meet him early tomorrow morning."

"That's a no-brainer. I just need to find out if I can get there by bus."

"I'll drive you. It's not that far. Did you eat?"

Nate came around to her side of the computer and checked the screen. "I had toast. Don't you have work in the morning? I'm sure I can catch a bus."

Emelie walked away, busied herself at the sink. "I can drive you. I'm not going to the studio."

"Oh, right. It's your day off."

"Yes, well, I'll have lots of days off, now." Emelie took a deep breath and turned around to face Nate. "Angie has closed the shop. So I'm temporarily unemployed."

Rick Cordell negotiated traffic on his way home from the station, his thoughts not on the cars around him but on the forensics report he'd been handed an hour ago. It wasn't conclusive; the skull had been in the water since the last century, but that only spelled twelve or thirteen years. The findings said it could have been much longer. Conditions around the breakwater, such as acidity, temperature, movement, etc., all played a part. The fact that the skull had been lodged in the rocks meant it was at least partially protected from erosion. The research admitted that it could have been down there for decades—loosened, finally, when the speeder collided with the breakwater; snagged on a piece of the wreckage that kept it from sinking to the bottom of the harbor forever.

What about DNA? Chuck was certain something would turn up. It would take a bit longer, since the discovery of the skull was technically classified as a potential 'cold case'; there were much more pressing matters queued up ahead of it.

Rick pulled into the driveway of his modest house and left the car outside of the garage, which was filled to capacity with junk. He brought the report with him into the house and spread it out on his kitchen table before grabbing a beer from the fridge. The photos were unpleasant, to say the least, but they revealed one very important fact. The owner of the probably decades old skull probably did not enter the water alive.

After a cheap but tasty dinner of macaroni and cheese with salad, Emelie loaded the dishwasher and smacked the 'on' button with her thumb. Already dressed in her workout clothes, she unrolled her mat in the living room and stepped onto it, closed her eyes, and straightened her shoulders while Nate watched from the couch. She took in a slow, deep breath, then pressed her hands together in front of her chest.

"Is it prayer?"

"Tadasana," she murmured. "Come."

Nate was tempted to look around in jest. She wanted him to join her? He couldn't help the grin but stood up and walked to face her on the mat.

"Like this?"

Emelie opened her eyes, then nodded. "Now, bring your arms out to the sides and up."

Nate took a breath and complied.

"Urdhva Hastasana. Good. Look upward, toward your thumbs. Let your shoulder blades slip downward. No, now stay aligned." Emelie lowered her own hands and placed them in the small of Nate's back. "Here. Come over to the wall. This will help you to feel what alignment should feel like."

"I never thought 'back against the wall' had anything to do with yoga," Nate quipped, but Emelie ignored him.

"Okay, now, you're going to bend at the hips and place your hands on the floor beside your feet. No, don't bend your knees. There, that's better. This is Uttanasana."

"How do you know all this?" Nate asked, his straight dark hair hanging down over his face.

Now Emelie smiled. "I took classes. I loved it. I got certified, then offered a job to teach it. You want more?"

"Sure. Bring it."

Emelie took Nate through the entire 'sun salutation' series of movements, ending back in the Tadasana position.

Nate was impressed.

"I feel pretty loosened up now," he commented, rolling his shoulders.

"You've never done this before? You did pretty well. I'm impressed."

"I stay pretty fit, but this...this is new. I like it."

Emelie sat down on the floor in front of the coffee table. "I just thought you could use a little limbering before you head down to that interview in the morning."

Nate nodded. He'd not thought about the job situation in, oh, ten minutes or so.

"Look, Hopi, no matter what happens, you are welcome to stay here as long as I have this place. I will also be looking for a new job."

"What's the rent like here? It seems like a pretty expensive neighborhood."

"It is. But the landlord is a friend of my dad's, so I get a discount. Even with that, though, it was going to be tough without the cash he was sending. Now, I'm getting zero. Rent's due in two weeks. I will be honest with you, I have about two hundred dollars left in the bank and I have almost five thousand in a savings account that I haven't touched in years. I don't have any other debt, because the credit card is his and he cancelled it. He'll pay it off. My car is also paid for. My car insurance is paid up for at least six months. We just need money to buy food and pay rent for now."

Nate wanted to say something but came up with nothing positive. Instead, he only nodded. Things had certainly taken a turn. He'd hoped to have met with Jack McKenzie by now; instead, he was going to bed hungry and contemplating homelessness.

Chapter 6

October, 2012

Jack stood by as Tim directed Rob Evans and his band mates aboard the U.S.S. Iowa battleship, permanently berthed in Los Angeles Harbor. This was exciting; the Iowa was the only ship in her class to serve in the Atlantic and Pacific oceans during World War II, and later served through the Korean War and Cold War before being decommissioned in 1990. It has just recently opened to the public and the film industry. A perfect backdrop for a portion of Evans' "California Love Song" video.

The ship's own movie production company was on board to assist with the thirty second contribution to the short film. Jack couldn't stop grinning as he watched the expert camera work, the unprecedented cooperation of the talent and Tim's infectious enthusiasm. The sun acted as the biggest and brightest spotlight, and the gentle breeze kept the warm October day comfortable.

Beside him, Todd nudged his arm. "Did you see that?"

"What?" Jack turned around to follow Todd's outstretched arm.

"That lighthouse out there. That's cool."

"Right. That's Angel's Gate. It *is* cool." Jack squinted as he took in the small lighthouse, perched on the end of the harbor breakwater. "I looked into filming out there, but it's just not open to anything. It's a shame; I thought it would be perfect."

"What about on the breakwater? With the lighthouse in the background? Would they let us do that?" Todd asked.

Jack considered Todd's suggestion. "I don't know. It's

dangerous, what with the waves slamming it all day long. Used to be open to fisherman, tourists and stuff, but they closed it because people kept getting swept off."

"You should still try."

Later, Jack got on the phone to ask the questions he'd been asking all over town. What would it take to get permission to film? He expected the safety factor to be an issue. He already knew the lighthouse was closed to the public. What he didn't foresee was that Angel's Gate was currently classified as a crime scene.

"You're kidding me. A murder investigation? Wow. That's, uh, that's bizarre. But we only want to film on the breakwater. We wouldn't go so far as the lighthouse. We just want it visible in the background. We do have insurance, security, all that..."

Jack tapped his 'end' button with his thumb and slipped his phone into the pocket of his jeans. "Well, I don't have high hopes for that. Transferred about fifty times, then told they'll get back to me. Heard that one before."

No one was more surprised than Jack when, two hours later, he received a call from a local boosters club member who agreed to meet Jack out at the breakwater.

"You can see why they closed down this section!" his companion shouted over the din of the waves. "They got tired of fishing out the daredevils and crazies!"

Jack nodded, braced his feet. His jeans were already wet from the spray. "I think we'd better pass on this. Where I really wanted to film was the lighthouse," he called back.

"Maybe next year. Right now's not a good time. But I can give you a quick look if you're interested. Just for fun. Meet me over at the launch."

Todd's eyes were round as the small skiff approached Angel's Gate, and Jack squeezed his shoulder. "You stay glued to me, you hear?"

His stepson nodded, and the two followed the volunteer

up the rocks to the lighthouse entrance, where workmen were coming and going.

"I thought the remodel was done back in May?" Jack asked.

"We're just doing a little interior work, in advance of another big effort that will start next year. Maybe you can do another video, here, after she's finished," their guide said. "Try to steer clear of these guys; they're working hard to fix the place up. She's gonna sparkle when they're done, hopefully in time for her 100th birthday!"

Jack scoped out the interior of the lighthouse, with its narrow staircase snaking up the wall to the top. "Can we go up?"

"Sure. Just be careful."

The workmen were replacing rotted flooring and other woodwork on the second level. Jack nodded to them as he paused to look over their task. One of them, a young man wearing safety goggles and a short brown ponytail, stared as Jack continued into the tower. Jack looked back over his shoulder at the man who had pushed up the goggles and was watching Jack intently. Caught, he returned to his work, but Jack was discomfited by the worker's attention.

At the top, both Jack and Todd were in awe of the view. Los Angeles' busy shipping lanes, the harbor, the St. Vincent Thomas bridge, the varying depths of aquamarine and blue. Straight down, a short piece of yellow tape with black letters remained caught on the rocks. Todd busied himself with a cellphone camera as Jack took it in.

"Incredible."

"Yep. I think that every time I climb up here," the guide remarked.

"Those workers down there, do you know them?"

"No, they're hired by the general contractor. Nice guys, though. Skilled. Dedicated. I know they don't make much money, but they show up here every morning at 6:30."

Jack nodded. On his way back down the stairs, the worker who'd stared—glared?—at him worked intently and kept his back turned.

Nate turned over on the couch and tried to get comfortable, but this night sleep evaded him. He was tired enough, to be sure; the work at the lighthouse was tougher than he'd expected and his back ached from bending and squatting over the damaged flooring. Aspirin might dissipate the pain, but the memory of Jack McKenzie staring back at him was permanently etched. What were the chances that Jack would appear in the lighthouse?

"Unbelievable," Nate murmured, again tossing and punching at his pillow. Was this a sign? The work of some unseen force helping to throw them together? The job at the lighthouse had been auspicious enough. His first sight of the beacon, up close, had nearly taken his breath away. White, trimmed in black, with an octagonal base supporting a cylindrical tower, Los Angeles Harbor Lighthouse immediately intrigued Nate. Growing up in the arid spaces of Arizona left little opportunity to see such sights. Once inside, he felt a strong link to the structure, or rather, its aura. Almost like he'd been there before.

Nate smiled, thinking about Johnny. His long-time friend debunked all beliefs in the supernatural, the category under which much of the tribe's heritage could be found. Déjà vu? "You're nuts, Nate. No such thing. It's your own mind doing this," Johnny would say.

I know what I felt. The lighthouse, and its secrets, embraced me. The air was soft inside. Soft, and thick. Rich with past and happenings and... souls. It was as if every person that had ever slept there still occupied the space, somehow. Nate had to hide his excitement from the boss, the contractor leading Nate and his co-worker on the quick tour before they began working. He saw the keepers' sleeping quarters, the kitchen, and the gallery. The view of the Pacific, the shipyards, the harbor was like nothing Nate had ever imagined. The second floor, where he was assigned the renovation work, housed storage and the single bathroom.

The woodwork didn't fight him, and while strenuous, the repairs weren't difficult. Nate appreciated the quality of the original craftsmanship. He didn't remember the name, but was told that the lighthouse had won some kind of architectural award back when it was built in 1912. It didn't surprise him.

Would Jack McKenzie be back? Why had he come? The answers to his questions would appear, Nate was now certain. In time. Tomorrow was Saturday and he wouldn't go down to the harbor. Instead, he would help Emelie in her job search.

In the three weeks since he'd taken up residency on her sofa, Nate had grown close to Emelie in ways he never thought possible, discovering joy in their compatibilities. They shared similar politics and food choices, movie criticism and even spiritual beliefs. They both accepted the concept of a higher power without conceding to creationism or deity worship. As a friend, Emelie's devotion was unparalleled; she drove him to the dock each day so that he could board the water taxi for work. In the afternoon, she waited there with the car, a small bag of groceries in the back seat. They watched free movies on her laptop, and practiced yoga together at least every other day. She made him cucumber sandwiches which he hid from the other guys, but insisted he go for a beer with them once in a while after work.

In return, Nate kept a brave, sympathetic face when she complained of debilitating menstrual cramps. He helped with her resume and taught her how to make Paatupsuki, a meatless Hopi soup consisting mostly of beans, corn and hominy. He wiped her tears when she discovered her insurance had been cancelled and helped her come up with several new derogatory names for her father. Despite the fact that he was now making money, they were still short on the rent.

At five o'clock, Nate gave up on sleep and showered. He dressed and made a pot of coffee before heading out for an early morning walk, still thinking about Emelie's kindness. He wanted to do something nice for her, something really nice.

As he walked down the Third Street Promenade, Santa Monica's upscale shopping and restaurant district, he paused at the window of a jewelry store. The showcase was empty, of course; nothing would be left in view during their closed hours. Yet Nate envisioned a beautiful sapphire necklace he'd seen there before, and how perfect it would look hanging around Emelie's neck.

Who am I kidding? I can't even afford to pay attention, much less buy jewelry for my... my...friend. Is that what she is? My friend? Johnny was his friend. And Mari. And several other people back in Flagstaff, Winslow, and the mesa. But he'd never wanted to buy jewelry for any of them. Thinking of them did not bring on the rush he felt when he remembered Emelie's delving eyes and soft but wisecracking mouth. There were days when she would talk his ear off, and still he longed to hear her voice when she stopped.

As he continued on his walk, Nate pondered the direction his thoughts took him, and it was with much surprise that he recognized, finally understood, what had happened.

Nate Sinquah had fallen in love with Emelie de Maria Marin.

He splurged on a small bouquet of wildflowers from an early street vendor and put them into a drinking glass on the kitchen bar. The sound of water in the pipes meant that Emelie was in the shower, so he quickly threw together a double-sized omelet and dropped two pieces of bread into the toaster. Breakfast was hot and waiting when she emerged from the bedroom.

"Wow, Hope, you made nice! And I'm starved."

Emelie slid onto a barstool and picked up her fork just as her eyes lit upon the flowers. "Where did these come from?"

Nate quickly lifted his coffee mug to his lips, suddenly embarrassed.

"You bought these? For me?" Emelie put down her fork and took one of the blooms between her fingers. "How... how very thoughtful. I love them. Thank you," she said softly, "Nathaniel."

Nate shrugged and took a bite of his eggs, but Emelie's shining eyes stayed focused on him.

"I knew you had a romantic streak," she continued, finally turning her attention back to her breakfast. "I knew when we first met on the bus."

"One of your psychic episodes?" Nate asked.

"Nope. Just simple intuition."

"Can't figure it out. There was just something about this guy, Mad. He looked at me like he knew me. Almost like he was pissed off at me. And I swear, I've never seen him before in my life." Jack went to the refrigerator for milk. Across the room, Maddie's voice was guarded.

"Describe him again?"

"Well, couldn't say his age, I'm a bad guesser, but surely not over 28 or 29. White. He was wearing those big plastic glasses, you know, protective goggles, so I didn't see his eyes at first but then he pushed them up on his forehead. Dark eyes, dark hair, it looked like it was tied back into a queue or something."

"Oh my God, Jack, did he have a scar on his forehead?"

"Honestly, I didn't notice. The glasses covered part of his face. But he really looked like I'd done something terrible."

"The man at the funeral. He looked like that, remember? I told you about him. Kinda high cheekbones. Straight hair. And that scar."

"Too much of a stretch. This was completely random, me going into that lighthouse. He was already there, working since early morning, so it's not like he's someone stalking me. Just...weird. Probably nothing. Probably on drugs."

Maddie laughed. "It's always drugs. People can act strange without being on drugs, Jack. Maybe he just mistook you for someone else. He didn't say anything, so he probably realized he was mistaken. I say just forget about it."

"You're right. I know. It just rattled me." Jack went to his wife and embraced her. "You are my rock, you know that?"

"Well, this rock's gotta roll. It's Back-to-School night. I have to go own up to being Davey's mom."

"What about Duncan and Claire?"

"Let's just say being their mom doesn't have a ring of notoriety. Davey's teachers are the ones whom always seem to know us by name."

Jack grinned. "I understand. He is the McKenzie hellion. Tonight can we talk about L.A.?"

"If you want."

"I've been home for a week. I think it's time."

"There is supposed to be a meteor shower tonight," Emelie said, emerging from the bedroom just as Nate was putting away the last pan from the dishwasher. "I thought we might go up to the roof to watch."

"Good idea. Better get a quilt or something, it's cold out there tonight."

They spread a comforter on the flattest section of the roof and dropped on a couple of cushions from the couch, then lay back to watch the night sky.

"You should see the stars above the mesa. About a bezillion more than you can see here," Nate reflected.

"I'd like to go there some day. You say you still have family there?"

"My dad, his name is Sam, and my Uncle Robert. He's my mom's brother. Quiet guy. He's got a son named Jacob, my cousin, who lives in the East. That's all except for Sobo."

"Sobo?"

"My grandmother. She's eighty-eight and not doing too well. She's confined to her bed, her memory is spotty, you know, the usual old-people stuff. But she helped raise me, and I... I'm really going to miss her. I already miss her."

"I'm sorry. My grandparents are all out of the country. I've only met them a few times. Man! It is cold out here."

"Here." Nate moved closer to the edge of the blanket and beckoned. "Scoot over."

Emelie hesitated, then moved close to Nate while he pulled the excess blanket over them both. "That better?"

"Much."

Silence ensued while they watched the sky. Nate found himself missing the sound of Emelie's voice. "What are you thinking about?"

"Sam and Robert and Jacob don't sound very Indian to me."

"Well, there are these trends, you know, where people want to sound less like minorities and more mainstream. It helps on job applications and scholarships. They want a better life for their kids. Some of them have Hopi names also that they never use. My mom's name was Tiponi. Tiponi Pahana Sinquah, but everyone called her Tippi. My grandfather, her father, was named Makya, but we all called him Mako. The kids would tease and yell, 'Mako Taco!' at him all the time. He was a good soul, he just laughed it off."

"So sweet."

Nate closed his eyes. Emelie's closeness intoxicated, made him feel dizzy. Another couple of inches and they would be touching. Was this the right time? There was no reason to wait. If she wasn't interested, she would let him know.

"Still cold?"

"A little."

Without asking, Nate slipped his arm beneath her and pulled her close, so that her head rested on his shoulder. She immediately tucked her arm around his chest. They both sighed, and Emelie giggled.

"What?" Nate asked.

"Like we both weren't just wanting to do this."

Nate smiled in the darkness. Her hair tickled his face, and he luxuriated in the feel of it.

"I like hearing about your family and your life back there. Like, how did you get that funny little scar on your face?"

"Funny? You think it's funny?" Nate chuckled. "The kids at school think I got it from Lord Voldemort when I was a baby. They told me I'm cursed."

"You are much cuter than Harry Potter," Emelie assured him.

"Ha! Well, I have to say my life is a lot less exciting than his. My mom told me I was wearing a pair of her mocs, much too big, of course—I was only three. I tripped and fell and hit my head on a rock. Nothing as glamorous as a 'killing curse'."

"It sounds like you were very happy there. Makes me wonder why you ever left."

Her question sobered him. "It's kind of a long story. Complicated."

"Personal?"

"Yes, but—well, not too personal to share with you. You might think it's pretty weird."

"That's the best kind of story. Go for it."

Nate took a breath. Overhead, the first tiny, sparkling streak darted across the sky. "Did you see it?"

"See what?" Emelie answered. "All I can see right now is you. Now tell me your tale, Hopi."

By the time they'd gathered the bedding and descended the stairs to Emelie's apartment, Nate had shared the mystery of his mother's letters and had counted fourteen meteors. Emelie planted herself, cross-legged, on the couch as Nate retrieved the letters from the bottom of his backpack and selected one for her to read.

*"I hope this finds you well and happy. How are things there? Still hot and dry? I really wish you could come out here for a while and we could spend some time together. Things have really changed since the war years, when we first 'met.' So what do you think of our new president? Nothing like good old Harry S.—*Is he talking about Truman? Wow—*Here's a little something to make things easier. I wish it was more but you know how things are these days. Maybe in the future it will get easier.*

"It's been so long since I've seen you, I'm sure you've changed a lot. Just promise me you'll never lose that sweetness you inherited from your dear mother. Write me back, to the post office box, as usual. Much love, Gus"

Emelie's eyes widened. "Are you kidding me? Holy crap! That does sound like they had something going on, doesn't it? Man!"

Nate nodded his head slowly. "So... this Gus guy just died. But I'm thinking he could be my...my..."

"Your father? Oh Jesus. That could explain why you don't look so much like a redskin. And he's dead! What are you going to do?"

"Em. A *redskin*? Really?"

Emelie blushed. "C'mon. You know. Well, it's better than savage, right?"

"He has a son. Jack. I came out here this summer to meet him, but I bailed. I just got... scared, I guess. I mean, he seems nice and all, he has a big family, he works, he's well-liked..."

"You think he knows about his father and your mother?"

"Maybe. I don't know."

Emelie picked up the letter and turned it in her hands. "You were really close to your mom, yes?"

Nate nodded. "She was my biggest inspiration. She was so brave, fighting the cancer until the end. No one should have to go through that." He paused to redirect his thoughts. "But I feel like I have to know, about her and Gus McKenzie. I can't rest until I find out if he was truly my biological father."

"Well. I am not sure what this will gain you, my possibly one-half Native American friend, but I will help you to find out. I promise." She lifted her chin and stared at Nate with such warmth and determination that Nate lost all sense of restraint. Grasping her chin gently, he pulled her forward and kissed her on the lips.

What was he doing? He wanted to taste her, wanted to feel her tongue, the roof of her mouth... yet Nate stopped short, forcing himself to be content with just the feel of her lips against his. The warmth, the softness was like nothing he'd ever experienced. All the months he'd spent locking lips with Fawn disappeared from memory. He knew he should pull away, should apologize. Yet instead of retreating, he turned his head slightly and pressed his cheek against hers.

"Sorry. I don't know what came—"

"Don't. Don't ever say you're sorry for kissing me," Emelie whispered. "Unless you really are. I hope not."

Chapter 7

Jack spent a week helping Case at the marine hospital. Maddie balked about moving to Los Angeles, and Jack stressed over his desire to go.

"It's Friday. What do you say we knock off early and get a brew?" Case asked while pulling off his surgical gloves. "I need to get away from this place. I'll be here all night to keep watch on old Henry."

Jack admired his cousin's dedication, especially to an aging walrus that they both knew wasn't going to last more than a day or two. He nodded. "Sure. I'll get my coat."

It was too cold to sit on the deck at The Salty Pine, their usual hangout, but Donna seated them at the table in the rear window where the sun offered meager warmth.

"So, Mad's not ready to join the L.A. crazies?" Case asked.

"She makes *me* crazy. She's the one who suggested I go down there in the first place. But now she's all, 'I don't want to disrupt the kids' and 'You don't really want to work with *those* people, do you?' And here I just had the best time in my film career. What do I do?"

Case stroked at his trim beard. "I've never known you two not to work things out. One of you," he said, pausing to smile and lift his beer bottle, "will come around."

"That's helpful." Jack crinkled his face into a half-frown, half-smile. "Maybe we can compromise somehow."

"I hate to lose you, if that can make things any worse for you."

"You're just a wealth of support."

"Well, I try. How's Mom?"

Jack grew solemn. "Physically, she's fine. Blood

pressure's in check, heart is okay. Mentally... every time I go it's like, will she remember me this time? Or look at me like a stranger?"

Case shook his head slowly. "I'm sorry. And I feel bad that I didn't get down there before this...this turn. I just didn't foresee—"

"Nobody did. This Alzheimer's thing came on so fast. The good news, if you can call it that, is that she didn't really have to grieve when Dad died. She doesn't miss him because she doesn't even remember him. After fifty-five years of marriage."

"So unfair." Case let out a deep, dark breath. "They didn't deserve it. But then, the first fifty-three years weren't so bad, right?"

Jack mustered a grin. "Good point. We should be so lucky."

"You and Maddie—forever. Me, I can't even get Amy to the church steps."

"She will. One day. She's just taking her time, building suspense. Typical chick."

Case shrugged. "I don't know. She's the independent type. I thought maybe when Matt and Becca got hitched last year, Amy would realize that we were the last ones. But... no dice."

"She's worth the wait, man."

"Did Mad make you wait? Seems like you two got married fairly quick. Where did you meet, again?"

"In a park. She was there waiting for Todd to get out of some focus group at the studios, and I was walking Duncan in his stroller. Dunc launched one of his socks on the sidewalk and she picked it up and pursued me."

"Women have always pursued you."

Jack grinned. "I know, right? Anyway, we recognized each other from high school. So we had coffee together. Turned out she was in a loveless marriage with a self-centered egomaniac, and I was struggling with Kelly and Duncan, you remember, she wanted to take Dunc to New York with her? Man, those were tough times. Anyway, Maddie and Ray broke up, and, well, the rest is history."

"She's always adored you," Case observed. "If you want this bad enough, she'll move to L.A."

"You want me to talk to Aim?"

"What? About getting hitched? Naw. This is my problem."

Jack tilted his head, stared past Case out the window before placing his palm down on the table between them. "Get her a ring. Just do it. Get down on your damned knee and ask her."

Uncharacteristically embarrassed, Case looked around the restaurant, his face rosy. "You're joking, right?"

"Nope! I'm dead serious. It occurs to me that this is how you should do it. I mean, you've never formally asked her. Maybe that's what she's waiting for! Pick a time without interruptions. Surprise her. I think she'll be... enthralled."

"What if she says no?"

"Then you'll know. Right? You'll know she's not in this, not like you are. If she says yes, which I think she will, you'll be out of your misery."

Case smiled and shook his head. "I need to think about this."

"Think all you want, my man. But the sooner you get this off your chest, the better."

"Good advice for both of us."

Jack looked his friend in the eye and smiled. "True. So true."

Maddie was angry. Downright pissed off, if Jack read her correctly. The lips, thinned and in a straight line; the quick movements with her hands as she dipped into the grocery bag and placed her purchases on the counter.

"Look. This whole L.A. thing was your idea, remember?

You said you'd pack up the kids if I found I...needed to get back there."

His wife swept a shaker of seasoned salt off the counter and plunked it down on the pantry shelf. "*You* need. It's all about you. Don't worry about yanking the kids out of the only school they've ever known, dragging them into that sea of human dysfunction."

"Yanking? Dragging? Aw, c'mon, Mad. That's not fair. It's not like that and you know it. There are some great schools down there, private schools... although I'd rather they go to public... but that's not the point. It's not all about me, it's about us as a family."

Maddie stopped unpacking groceries, a head of cabbage in her hand. "Family? Our family is fine right here, Jack. This is home, now. This is where we agreed to raise our kids. In a natural environment without all the bad influences of L.A." She paused to fill her lungs, then exhaled. "I didn't really believe you'd want to go. I'm sorry if I misled you. I thought once you saw how much worse Hollywood was, you'd come running back."

Jack smiled, shook his head slowly. She just didn't get it. It wasn't like Maddie to be so contrary, so insensitive. Clearly, there would be no reasoning with her tonight.

"Let's talk about it tomorrow. I need to get some air." Jack lifted his jacket off the back of a kitchen chair and turned to go.

"At least we have *air* up here."

Nate moved through his work in auto-pilot, expertly inserting new wood slats and sanding rough spots. His hands knew the work, freeing his mind to think about other things. Things like Emelie. The woman who was now always pervading his thoughts. He couldn't stop reliving the kiss of a few nights ago.

Go slow. Take it easy. You might be rushing into the

wrong thing.

"Ready to break for lunch?" Frank asked, wiping the sweat from his brow as he stood from the floor.

"What? Oh, yeah. Sure. I'll be right out." Nate took a rag and wiped the wood clean of the fine layer of sawdust, then inspected his work. Not too bad. Stain and varnish, and this job would be done. Getting to his feet, he leaned back and stretched; he'd been sitting too long. Overhead was his next task: a light fixture that was in danger of falling from the ceiling. It wasn't his normal forte, doing electrical, but this was a simple task that wouldn't require any wiring work. At least he didn't think so.

Curiosity piqued, Nate retrieved a ladder from the side of the room and set it up beneath the ailing light, then climbed up to get a closer look. The fixture had definitely seen better days and nearly fell into his hands when he touched it. He wondered when the lighting had been updated last. Without too much coaxing, the cylindrical predecessor to the "can" light came loose and freed an accrual of dust and bugs which fell to the floor in various pieces. Nate figured he might as well clean out all of the muck and stuck his rag up into the opening to brush away more cobwebs and dirt. He was surprised when his fingers snagged something small but more substantial than the dust bunnies that had already fallen out. A small bag with a drawstring top dropped to the floor with a decided "clink."

Nate descended the ladder and picked up the velvet bag, originally dark red but now gray with dust. It was about the size of his palm and heavy.

"Hmm." Carefully grasping the edges of the bag with his fingertips, Nate pulled it open and turned the bag upside down into his hand. Five gold coins, each about the size of a silver dollar, slipped onto his palm. Nate's mouth opened at the sight, but before he could register the magnitude of his discovery, Frank appeared in the doorway.

"Hey, you comin'?"

"Yeah. Sure." Nate casually slipped the bag, and the coins, into the pocket of his jeans and went to retrieve his lunch.

"What was that?" Frank asked.

"What was what?"

"What were you just looking at? In your hand?"

"Oh, nothing. Just checking my coinage. Gotta do laundry tonight."

Frank stared at Nate for a moment before nodding. "Right," he said. "I hear ya. Hate doing it myself."

The two sat outside together to eat their brown bag lunches. The weather was sunny and cool, the salt spray tickling Nate's face from time to time. He ate slowly, trying to remain calm and relaxed while inside, his mind raced. What kind of coins had he discovered? Were they real gold, and if so, how old might they be? How long had they rested in between the floors of Angel's Gate Lighthouse? He couldn't wait to get home and look at them with Emelie.

The coins lay evenly spaced on a paper towel beside the laptop. Nate and Emelie sat together on the floor behind the coffee table, comparing each coin with the ones on the computer screen.

"It's that one. I think," Emelie said, pointing to the photo on the coin website.

"No, no, it's older than that. Scroll down." Nate took a bite from his burrito and focused on the screen as Emelie brought up more photos. "Stop. That one. Can you zoom in?"

"It's a 1933 Double Eagle. Worth... oh my God."

"Over seven million dollars? Are you kidding me?" The bite he'd just taken lodged in Nate's throat. "There's got to be a mistake. Maybe it's a fake. Or a replica. Something like that."

Emelie turned to look at him, her eyes wide. "But what if it's real? It says here there are an unknown number of them because they were supposed to be all melted down. Then a few of them resurfaced because..." Emelie squinted at the screen. "Because someone stole a bunch of them before they could be converted to gold bullion bars."

"Do you think *that* someone is the one who hid them in the lighthouse?"

"Crap, I don't know. What about the other coins?"

After more careful research, Emelie determined that the remaining coins were rare but of lesser value than the "Saint-Gaudens Twenty Dollar Gold Piece," also known as the Double Eagle. Nate picked up the coveted coin and delicately turned it over.

"It's pretty nice," he murmured. "We need to get it looked at."

"But can we trust a coin dealer? I mean, what if it's the real thing? They might try to steal it, or they might call the authorities. Maybe it belongs to the Lighthouse, or the Harbor, or—"

"Whoa, whoa... you're getting ahead of yourself. There's probably a way to find out. But just in case, do you have a safe?"

"A safe? I do not even have a working garbage disposal, Hope."

Nate grinned, amused by her latest nickname for him. "Well, I'm sure you can think of some place secure to keep them. Tomorrow, we'll look online for a coin appraiser."

"Okay. And maybe we can find out if they are listed somewhere as lost. Or... stolen."

"One thing's for certain; they've been hidden up there for a very long time," Nate mused.

Later, he watched as Emelie made her nightly rounds, turning the lock on the front door. She checked that the stove was off; that the computer was shut down and the cell phone plugged in.

"Well, goodnight. See you in the morning," she finally said, standing in the doorway to her bedroom.

"Sleep well." Nate stared across the room, waiting for Emelie to close her door. When she didn't, he looked away and picked up his blanket from the couch.

"You, too." Emelie smiled briefly before taking the doorknob in her hand and slowly pushing the door closed.

Nate exhaled and sat down on the couch. With the discovery of the coins, his mind teetered on overload. His original goal of finding and talking to Jack McKenzie had just slipped farther down the list, after figuring out what to do with the coins, and telling Emelie he loved her.

Chapter 8

Jack toyed with the cell phone in his hands. Tim Cole had called to say he'd be a few minutes late and that Jack should start without him. Little did Tim know that Jack had, indeed, already started without him, having just ordered his second St. Pauli Girl. He wasn't exactly drowning his troubles, but he certainly needed to wet them down some after the horrendous row with Maddie.

Case had talked about compromise. Maddie accused Jack of egotism and self-servitude. Did he really put his own needs before that of his family? Would moving back to L.A. be such a bad thing?

"Pshh." Jack shook his head and ran the lip of the beer glass across his own, letting the foam drag across his stubble. He and Maddie had never fought before. Disagreed, yes. Challenged each other's logic. Argued over paint colors and car makes. But never to the point where she'd slammed the door in his face, like she'd done yesterday morning when he tried to say goodbye.

"Be that way!" he'd shouted, like a disgruntled teen. He might as well have threatened to withdraw her best-friend status. But he was angry, hurt, disappointed. After all, she'd gone back on her word. She'd said she would move to Southern California if he wanted to, and now that he wanted to, she wouldn't budge.

Jack took another draught. Tim's invitation to view the pre-screening of the Evans video thrilled Jack, made him feel important again. Not that hand-feeding sardines to a seal wasn't important. Yet Tim had another deal in the works, another rock video he swore would be a slam dunk for Jack. With Maddie's obstinacy fresh in mind, Jack couldn't wait to find out more.

The Evans band video rocked. The grin never left Jack's face throughout the four minute, five second film. He nodded to himself at each new locale visited by the musicians, and the memories of the days spent filming. Tim had shared so much, inviting Jack to learn more about video direction and cinematography. Now, Tim was offering Jack the director's chair on a new project.

The film would take six to eight weeks to shoot. The subject, a young female country singer; the angle, a runaway girl in a roadside motel, lamenting the boy who also ran away and then shows up at the end of the video. Jack liked the concept immediately. His first thought was to call Maddie, to share his good news. He changed his mind when he arrived back at Matt's Hollywood digs and listened to Maddie's phone message on his cell.

"I hope you're thinking about us, Jack, up here alone. Duncan's got a book report due in the morning, Davey came home with a black eye and Claire has a sore throat. Of course Duncan hasn't read the book, and Davey will probably be suspended for fighting. I can't do this by myself. Todd's over helping out at Case's, they got in a pair of otters or something that need help, I don't know. I just know the boys need you here. I need you here. Call me."

Jack didn't want to call. He didn't want to listen about the kids' problems, or hear the disappointment in Maddie's voice. If they'd come down here with him, like he'd asked, they would all be together and he could help. He wanted, so badly, to share his joy with his wife. To have her laugh and be a part of his success. The opportunity to direct? His dream come true. A foothold. A new direction. Book reports and playground fights were small stuff. They could wait, just a while, right?

No, not really. With a heavy sigh, Jack dialed his wife's cell number and waited while it rang and eventually went to voicemail. He cleared his voice.

"Hi, it's me. Just got in, sorry, had a late meeting with Tim. He's asked me if I want to direct the next one. The next video, it's for Shannon O'Malley. New country singer. Anyway... look, I'm sorry about all that crap with the kids. I'll talk to Davey tomorrow. We need to take away some privileges. No Facebook, no video games. Christ! He's only six years old. I'll meet with the principal, okay? I just—just need a few more days then I can come home for a couple."

Jack sighed again as he stared out at the night beyond the picture window, the city spread before him like a blanket of stars. "Don't be so hard, Mad. Try to get this. This is what I've wanted for a long time. Finally, the chance to—never mind." It wouldn't matter to her, right now, with all the domestic challenges she faced. "Just don't be mad. I love you. I'll talk to you tomorrow. Tell the kids I love them, too. And dammit, Dunc knows better than to wait until the last minute on that stuff. Jesus. Call me if Claire gets worse."

Dropping the cell onto the coffee table, Jack fell back onto the couch and stretched out. He dreaded telling Tim he had to go back to Nor Cal so soon, but what could he do? He couldn't leave Maddie to take care of it all, not in the frame of mind she was in. Todd was going to have to help with his little brothers, especially the hellion. Maybe Amy could tutor Duncan. It would free Maddie up to tend to Claire for a few days. Jack groaned, fighting the guilt that swelled within him. Maybe he was wrong to want this. Maybe he should get his butt into the car and head north, apologize to his wife and get back to his 'normal' life. Resume his duties as a father and husband.

With a groan, Jack laid his arm across his eyes and tried to fight the exhaustion that threatened to knock him out. He'd think about all this tomorrow, after a good night's sleep. He hoped.

Emelie turned over and punched her pillow, cracking one eye open to view the clock on the nightstand. Normally, she'd be up and dressed by six o'clock; Nate had to be dropped at the dock by 6:45. But today, she had orders to sleep in because Frank Danvers was picking Nate up.

"I really don't mind," she'd told Nate after dinner the night before, her back turned so he couldn't see the disappointment on her face. "I'm up anyway."

"You do way too much for me already." Nate, preoccupied with packing his backpack, responded softly. "You get some extra z's, will you?"

But she couldn't. Not only did she miss driving her best friend to work, she worried about him. Worried because of the vision. Or, *visions*.

They'd started just after Nate's discovery of the coins. Emelie wasn't sure, at first, if the feelings were just normal anxiety or precursors to a clairvoyant episode. When Nate came home with a bleeding finger—a work injury—and she'd tended the wound, contact with his flesh sent a vivid photograph before her mind's eye. In the picture, Nate lay on the floor in a dark room, and while he might have been sleeping, Emelie knew he was not. Something was wrong with him, something far greater than a nick on the finger.

Her visions didn't always come true. Once, she'd "seen" her mother slap her father, which she would never do. Of course, Emelie had assumed the man in the vision was her father, even though his face was not clear.

She didn't tell Nate about the vision; experience taught her that most people called her crazy when she tried to warn them. But the lingering feeling, the certainty that Nate was in some kind of danger rattled her. Throwing back the covers, Emelie bounded from the bed and went to the kitchen in search of coffee. What she found was a note on the coffee maker.

"You'd better be reading this after nine, Em. See you

around six. Let's go out for steak."

Emelie smiled. *As if.* She poured herself a cup of coffee and sat down at the breakfast bar. *Oh, Hopi. You don't even know what you do to me. Even when you're not here.* Emelie felt warm, happy inside at the thought of Nate; the imaginary steak dinner out, with Nate in a fancy suit and herself in a beautiful, fluttery dress, glasses of wine in their hands as they laughed about nothing in particular. They would have no cares, no worries, just each other. And afterward, they would dance.

Emelie's fantastic daydream disintegrated quickly when she realized that there would be no steak, no wine, no dancing. Dinner would be meatless spaghetti at best. They just weren't making it on Nate's pay alone.

They? Since when were they a couple? Sure, she'd invited Nate to move in, to stay until he could support himself. Yet in reality, he'd instead begun supporting her almost immediately. Her own job search continued to yield nothing.

A melancholy sigh escaped as Emelie toyed with Nate's note. Tomorrow, Saturday, they would take the coins to the shop they'd chosen and find out if they were worth anything. Maybe she wouldn't have to worry about a job. In her practical heart, she doubted the "gold" was more than a collection of cheap replica coins. Still, she was anxious to find out. Ready to stop wondering, stop worrying about protecting the small velvet bag that today was stuffed under her mattress.

The doorbell brought her out of her contemplation. She was surprised to see Angela outside her door. After a heartfelt hug, the two women stepped into the living room.

"I brought you these. I thought you might have some use for them. I sure don't." Angela dropped a bag containing two rolled up yoga mats and several foam blocks onto the floor. "I've liquidated everything else and honestly, these weren't worth selling. There are also a couple of CDs in there."

"I'm so sorry, Ang. I've thought about you so much, but... I don't have a phone anymore, and I'm still not working anywhere to use a phone. What are you going to do?"

"I'm leaving town. I've got some problems, Em, I got some people after me for money and I just—I just can't find any way out. I'm going underground for a while. I won't tell you where so that when they come asking, you won't have to lie."

"Oh." A chill passed over Emelie's body. "That sounds serious. You aren't in any...danger, are you?"

"Physical danger? God I hope not. No, this is legal stuff having to do with an ex-employee. Again, I don't want to involve you. I should go."

"Can't you stay for a cup of tea or something? Just for a bit? I am going stir crazy here by myself. And since I don't know when I'll ever see you again..."

Angela smiled gratefully. "Okay, just for a bit, as you say."

Emelie quickly put some water on to boil and got out two cups. In the fridge was a half loaf of raisin bread and she dropped two slices into the toaster. Angela propped herself onto one of the barstools. "So what have you been up to?"

"Periodic job seeking. You remember my father sliced me off."

"Cut you off? From what?"

"Money. Insurance. Credit cards, cell phone."

"Ah babe, I'm sorry to hear that. My shutting down didn't help one bit, did it? You still seeing that nice guy?"

"He's the only thing keeping us from the streets. He's working down in the harbor. Hard work that's really below him but it's all he could get."

"Tell me about it."

"I usually drive him down to the docks in the morning,

and pick him up later from the water taxi slip."

"Hmm. He doesn't have a car?"

"Nope."

Emelie prepared their tea and buttered the toast. "We have one possible save. Nate found some coins that might be worth some money. They don't seem to belong to anyone, so we think we can sell them for whatever they're worth."

"Really? That's—that's interesting. My ex-husband used to collect coins and stamps. Never had anything really valuable, though. Mostly just stuff worth under a hundred bucks. I donated it all when he left."

"There's good revenge," Emelie observed. "I have a feeling these coins are just junk, too, but you never know."

Angela nodded, then took a sip of tea. Emelie watched as Angela's hand trembled slightly while holding the cup. Something was off. Maybe just the threat of her money issues and legal problems.

"You want to see them?" Emelie asked, hoping the distraction might be good for her friend.

"Heck, yeah! I'm no expert, but it'd be fun to just look."

Emelie retrieved the coins from her room and placed them on the kitchen counter, careful not to touch the large one with her fingers. Angela's mouth opened.

"These are stunning. Wow. I wouldn't leave these babies lying around. Get 'em appraised and get 'em sold."

"That is the plan, yeah. I keep moving them around. I don't really know where to hide them."

"I've got a couple of ideas. I mean, most thieves are gonna look everywhere. But at least you've got a chance if you get creative. I once hid a sapphire ring in my daddy's garage freezer, wrapped inside some ground round. You can also tape one to the inside of the ceiling light fixture. Behind or above the bulb, so it won't make a shadow."

Emelie stared at her ex-boss. "Really? Wow, you seem like you are quite well versed in this hiding-of-things."

Angela laughed. "I had to get good at it when I lived with Zayne. He was always digging into my stuff. What a jerk he turned out to be. But anyway, don't forget about the toilet tank. That's another good spot."

It wasn't long before Angela took her leave, embracing Emelie for several moments. "You take care. I'll be in touch, someday."

Once alone, Emelie went to her bedroom and slid her fingers between the mattress and the box spring, snagging the tiny drawstring and pulling the bag out. It occurred to her that should a thief find the coins, they'd easily get them all. She decided to split the coins into two groups and hide them in different places. Carefully drawing the bag open, she dumped the coins onto the bed and was again taken aback by their beauty. She didn't look long, however. Having the coins out in the open made her nervous. Frowning, she quickly divided the coins into two groups of two and three. The largest coin, the Double Eagle, caught her attention and she paused, drawn to its beckoning aura. Unable to resist, she picked up the heavy coin and held it in the palm of her hand. Her eyes closed, involuntarily, and the gold piece began to radiate warmth.

The vision came quick, dark, in and out of focus. A man in a uniform, and another, in a different uniform. They were fighting. She felt connected to only one; blood in his mouth, pain in his head. Angry voices, a heavy blow, then blackness. Cold. Muted sounds. Sinking. Silence.

Emelie drew in a gasp and opened her eyes, then dropped the coin onto the bed. Her breath ragged, she stood and stared down at the five gold pieces, reeling from the vision and its overwhelming portend of impending death. Looking around, she sought a basket of clean laundry and selected a sock, which she used to pick up the coins. The Double Eagle and one of the other coins dropped into the sock, and the other three returned to the velvet bag. The latter went back under the mattress, and the sock was dropped unceremoniously into her lingerie drawer.

This time she would tell Nate about her vision. Shaken and confused, she vowed she wouldn't touch the coins again.

Chapter 9

Nate gave Frank a sideways glance as the pair drove home from the dock. His workmate's sudden interest in Nate's life wasn't particularly welcome. That, and the fact that Frank had made them almost an hour late leaving the lighthouse, annoyed Nate.

"Yeah, Arizona's cool. Been there a few times myself," Frank was saying. "Grand Canyon. With my first wife and kid. Ha! I shoulda left her there."

Nate chuckled politely, wondering if perhaps Frank's wife should have left *him* there.

"So you and the brunette been together long?"

His jaw working, Nate shook his head. "We're just friends. We met on a bus. We're sharing expenses for a while."

"Ah. That's cool. You two just look like, a couple, you know. She looks at you, when you get in the car, you know."

"Looks at me, how? I'm not sure what you mean."

"Just, like, she likes you, you know. No big deal. I just noticed. She's hot, too."

Frank's comment distracted Nate from his irritation. Did Emelie really look at him with affection? If so, he hadn't noticed. Or maybe he was afraid to notice. But Frank was still talking.

"I was thinking, maybe we'd get some dinner together. I'm seeing this blonde chick from Hollywood. What 'ya say we get some tacos and Coronas? Maybe later tonight? It's Halloween, in case you forgot. We're going as Bonnie and Clyde."

Nate wet his lips. "Not sure that'll work out. I'd need to check with Em."

71

"So, call her. She's probably sittin' around on her ass anyway, like most broads do, right?"

His good nature tried, Nate grinned out of frustration. "Emelie is no broad, Frank."

"Aw, sorry. I didn't mean no disrespect. I'm sure she's quite a little lady. So call her."

"Can't. I, uh, forgot my cell."

"Use mine."

"Look, we'll be there in fifteen minutes. I'll just ask her then. I can call you later. Deal?"

Frank looked over at Nate, peering so long that Nate feared he'd lose control of the car. Finally, Frank grinned and returned his eyes to the road. "Yep. Okay. You call me later. Me 'n Sheila will be going anyway."

When Frank stopped the car in front of Emelie's apartment house, he got out and walked around to the sidewalk. "I'll just stop in to say hi. I feel bad about my comment."

"Frank, dude, she didn't hear you. She's funny about strangers coming into the flat, so..."

"I get it. Okay. Look. We'll be at Garcia's Cantina if you two want to show."

"Great. Have a good time, in case we don't, you know, come by." Nate stood on the sidewalk until Frank drove away.

Emelie sat on the couch, knees drawn up to her chin, her face towards the apartment door. She hadn't moved in thirty minutes, except to nibble away her thumbnail, which was now uncomfortably short. When she heard the key in the lock, she bolted from the couch and leaped onto Nate before he could close the door.

"Trick or Treat—whoa!" Nate stepped back in order to steady himself. Emelie buried her face into his shoulder and tried to stifle the onslaught of tears.

"Em! What's the matter? What happened?" Nate kicked the door closed and carried Emelie back to the couch. "Are you okay?"

Emelie nodded, her face still hidden. "You're so late. I thought—I thought something had happened to you!" Her voice, muffled by his coat, broke with relief and embarrassment.

Nate chuckled and gently turned her head with his hands. "I'm fine. Frank made us late. I'm sorry you were worried. I wish we had a damned phone."

"It's all right. I am fine. I get unreasonable sometimes. It's just that something happened today, with the coins, and I got scared."

Alarmed, Nate's eyes widened. "What happened with the coins?"

"Well, nothing really *with* the coins, but I was just checking on them and I had this stupid vision. Oh Nate, it was just awful."

Nate gently brushed the hair from Emelie's damp cheek. "Tell me about it. Tell me all about it."

Her traumatic incident wore Emelie out and she fell asleep on the couch while watching television. Nate indulged himself with one of the few precious beers he had left and sat down at the end of the couch, taking care not to disturb Emelie as he gently lifted the remote from her hand. The tube held little interest, but he lowered the volume and surfed the channels anyway. An old Western caught his eye and he settled in, sipping the beer and periodically looking over at his roommate.

Emelie's vision clearly terrified her. Not having experienced anything like it, Nate could only guess at the impact witnessing someone's death would have—especially from inside the victim's mind. She described in deadly detail the pain of the blow, the darkness, the sensation of falling and the inability to breathe amidst the depths of an icy grave. No wonder she was so shaken. He'd done what he could to comfort her, all the while acutely aware of his own obsessions, his deep desire to hold her close and never let her go.

The beer calmed him some. John Wayne was rounding the bend on horseback, gun drawn, shooting randomly at the grim-faced, retreating Comanches. Nate frowned, the wrinkles in his brow eventually smoothing into a tentative grin. The 1956 film cast real Navajo actors and portrayed Navajo customs and beliefs, calling them Comanche traditions. Nate had heard about *The Searchers*, and now, the nearly sixty-year old movie seemed more comical than offensive. Maybe he'd be more offended had the Hopi been portrayed so blatantly wrong.

Emelie stirred beside him. As he stared down at her small feet tucked against his thigh, he envisioned himself stretched out next to her. His arms fairly ached to wrap themselves around her, to protect her from the nightmarish visions that plagued her of late. Maybe he could... just... slip himself between her body and the couch back... after switching off the TV and letting the remote drop to the carpeted floor.

The room fell into near darkness, the lighted businesses on the street invading through the back windows. Nate wedged in behind Emelie's sleeping form, settling in and draping a tentative arm across her tummy. She moved again, adjusting herself, turning slightly to rest her head beneath his chin. Nate exhaled slowly, eyes closed, hoping she wouldn't be mad when she awoke and found him beside her.

Even if she was, it would be worth it, he decided.

November 3

Jack never thought the odor of the men's locker room

would smell so sweet. As he bent from the bench to lace up his skates, he chuckled at the sound of his buddies arguing over whether or not the L.A. Kings could win another Stanley Cup.

"You guys are all wet. You *know* the Canucks have it in the bag."

Matt Farralone, in town for the weekend, shoved Jack in jest. "You're full of it, you know that? You hate the 'Nucks as much as anyone here. Maybe more."

Jack stood and reached for his hockey stick. "That so? Hmm. You may be right. Maybe even more than I hate the Ducks."

"Or the Wings," Matt suggested. "L.A. has no love for Detroit."

"True. Then there's the Sharks."

A collective groan resonated in the locker room as Jack and Matt headed out to the rink.

The skate went well. Jack wasn't at all sure he could still maneuver the puck but was pleased to find himself beating out the goalie several times. Matt was better than Jack remembered, but neither had played for a couple of years. Afterward, the friends grabbed some lunch and then stopped in at a big box electronics store to replace Matt's cell phone.

"I only had the damned thing for six months," he complained to the salesman. "Craps out almost on cue, every time I really need it. Just sell me something reliable. You'd think for the price of these things they'd work."

While Matt negotiated his way through iPhones and Androids, Jack wandered to the impressive display of tablet computers. Todd had been asking for an iPad, and Jack thought maybe it was time to fund one. As he perused, his ears picked up on a nearby conversation between a customer and a clerk.

"Just something I can use in an emergency. You know, cheap. No service plan."

"You want a pay-as-you-go phone. I can help you with that."

"Thanks. I'm uh, not very cashed up at the moment. But my, uh, girl, uh, girlfriend had, um, an accident the other day, and I couldn't—"

"Say no more, sir. This will work just fine."

Curiosity piqued, Jack casually turned to see the cash-strapped young man behind him. To his shock and amazement, there stood the workman from the lighthouse. Right there, not ten feet away. Jack quickly turned back to the device in his hand and pretended to examine the screen. How could it be? The same kid! The one who'd stared him down like a criminal. Was it possible he *was* being stalked? That the stranger at the funeral was truly the same guy? Impossible, he reminded himself. The trip to the lighthouse had been spontaneous. No one could have possibly known Jack would visit that day at that time because he didn't know himself.

Maybe I should confront him. Maddie would tell me to do that. She would just march herself right over there and ask. Jack put the tablet down and walked unhurriedly around the table, so that he was now facing the spot where the young man had stood... but now did not. Surprised, Jack looked around but could not see the man anywhere in the store. He flagged down the salesman.

"That guy you were just helping. Did you see where he went?"

"Uh, he left the store, sir. He bought a phone and left. Paid cash, so it was quick. Why? Did he drop something?"

"No, no, I just thought I recognized him and I, I was going to say hello. No big deal. Thanks."

Matt returned as Jack tried to reason with himself.

"You looking for a new phone, too?" Matt asked, holding up his store bag. "I went with the new iPhone."

"No, I'm okay with my Samsung. Did you happen to see

that guy that was just here? Longish dark brown hair in a ponytail? Dark eyes? A scar on his face?"

Matt frowned. "No, I didn't. Why?"

"Never mind."

In the parking lot, Matt pressed the button on his key fob and the lights on a silver Lamborghini flashed twice. Jack stood for a moment to check out the parking lot. Just as he was about to slide into the low profile seat, he saw a small, late model Toyota waiting at the exit for the light to change. The man behind the wheel turned and stared at Jack, his face flushed with surprise. The young woman in the passenger seat fiddled with a small pocket phone. Jack focused intently on the couple until at last the light changed and the little car sped away.

"Someone you know?" Matt asked when Jack joined him.

"Maybe," Jack muttered. *I need to call Maddie. She would want to know.*

Emelie pretended to dial on the new phone and then put it to her ear. "Hello, Daddy? I just wanted to let you know that I am fine. Do you hear? I am fine. I am not going to roll down and ask you for help."

"Roll over."

"What?"

"It's roll over. That's what you're not going to do."

Emelie smiled. "Right. Roll over. And if I had rolled over last night, I would have ended up on the floor."

"Mm hmm." Nate blushed, causing Emelie to recall again the feeling of waking up beside him on the couch. So filled with joy, she'd kissed him on the cheek before dancing off to her bedroom. He'd blushed then, too. She never asked how he came to be with her in the first place, but his closeness delighted her regardless of whether he intended to be there or had just, like herself, fallen asleep.

It wasn't far to the Triple A Gold Exchange. Nate pulled into the tiny, off-street parking lot and edged into a narrow space. Once the car was parked, he sat back in his seat and stared out the windshield at the backside of the building.

"Ready?" Emelie asked, opening the glove box. "You'll have to carry them in. I'm not touching them, ever again."

Nate didn't respond for a moment. Finally, he turned and stared at Emelie. "What's wrong? Change your mind?"

"No, nothing like that. I am fine. Let's go."

Emelie watched closely as "Abe" examined each coin in succession and made notes. He wore a jeweler's loupe and carefully scrutinized the gold.

"What are you looking for?" Emelie asked, leaning forward to get a better view.

"What we do is attempt to establish a grade. This means looking at the condition, like wear, blemishes, purity, etc. High grades, for example, are called "investment quality" and the like. There's a lot of debate about whether what we do is an art or a science. Are we subjective, or is there a true scale we can use to appraise? Capiche? Understand?"

Emelie nodded vigorously and Nate grinned. Abe seemed like an okay guy, so far.

"So, Abe, what do you think? Are they real?"

Abe put down the last coin, the Double Eagle, and looked Nate in the eye. "Oh, they're real all right. Might I ask where you got these?"

"Well... I found them—"

"In the closet. His father's closet. That's where," Emelie announced. "Yup. In an old shoebox."

Nate frowned and stared at Emelie, who returned her most engaging smile.

Before Abe could continue, a younger man with curly black hair and glasses approached and whispered something in his ear. Abe nodded and then sent him on his way.

"Sorry, my son. The worrier." Abe gestured dismissively

toward his son's retreating back. "Now, back to these. That's very interesting that you *found* these coins. We don't see many of these anymore. And since I know what your next question will be, yes, they are worth a lot of money. Especially this big boy here. But there's a problem with that."

"Problem?" Nate echoed, almost as if he had already prepared the word on his lips.

"Problem. There aren't supposed to be any more of these. Government minted almost a half million of them, back in 1933. Same year, Uncle Sam discontinued the gold standard, so they melted 'em down. Only a few, a very few, remained out there, and those were all stolen. Periodically, they would show up, and the feds would confiscate them."

"Why?"

"Because technically, son, they belong to the United States Treasury. If you try to sell it, believe me, they'll be watching. You are actually duty-bound to turn it in. They'll put it in Fort Knox."

"Seriously. You're serious?"

"Absolutely. You go home and do a little research. You'll find I'm right. Now, these other coins are a different story." Abe slipped the Double Eagle into a small plastic coin sleeve, then picked up one of the remaining four coins. "These are 1878 Coronet Type Liberty Head Quarter Eagles. Originally worth two and a half bucks. Two of them are a little shabby, one is good and this one... is excellent."

Nate's head still swam with visions of the men in black dragging him and Emelie off in handcuffs. Abe bent over the last coin with his loupe, and Nate felt Emelie take his hand.

"This one's worth, oh, two, maybe twenty-five hundred. These others, probably around four grand all together. You'll get around sixty-five hundred for the lot."

Emelie's gasp brought Nate around. "Really? I mean... *really*?"

"Well, it might be a little less if you don't have any documentation, you know, papers. Proof of ownership. Did your "father" write anything down, or leave any receipts or such?"

"Uh, I'll have to look. Thanks. Thanks so much."

Emelie was squeezing his hand so tightly Nate thought he might lose circulation. Abe bagged the four coins back up and handed them to Nate, along with the larger coin in its sleeve. "Here. The number to call about turning that coin in is on this card. And by the way, it's worth over eight million, so take care of it. When you're ready to sell the others, I hope you'll consider working with me."

"You bet, Abe. Thanks again."

Nate could barely get a word out once in the car. "Did he really say eight million dollars?" he croaked, turning the key in the ignition. "For a coin we can't legally sell?"

Emelie giggled, reached over and gave his ponytail a little tug. "Did you not hear what else he said? The others are worth gobs of money, Hope! We're rich! We can pay rent, and buy gas, and go out for a steak dinner!"

"But what about documentation? And what was all that bullshit about my father leaving me the coins? Now I'm more curious than ever about who stashed them at Angel's Gate."

"The point is, it doesn't matter. So, we don't have any stupid papers. We get six thousand instead. So what? It's all good!"

She was startled by the sound of someone knocking on the car's passenger window. She lowered it and the young man with the black hair handed her a small card.

"You dropped this. The number to call about the Double Eagle." His expression was grave. "You live around here?"

"Actually, just down the street, at the Tradewinds."

"Okay, good. Hate to think of you driving around with that kind of asset. Watch your back." The man patted the door frame and turned to go back into the store.

"We gotta turn in that coin, Em. I want to take some pictures of it first, just for fun. We'll call the number tomorrow. The sooner we're rid of it, the better."

Now sobered, Emelie nodded. The eight million dollar coin carried a bad aura. Someone died, either because of or for that gold piece, and she didn't want anything more to do with it.

Chapter 10

November 5, 2012 – Monday

Nate stood up and viewed the job he'd just completed. Hands on hips, he turned a slow circle, noting once more the fine craftsmanship of the original construction. Unless he was missing something, the lighthouse project was now complete. A contented sigh escaped, capping his satisfaction but also punctuating his regret that the end of the job meant the end of employment. He'd be back pounding the pavement tomorrow or the next day. Lifting his gaze, he peered at the recently reassembled light fixtures. With the astronomically valued coin still at home, he wondered for the *Nth* time if paperwork did exist.

On a whim, he grabbed a ladder and ascended to the fixture, carefully pulling it open. He stuck his hand up inside the recess and felt around but discovered nothing. After stowing the ladder in the store room, Nate wandered outside to where his boss sat talking to Frank. The two stood quickly, and the boss ran a gloved hand over his bald head.

"I'll have your checks ready tomorrow if you want to come by the dock. You guys did a badass job out here. You did the old lady proud." The three men turned to look up at Angel's Gate's freshly painted, black and white tower.

Nate nodded. "It was an honor to work on her."

"Yep. That," Frank agreed. "I think we need to celebrate. You game for a beer or three?"

It was the last thing Nate wanted to do. Their boss had turned away, preparing to carry his gear down to the waiting boat. Frank prodded.

"C'mon. Last time. This might be it for us, and I've

enjoyed working with you. I can run you home after. Just a couple of brewskis?"

Nate shrugged. He could also celebrate, privately, that it would be the last time he'd have to put up with Frank's coarse language and redneck attitude. "Sure. Okay."

Frank seemed inordinately chipper on the way back to the shore and he laughed easily at almost everything Nate said. Once in Frank's car, he drove Nate away and through the streets of San Pedro, passing all the spots he usually frequented.

"So, where we headed this time? A new bar?"

"Someplace special," Frank said with a grin. "We have a lot to talk about, and I don't want any interruptions, if you know what I mean."

Nate felt the back of his neck tense up. Something didn't feel right.

The sound of the pendulum on the wall clock seemed loud, ominous. Jack stared at the ceiling above his bed and tried to figure out what had happened between him and Maddie. He thought back to the days before they were married, when she'd been caught up in the mystery surrounding the disappearance of Thomas LaForge—Todd's biological father—and Jack had almost lost her to her past. The thought of Maddie choosing the older Frenchman over himself had nearly killed him. Things had worked out in his favor, though; Thomas had been arrested and incarcerated, Todd accepted Jack, and Maddie became the most beautiful bride ever.

Sadly, Duncan's mother had slipped on some ice in New York City and had succumbed to a serious head injury, paving the way for Jack to take custody of his young son. Davey was born just months later, and their instant family made life complete. Claire soon followed, just before the move to Northern California. It seemed right at the time.

Now, it was all coming down around his ears.

Maddie was terse on the phone. She didn't seem to care about Jack's encounter with the lighthouse guy. She no longer asked him to come home, didn't share what the kids were up to. Punishment, Jack decided. *She's shutting me out because she's angry.* The more he thought about it, the more annoyed he became. Weren't they a couple? Didn't he deserve some consideration for what he wanted? His career? He'd certainly show caring and compassion if she wanted to make a move. In fact, he now remembered, it was her desire to move up north in the first place. She was weary of L.A., tired of working in the law office, disappointed in the school district and fearful of the crime and the traffic. Case had mentioned how much he and Amy liked living in Grogan's Head, so Jack and Maddie had gone for a visit. Maddie fell under the spell of the serenity, the peacefulness of the forest where it met the ocean waves. So in love with the idea of pleasing her, Jack walked away from the studios and learned how to swim with the dolphins.

He thought about pouring himself a drink. Maybe something with a deep punch, like bourbon. Maybe a little Scotch whiskey, his father's poison of choice. *Ah, Dad.* Jack once asked his mother if Angus had always been a drinker. She deferred, saying his father didn't have any bigger problem with alcohol than other survivors of the Big One. She hinted at some particular trauma that might plague the old man, but Jack habitually put her intimations aside. Now, quiet, reflective, he wondered at the possibility. Had Angus suffered at the hands of the enemy? Seen too much death in the trenches at Normandy? The elder McKenzie spoke fondly of the Allied win but told little about his personal experiences overseas.

Maybe I should have cut him some slack, Jack thought, frowning as the room grew darker. Who were his friends? Such a different world. He imagined himself tramping across a muddy field, carrying a rifle, his pals Case and Matt alongside. Walking into an ambush. Case or Matt getting shot. Or both. What would that do to him? How could he have survived such a horrific experience?

Jack shuddered a little as his mind tried to shrug off the gruesome imagery he'd conjured. War, as archaic as it was, still existed. Would a day come when Todd, Duncan or Davey could be called to defend freedom? His respirations picked up; he remembered a time when his father had accused him of sliding through life without responsibility. *"You don't know what heartache is. You don't know what it's like to lose everyone you love at once."* At the time, Jack-as-surly-teen had waved off his father's admonitions as the ramblings of an angry, self-important man. In retrospect, Jack now allowed that his father certainly had suffered, the way he himself would suffer if he lost "everyone he loved at once." And whom did he love? Maddie. Todd. Duncan, Davey and Claire. Case, Amy, Matt and Rebecca. His beloved mother.

Jack swung an arm across his rapidly filling eyes. "I'm sorry, Dad. I wish... I wish I had asked. I wish I knew who it was you lost and how you lost them." *Could I have helped him, somehow? Made his burden easier? Gotten him to talk about those days, so long ago, when life was so tenuous and responsibility so strong?*

He couldn't ask his mother; on her best days she had trouble remembering Angus's name. On her worst, she didn't even remember her own. But Dad had friends, living friends who'd served with him. Jack remembered how they'd clamored around him at the funeral. The drunk guy, in particular. What was his name? Floyd. Floyd... Holmes.

Moments later, Jack found himself searching his cell phone for Floyd's number. The old man's daughter had called for directions back in June.

It took several minutes before Floyd could get to the

phone, but Jack remained calm. The senior sounded bright and alert.

"Of course I remember you. You know you're a spittin' image of your dad."

"So I've heard," Jack said with a smile. "This might sound like an odd request, but can you tell me anything about Dad's other friends? During the war, I mean."

"Most of 'em are gone, son. We ain't gettin' any younger! Ha!"

Jack chuckled politely. "Well, I'd like to know about any that might have been lost during the war, you know, like in battle. Someone close to him, maybe?"

Floyd took a moment, and Jack thought perhaps he shouldn't have asked. "There were so many. But close to Gus? I don't know. We only met as enlisteds. Any friends prior to that, I didn't know. But there was a girl."

"Lucille. My mom."

"No, weren't Lucille. Not this girl. He showed me her picture once, he carried it with him like we all did back then, you know, most of us had sweethearts back home."

Dumbfounded, Jack narrowed his eyes as if Floyd could see his confusion.

"How do you know it wasn't Mom?"

"Because your Mom is not a Jap. Not even close."

Emelie looked at the clock for the tenth time in as many minutes. Eleven fifteen. P.M. She stared at the phone in her hand with chagrin. What good was a damned cell phone if you only have one? *"I can always borrow a phone to call you. Or use a payphone. You can't. So you should keep it, and I'll find a way to call you if the need arises,"* Nate had decided.

Now, it seemed like a stupid idea. Why hadn't he called? Was there no one around him with a working phone? No phone at a business he could borrow? At the yoga studio, people often asked to make a call, and Ang always let them. No, something was wrong, for real this time. Nate should have been home hours ago.

Every noise, no matter how miniscule, brought her to her feet and anxiously waiting for the front door to swing open and Nate to walk through. This time, she vowed, she would do more than just hug him. She would kiss the daylights out of him and demand that he carry her to the bed. She would show him, at last, just how she cared. How much she'd grown to love his dimpled smile, his soulful eyes and that cute ponytail. How dependent she'd become on his solid wisdom and clean humor. She'd offer—beg!—to have his babies and swear to take care of him forever. And ever.

If only he would walk through that door.

When a soft glow began to appear in the south-facing windows, Emelie lowered her head and began to cry. Her call to the L.A.P.D. had produced nothing more than a "He'll probably show up with a good excuse," response. They were courteous, took some basic information, but she didn't have much of what the "Adult Missing Persons Unit" wanted to know. No phone, no email address, no friends, no family contacts. They suggested she check with local hospitals, shelters, coroner and morgue websites. She couldn't even go there in her mind.

She waited until eight o'clock before forcing her fingers to dial the long-familiar phone number she hadn't used in months. Her father answered on the third ring.

"Hello, Father. It is me."

"Me. Is that the way you identify yourself?"

Emelie bit her lower lip and swiped at a tear. "This is your daughter, Emelie de Maria Marin. I need...your help."

It galled her to ask; she had nowhere else to turn. She heard her father sigh but he said nothing.

"My... friend is missing. I think he's in some kind of trouble."

"Why does that not surprise me? Do you have any reputable friends?"

"Papa... I am serious. He is a good man. I think he may have been abducted. Or hurt. I cannot get any help from the police."

"Perhaps this man does not want to be found. Perhaps he is hiding in his house and does not want a clinging girl around. If he wants to see you, he will call."

"You don't understand. He doesn't have a house, or a phone, he—"

"You are seeing a homeless man, Emelie? Is this how far you have fallen? And you, with so much potential. Throwing away yourself for what? A man who runs from you and lies about where he lives?"

"Papa! You're not listening! He—he lives here. With me. He has no phone because we could afford only one. He gave it to me! Papa, please!"

"With you? You are sleeping with this homeless man who has now left you? Are you with child?"

Emelie groaned in frustration and stamped her foot. "No! Goodness no. Papa. Nate would never just leave. He cares about me. And for the record, I am not sleeping with him, not that it is any of your business!"

"You are correct. None of this is my concern."

"Could you at least call in a favor? With the police? I know you know people there."

"Emelie. Listen to me. I re-extend my offer, although I said I would not. Your bedroom is still here, your clothing, your books. The door is open for you to walk through, when you are ready. When you come to your senses. But you will return to school, you will live by my rules, our family rules, until you graduate with a degree and some sense of reality. It sounds like that time is not now."

Emelie gulped air. The tears returned, dropping into her lap as she tried to talk.

"Daddy, please..."

Her father was quiet for a moment, and when he spoke, his words were determined but tinged with sadness. "Adios, *Mija*. I hope your young man comes home. Truly."

Hurt and exasperated, Emelie threw the phone down onto the couch and stomped around the apartment, shouting expletives in Spanish as she played out her tantrum. And when she had expended the last of her fury, she sat down and ran her fingers through her tangled mass of hair. There was one person, and one person only, left to call. The man responsible for her meeting Nate in the first place, the one he'd come to Los Angeles to meet. The man who could be the key to Nate's past.

Rushing to the closet in the hall, Emelie hoisted Nate's heavy backpack onto her shoulder and brought it to the kitchen table. Inside, she sought his small black notebook, the one containing all his notes and phone numbers. Quickly she tore through the pages, seeking the name she needed. She didn't have far to look; there, at the top of the third page, was the name "Jack McKenzie," underlined twice. Now, all she had to do was find him.

Chapter 11

November 6 – Tuesday

Jack filled a Thermos container with hot coffee and threw a couple of bagels into a paper bag. His need for sun and heat pushed him into the car and toward the beach. California's predictably unpredictable weather brought warmth to the early-November day and Jack didn't mind a bit as he sat down in the sand near Santa Monica Pier.

The bagels weren't fresh, but he gnawed on one anyway. As he watched the waves rush toward him and then retreat, he tried to envision his father as a young soldier. Sure, he'd seen photos of Angus as a G.I., one in particular his mother had on her dresser at home. But the notion that he was seeing a Japanese girl boggled the mind. Floyd was certain, absolutely positive, about the snapshot Gus carried with him into battle.

Jack chuckled in ironic remorse. There was no one left to ask. *No one left living who could tell me more about the photo Floyd remembered.* Even if his mother had one of her rare moments of clarity, he couldn't risk hurting her over something that she might not know about.

I'll just have to let this one go.

If his dad didn't want him to know, maybe there was a good reason. Still, it would be a long while before Jack could put this one on a back burner. The shock of learning about his dad's lost love had all but eclipsed his own marital discord. If Angus had truly loved this Japanese woman, this daughter of the enemy, how did he feel about Lucille, his eventual wife? Was Jack's mother just a rebound love, a second choice?

Jack groaned and lay back on the blanket he'd spread beneath him. The midday sun blazed across his closed eyelids.

Who was she? How—and when—did she die? If she was dead...Questions flooded his mind, ugly questions he didn't want to ask. The ringing of his cellphone from his pocket was a welcome respite from the barrage of painful thoughts.

"This is Jack," he responded to the woman on the phone. "Who is this?"

"My name is Emelie Marin. I'm a friend of someone, someone who needs your help."

Jack sat up, pressed his hand against his other ear to close off the roar of the waves. "Who needs help?"

"It's—it's complicated. Can you meet me?"

"Well, I'm a little hesitant to just meet someone without knowing... who is this someone? Is it a mutual friend, something like that?"

"He is, maybe, someone related to you, Mr. McKenzie. He is in serious trouble, I don't know where he is—" The woman's voice broke and Jack could hear her quiet sobs.

"Hold on, calm down, what kind of trouble is this guy in? Do we need to call the police?"

"I tried that. You're the only one I have left. Please. Could you just come? I promise that after you hear what I have to say, you can just go on your way if you want."

She sounded harmless enough, and clearly upset.

"Where should I meet you?"

"Do you know the Starbucks on Santa Monica Blvd.?"

After ascertaining *which* coffeehouse she referred to, Jack rolled up his blanket and headed for his car. Traffic was slow and uncooperative, but Jack could only think about the strange phone call and the girl he was about to meet. Could be a prank, he thought, scanning the street for a parking space as he neared the Starbucks.

It took no time at all to identify Emelie Marin. Young— maybe mid-twenties. Chestnut brown hair, pulled back into a hasty ponytail. Pink nose propping up sunglasses that undoubtedly hid her swollen eyes. This was no prank. Jack slid into the chair opposite.

"I got you a coffee," she said, timidly pushing a paper cup across the table. "I thought it was the least I could do."

"Thanks. It wasn't necessary. Tell me about your friend."

Emelie moistened her lips and took off her sunglasses. "Do you want to know about how he might be your brother, or how he might have been abducted?"

Jack stopped, the coffee halfway to his lips. His eyes focused on hers, his brow furrowed. "That's impossible. I have a brother, one brother, named Sean. That's it. What makes you think this...this..."

"Nate. Nathanial." Emelie reached for her bag on the floor and brought it to her lap. From inside, she drew a letter, a thin envelope with the words "AIR MAIL" printed across the blue striped bottom. Her hand shaking, she handed the envelope to Jack. "When his mother passed away recently, he found several letters hidden away in her dresser. They are signed by Angus McKenzie."

"Okay, well, that's a common enough name, especially in the U.K. Obviously someone else."

"Please, just read this one."

Jack carefully withdrew the onion-skin sheets and stared at the handwriting, not reading the words as he examined the familiar script. Incredulous, he glanced back to Emelie before returning his eyes to the top of the page. "Who is she again? What is... was her name?"

"Tiponi Honanie Sinquah. Nate says they called her Tippi. She was only sixty when she died."

"Sinquah? What kind of name is that?" *Certainly not Japanese.*

"Hopi. Nate's family is Native American."

"This is crazy. My father didn't... well at least I didn't..." Jack paused, took a gulp of coffee and found it almost gone. "Look. I need more coffee. You want anything?" He noticed his companion drank only water.

Emelie shook her head, but Jack returned with a mocha latte and scone for her and a fresh coffee for himself. He sat quietly while Emelie, despite her admonitions, dug into the pastry. She was hungry.

"Let's just set this aside for now. I can't even wrap my mind around this thing. Tell me what happened to Nate."

Emelie swallowed hard and took a gulp of the hot latte. "Mm. This is so good. Yesterday, Nate didn't come home from work. Usually, I pick him up at the dock but this time, he said he would get a ride home from his co-worker because it was the last day of the job. He didn't know what time he would get off."

"Did he call you?"

"No. He does not have a phone. We only have one, and he told me to keep it because he could always borrow Frank's phone to call me. But I don't have Frank's phone number."

"You said you thought he was abducted."

"A week or so ago, Nate found these coins. Five gold coins. We found out they are worth a lot of money. I think Frank saw the coins and maybe he is trying to steal them from Nate. Frank is not a nice man."

"Where are these coins now?"

"At the apartment. I hid them there."

Jack chewed his lower lip. "Where did he find the coins?"

"At work. They were hidden in the ceiling."

"Work? You mentioned the dock. Are they dock workers or something like that?"

"They worked at the light—" Emelie's words were

94

clipped by the ringing of Jack's cell.

The caller I.D. photo gave him pause. "I really need to take this call," he apologized.

"No problem, should I?" Emelie gestured over her shoulder, but Jack shook his head and then answered the phone. Maddie was calm but aloof.

"I hope I'm not disturbing you."

"Could I call you back in a bit? I am with someone at the moment." Jack cringed inwardly at the implication.

"I have tickets for Paris, leaving in the morning. We're going to visit Monique."

"What? Are you joking? You can't just leave like that."

"I'll call you in the morning so you can say goodbye to the kids."

"Maddie. Stop. I don't know what's going on with you, but this isn't right. Let's talk this over."

"With you there and me here, talk means nothing. We need a break."

Jack shook his head. "No. Absolutely not. I will be there in the morning. You wait. Just sit tight, Mad."

The phone went dead. Jack quickly checked his signal, which was strong. Maddie had hung up on him.

"Damn." Emelie momentarily forgotten, Jack angrily shoved his phone back into his pocket.

"I'm sorry. If you need to go—" Emelie began, reaching for her bag.

"No. It's—it's fine. I'll deal with her later. Let's get back to these coins. Did you tell the police about them?"

"I didn't because at least one of the coins is stolen from the United States. This man who appraised the coins said we could get into a lot of trouble if we don't turn it in."

Jack's eyes widened. Could this story get any more bizarre? One car, one phone, a girl who voraciously goggled up a tasteless Starbucks scone. These kids were broke, and when they happen upon a fortune, they're robbed in one way or another. "Look. I have a friend who's with the D.A.'s office. He can put a little muscle on the cops to do their job. You might have to tell them about the one coin, at least. Do you have a description of this Frank guy? A last name, even?"

"I've never met him. I don't even know their boss's name. I'm sorry, I'm worthless."

"No, you're not. I'll bet you have a photograph of Nate, right? Tell me you have a snapshot or something?"

Emelie brightened. "I do. We met on a bus, coming from Arizona. He was coming here to meet you, only he never got up the nerve to talk to you." She began digging in her bag again. "I have my old iPhone, it does not call anymore but it still has its camera. I took a picture of him, he doesn't even know I did it. He was so cute with his ponytail and those dark, soulful eyes." She scrolled through the photos on the phone, finally selecting one. She turned the screen toward Jack. "Here. Nathanial Sinquah. The man I love."

Jack leaned forward to focus on the photo and felt his jaw drop.

Chapter 12

November 7 – Wednesday

Jack settled himself on the living room floor, cell phone in hand. He'd already brought Matt on board to ruffle some feathers at L.A.P.D., and had left Sean just as perplexed about their father as he was. The notion of Angus dallying with a Japanese girl and a Hopi woman boggled the mind. But right now, Jack's most pressing matter was his wife.

The house phone rang four times before Todd's voice came on the line. "Mom's busy. She's packing and stuff."

"Packing? Is she really planning to go?"

"Hang on."

Jack waited for Todd's return. "Sorry. I had to go to my room. Mom's acting all freaky. She's taking the kids to France in the morning. I told her I'm not going and she's, like, ok, fine. Stay here then. She's all weirded out."

"Huh. So it's not just me? How long has she been like this?"

"I dunno. Maybe a few weeks. She's, uh, not like Mom. Like some alien took her over or something. Can you come?"

Jack huffed out a gut-wrenching sigh. "Yeah, I'm coming. Stall her if you can, I'll get there as soon as humanly possible."

Jack let the phone drop from his fingers as he fell back against the front of the couch. There was no good way to get to Grogan's Head... unless he asked another favor. Matt had a HondaJet that could take him directly from Van Nuys to Crescent City, where he could pick up a rental car.

Rick Cordell stared at his computer screen and blinked, then rubbed his eyes. The data was old, stale, useless and uninteresting. He wanted to blow a raspberry at the monitor, but opted instead to just stand up and stretch his back. No small feat, he was reminded, as he struggled to get to his feet with the help of his nearby crutch. Damned leg. Damned thief. Damned bullet. He contemplated, once again, his actions on October 1st, the night the liquor store heist had gone bad and he'd lost the use of his left leg. Could he have better anticipated the little creep's move, maybe dashed to the side to avoid the stupid pansy-ass .22 that pierced his back and nicked his spine?

I have to stop thinking about that. Can't do anything about it now.

His phone rang and he reached across his desk to pick it up, only to lose his balance and fall awkwardly back into his chair. He was still scrambling to grasp it when the phone stopped ringing, just after he knocked a small stack of files to the floor.

"Damn it!" Rick leaned over the side of his chair, dropped his crutch and managed to scoop up three or four folders and smack them back onto the desk.

Cold cases. Stuff so old it had grown moldy with forgotten, dead-end details that no one cared about or remembered. Rick blew out a breath. No, *someone* remembered; the victims' families, those who still called once or twice a year to see if anything new had come up. They remembered, and he owed them at least a look-through on each file.

He shouldn't be so negative. It wasn't their fault he'd been relegated to a desk job after fifteen years in the field. It was that or leave the force completely, and that wasn't about to happen. It was his career, and he'd stick with it despite his bum leg.

Rick picked up the next file and he brightened. The

Angel's Gate skull. He thumbed through the few pages of information he already knew. No one had followed up once it was determined that they had no leads. As he browsed the now-familiar report, it occurred to him that a return visit to the site had not been made. He reached for his phone.

"Hey, Mert. What would it take to get a diver to take a second look on a cold case?"

November 8 — Thursday

Rick found it fortuitous that he and Chuck had the same day off that week. When the department balked at getting a dive team out to Angel's Gate, Rick found a local guy willing to take a look in return for some positive press if they found anything. The three of them took a motorboat out to the lighthouse on Thursday morning with SCUBA equipment and a bag of tacos and burritos.

"Miss me?" Chuck asked as he and Rick waited for the diver to return from the depths.

"Miss you? Like a bad case of the runs. How's the new partner working out?"

Chuck grinned. "The kid ain't so bad, pretty green, he'll make a good cop someday."

"Yeah." Rick looked away, scanning the Pacific's slate blue horizon. "What does that mean, 'good cop'? You mean one that knows how to get his damned ass out of the way when someone shoots at him?"

"Aw, man, don't go there, Rick. It could have happened to either of us. Neither of us thought that jerk was going to actually shoot."

"We're trained to expect that. I got lazy. I thought he was going to drop it. Just a half a second was all I needed to move to the side. Now I'm a damned cripple."

"Not necessarily. You have that surgery coming up, doc says he might be able to fix—"

"Yeah, yeah, yeah. *Might*. Not likely."

Chuck looked down, unwrapped another taco. "Well I miss you, too."

"Sure." Before either could think of something else to say, the diver emerged and climbed up from the breakwater.

"Find anything?" Chuck asked, getting to his feet.

"You won't believe this. Check it out." Their aquanaut held out his hand; something small and gray covered his palm. He wiggled his fingers, letting a portion of the item drop and dangle from his hands. A set of military dog tags.

"What the hell?" Rick held his hand out and the diver draped the corroded chain across it. "This should clean up enough to read the name!"

"That's not all. Here's the real treasure." From his belt bag, he produced a gold coin, which he handed to Chuck. "Pretty cool, huh?"

Chuck squinted and examined the coin, then looked up. "This is awesome. This looks like the real thing. Where'd you find it?"

"Just a foot or so away from the tags."

"Only one?"

The diver smiled. "Well, I can't remember now. There may have been two..."

Rick shook his head. "Funny thing about memory. Well, I only see one coin. Let's leave it at that."

At the precinct, Rick was the man of the hour. The L.A. Port Police even sent out their dive team, who recovered a pair of wire-rimmed glasses and key ring with two keys still attached. Because they weren't discovered at the same time or by the same diver, the skull could not be definitively linked to the tags, eyeglasses, keys and coin; at least not yet. Rick was determined to make that connection. As the diver predicted, the dog tags had cleaned up nicely, revealing the name of Coast Guard Ensign Joseph A. Halleran, missing since February, 1942.

The trip was brief. Jack nodded off several times, never quite reaching any kind of restful sleep. More tired than ever, he took a moment to call Emelie.

"You'll be getting a call from my buddy. Matt Farralone. He's a deputy district attorney, and he's already been in touch with the police in Santa Monica. You'll need to somehow get him that photo of Nate, okay?"

"Yes. Of course. Maybe I can print it out."

"He's also making calls to the people Nate worked for. They'll get a name for this co-worker so they can confirm if he's involved or not. Cops are checking hospitals and their own jail, too. It's all moving."

"Oh, thank you so much, Jack! I'm so sorry for what you're going through. I hope you can fix things up with your wife."

"Not to worry. After you take care of getting Matt what he needs, you should get yourself a little nap. Just turn up your ringer and it will wake you up if he—or anyone else— calls. And don't hesitate to call me if you need to. I'll be back...soon. I just have a few things to button up here." Jack peered out the window of the jet as the Crescent City airstrip came into view.

Jack steered the rental car onto the highway, a fresh cup of coffee propped into the drink holder. Tapping an icon on his cell, he waited for the hands free call to connect. Todd answered, his voice glum.

"Sorry I missed your call, dude. I was in flight. Everything okay?"

"They left. About an hour ago. You missed them."

Jack thumped the steering wheel with the heel of his hand. "Dammit. She just couldn't wait, could she?"

"She had a morning flight to SFO, then to Paris. Claire and Davey were excited. Dunc didn't want to go."

"Okay. Look, I'm only a half hour away. You dressed? Let's get some breakfast."

Jack took his stepson to the Salty Pine.

"Maybe you could still stop her," Todd suggested, dripping ketchup onto his eggs.

"Nope! Not interested. There comes a time, my boy, when a guy's gotta just let stuff go. She'll be back. She obviously needs some space."

The two grew quiet, finishing their breakfast in an uncomfortable silence. Jack pushed away his plate and rubbed his eyes. "What I wouldn't give for a solid eight hours."

"What are you going to do?"

"I dunno. What do you want to do?"

"You should call Mom, talk to the brats, find out when she's coming back. Then we'll close up the house and head back to L.A. You got a new gig, right?"

Jack stared at the young man across from him. When had he grown up? "Okay, and yes. We'll drive Mom's SUV down there. You're going to need a car. And it'll give us time to talk; I have a lot to tell you."

Chapter 13

November 9 — Friday

Rick couldn't wait to open the envelope on his desk when he arrived Friday morning. Who knew the Coast Guard kept dental records so far back? Sliding the report out, he quickly scanned the data filled in on the familiar form. The teeth did, indeed, belong to Joe Halleran.

"Well, yippee yi yo kayah." So the tags, the skull, and now likely, the keys and glasses all belonged to the twenty year old service man who went missing the night the Japs almost bombed Los Angeles. But what about the coins? Or coin, he reminded himself. One thing at a time; next up was to find out if Halleran had any family members still around.

He was surprised to see Chuck walk into the room. "What you doin' here, champ? Where's the boy wonder?"

"Mandatory training exercise. And I got a present for you." His ex-partner handed him another group of paper-clipped pages.

"What's this?" Rick quickly looked over the top sheet, a police report from February 24, 1942. Details surrounding the theft of eight vintage U.S. gold coins from a collector in Hawthorne, California. Included were rudimentary photographs of the stolen coins and the broken window and door lock on the collector's shop. "Wowzers. You think?"

"Pretty sure, yeah. The coin the guy brought up matches one of those."

"Praise Jesus, Mary and Joseph. This Halleran guy was a thief?"

"Looks that way, pal. But I gotta run. Keep me in the loop!"

"So Grampa was a chick magnet."

Jack chuckled, shook his head. "Well I don't know about that. Suffice to say, he was more than we thought he was. I think we'll stop for gas in Ventura."

"Does Uncle Sean know? About Grampa Gus?"

"He's just as clueless as I am. I gotta say, this has been the strangest week of my life. When she showed me the picture of this guy and I see it's the same guy I saw in the lighthouse, the same guy I saw at Best Buy, and probably the same guy your mom spotted at Dad's funeral, I about choked. But what's so weird is, he didn't plan to see me at the lighthouse, and my seeing him at the store was also a complete coincidence."

"Some things are just meant to happen. He couldn't get up the guts to go see you, so fate was, you know, like moving in."

"You're probably right, although I don't generally believe in that stuff. Anyway, as soon as we get into town, I should call her—Emelie—and see if she's heard anything back. She's really upset. I guess this Nate guy is a pretty cool dude."

"He could be. He could be your bro."

"I still can't get a grip on that. Maybe if I ever get to meet the guy, and we can dig through the past... I don't know."

Emelie's heart cinched painfully when she awoke to the sound of the little cell phone beside the bed. Answering quickly, she tensed to the sound of Matt's voice.

"We've had Nate's photo out on the net for 48 hours. A couple of street cops are still canvassing the docks, talking to people who might have seen him arrive and depart. And I'm waiting on the name of the contracting firm he worked for. Should have that momentarily. You doing okay?"

Emelie nodded, as if Matt could see her. "Yes," she finally added. "But I need to get out of here."

"Have you heard from Jack?"

"He's home. He's taking a much needed rest after driving back. I don't want to bother him."

"Can you meet me and my wife for lunch? I'll buy."

Emelie did her best to dress up, as Matt and Rebecca were meeting her at a swank lunch place at Third Street Promenade. They made a handsome couple, both tall and sophisticated, but also warm and gracious.

"So how do you know Jack?" Rebecca wanted to know, squeezing a lemon slice into her tea.

Matt interrupted. "Remember I was telling you about how this guy came to town, claiming to be Jack's younger brother? The guy, Nate, is Emelie's friend."

Emelie smiled. "Well spoken. It's all very bizarre, I know. When Nate found the letters from Jack's father, he couldn't rest until he found out if his mother had actually, you know, known Angus McKenzie intimately."

Rebecca's eyes widened. "That's my kind of mystery. And what's this about a lighthouse?"

Emelie cleared her throat. "Nate was working out there, at Angel's Gate, when Jack just walked in one day. They didn't know each other would be there. A weird quark of fate."

"Quirk. I'll say," Matt commented. "Yeah, Jack's pretty wound up about this whole thing. And that's where Nate found the mysterious coins, right?"

Emelie nodded. "He loved working there."

Rebecca chuckled. "We know a little bit about lighthouses, don't we, babe?"

"Could say." Matt nodded. "Not always the romantic beacons people think they are."

"Jack thinks the coins might be behind Nate's disappearance," Emelie continued.

"Well..." Matt began, "I have news on that front, anyway. I guess the feds have been called in. Port police found another one of those coins, in the rocks, in the water beneath the lighthouse. Right next to where they found a skull a few months back."

Emelie's lips parted in surprise. "Another coin? Like ours? Why would the federal government care?" As soon as the words left her mouth, Emelie realized just why the U.S. would be interested. It was the Double Eagle.

"One of our detectives found an old cold case about a set of coins that were stolen back in '42. Around the same time the guy whose skull they found went missing. They're thinking that this guy, named Hallman or Hallerman or something, he stole the coins, stashed some of them in the lighthouse, then got himself offed. One of the coins is a U.S. Treasury 'item of interest'. Hence the feds."

"Oh." Emelie felt her face grow hot despite the ice in her veins.

"Are you okay?" Rebecca asked, gently grasping Emelie's arm. "Maybe a sip of cold water?"

"I didn't know about any skull. I wonder if Nate knew about that."

"Doesn't really matter since the two were completely unrelated until this morning. Anyway. We've got Chuck Beeman riding point on Nate's disappearance, and Rick Cordell is heading up the investigation of Halleran's remains and the coins. When we're done here, we'll follow you back to your apartment to retrieve the coin the feds want. Does that work for you?"

"Hell, yes," Emelie murmured. Then more loudly, "I can't wait to get rid of it."

The three climbed the stairs together to Emelie's second floor apartment. Once there, Emelie felt like she was walking into a crime scene on a movie set: the door stood ajar about three or four inches, its lock and doorjamb broken.

Matt held the two women back and listened at the door. "L.A.D.A.!" he called out before pushing the door open and stepping inside. After a quick look around, he returned for the women.

"Place has been tossed, but whoever did it is gone." He turned to Emelie, touched her shoulder. "Can you tell me if the coins are gone, too?"

Jack woke with a start. He smelled smoke, bolted upright from his bed and dashed from the room. Todd stood in the kitchen, trying to force open the window over the sink. "Sorry," he mumbled, as Jack examined the smoking frying pan in the sink. "I was texting."

"Knucklehead," Jack said, smacking Todd gently on the back of his head. "Trying to burn Matt's house down? And me in it?"

"Your phone's been going off. I was just going to come in and wake you."

"You, and the fire captain?" Jack chuckled and retrieved his phone from the counter. Numerous missed calls. Matt never did have any patience.

"I've decided I need to start packing heat," Matt said. "Somebody trashed Emelie Marin's flat. Took the coins. We were just going there to retrieve them."

Jack said nothing, shook his head.

"She's pretty shook. But we finally got a name, and we put out a BOLO on this Frank Danvers. Got a couple of witnesses who saw Nathaniel Sinquah get into a car with Danvers driving."

"No shit."

"Yep, shit. And more of it. Danvers' girlfriend reported him missing this morning."

"Sounds like he's your guy."

Matt paused before responding. "Can't be sure, just yet. You, uh, wanna come down here and get this little gal? She's pretty torn up. Can't go back to her place. Is Maddie coming down anytime soon? Maybe they could hang together."

"Maddie won't be coming down anytime soon. No. But I'll come down there and talk to Em. Where is she, exactly?"

"Right now, she's sitting with Rick Cordell."

"Okay."

"So, Mr. Farralone used to live here?" Emelie asked, turning a slow circle in the middle of the living room. "He's such a nice man. And his wife. Have you known them long?"

"Matt, I've known for many years. He used to be a private attorney. His bucks-up grandfather left him a bunch of cash and a mansion, but then he took the job at the D.A.'s office out of boredom. He also wanted to get more exposure to criminal law. I don't think he'll be there long. Doesn't like the hours."

"I don't blame him. I sensed something about him. He is uncomfortable about the lighthouse connection."

"You're spot on with that. He and Bec had a sort of... bad experience up north with an abandoned lighthouse. Claimed it was haunted. I don't put much stock in it, but they were deeply affected."

Emelie looked down, whet her lips. "Someone important died in the lighthouse."

"They tell you that? You want a soda or something?"

"No. No soda. And no, they didn't tell me. I just felt it when Rebecca touched my arm. It's deep. With both of them."

"Oh, yeah? Are you a psychic or something?"

"As a matter of fact, yes."

Jack smiled, shook his head. "I'm sorry, I don't have much experience with that. I think people believe what they want to believe, and sometimes it's true, and sometimes, well..."

"I can show you."

"Show me what?"

"I'm very sensitive right now. It's because of Nate. He connected me, somehow. Here, sit down and give me your hand."

"Naw, that's okay."

"Afraid?"

"Afraid of what? That you'll tell my fortune? Tell how I might die someday?"

"No. Not like that."

Jack considered, then sat down. Emelie joined him, and Jack turned his hand palm up. "Okay, but I really don't want to disappoint you."

"You won't. Trust me." Emelie pressed Jack's hand between both of hers and closed her eyes. Warmth preceded the vision.

"Should I close my eyes, or what?"

"No. Unless you want to." Emelie smiled. She saw, through Jack's eyes, a stunning woman in white, standing in brilliant sunlight. "Madeleine was a beautiful bride." The pictures changed, floating in and out of Emelie's internal vision. Babies born, children growing; job changes; scenery that moved from warm beaches to cold forests. "You have something in your pocket that she recently touched. May I have it?"

Frowning, Jack pulled Maddie's car key fob from his jacket and pressed it into Emelie's hand. "She was a beautiful bride. An easy assumption."

Emelie layered the fob between her hand and Jack's. "She didn't really want to go. She almost turned back when she got to San Francisco. A boy, Duncan, I think, won't talk to her. A little girl with blonde curls is crying." Emelie paused, letting the scenes unfold. "Your wife has been ill. She didn't want you to know. She is taking some kind of pills to help her to... to... concentrate, but she can't control her negativity. The doctor won't... give her any more pills, so

109

she thinks maybe in Europe she can get more..."

Incredulous, Jack pulled his hand away. "Are you crazy? Maddie, an addict? That's—that's ridiculous. She's a responsible, solid, good wife and mother. She knows better. You got something wrong here, Em."

Emelie opened her eyes. "She loves you with all her heart. She didn't mean to hurt you. She is visiting a man in prison, though."

"Thomas. How did you know about him? I never said anything." Jack stood and paced to the picture window. "Was there anything else?"

"She is grasping a silver necklace inside her shirt. It is some kind of intricate symbol. You gave it to her."

Jack spun around, once again stunned beyond belief.

Chapter 14

November 10 – Saturday

Jack leaned back in his seat and closed his eyes. Having Matt drive him down to West L.A. was the best decision he'd made all week. Plus an extra pair of eyes wasn't a bad idea, either. With Rebecca keeping an eye on Emelie and Todd off with old friends at the movies, Jack could take the time to pursue at least one of his issues.

The storage unit was only half-full. After his father had passed and his mother moved into the assisted living home, Jack and Sean had managed to clear out a lot of unnecessary junk; the accrual of a fifty-plus year marriage. He didn't exactly know what he hoped to find. Maybe proof, or even the strong suggestion, that the Japanese girl was a myth; that the Hopi woman was some kind of bizarre friendship.

"Right," Jack muttered, shifting his position. Could he be so lucky? That something would go right, for once?

"You say something?" Matt asked, glancing over.

"No. No, just the inane ramblings of a troubled mind."

"Well, look at it this way. If there were other women, at least neither of them came forward to demand money, right? Unless you think this Nate Sinquah wants something."

"No, I don't get that impression from his girlfriend. Hell, if I were him, I'd want some answers. I want the same answers, actually. It's tough when you didn't really know your own dad very well, you know?"

"Yeah. I knew my dad. But he died at his desk. It was my granddad that threw me for a loop. And my poor old Uncle Russ. Great-uncle, in reality. All those years, him, a murderer, right under our noses. And granddad knew it."

Jack nodded. "That's right. That was a blow-mind. How's your uncle doing, anyway?"

Matt shrugged, turned into the storage facility and punched in the security code at the gate. "He's still alive."

Once Jack had opened the unit, the two set about sifting through boxes of letters, albums and keepsakes. Jack had to force himself not to pause over old report cards and snapshots. "Here's a gem: me, Sean and Case on my twenty-first birthday. Man, were we sauced. Look at our noses! Those were the days, as they say. My friend."

"We thought they'd never end..." Matt sang, holding up an envelope to the light. "I shoulda been there."

"Hadn't met you yet, had I?"

"Mmm... Not sure. What about this?" He handed a small, yellowed photograph to Jack. "Looks like a wartime shot."

Jack took the small, square picture and squinted. Two G.I.s, flanking a young, Japanese girl. A very beautiful girl. One of the soldiers was undoubtedly Angus McKenzie. The other one had his arm around the girl's waist. Angus stood slightly apart.

"There. There! Damn! She wasn't his girl! Clearly, she's with this other guy. Is he Japanese, too?" Jack handed the photo back to Matt.

"A Japanese soldier in the American Army? I think not, amigo. No, he looks... Hard to tell. It's dark and blurry. Maybe Pacific Islander? Or... Mexican?" Matt turned the snapshot over. "Only a date, in pencil. 'February 22, 1942'."

"Dad shipped out around March 5th, I believe. Wow. This stuff is more intriguing than I thought. So he goes off to France with a picture of this chick in his wallet. But, she's with this other dude. Is that what you get?"

Matt chuckled, shook his head. "Can you imagine Duncan one day trying to unravel all your previous relationships? Or better, Davey?"

"You think?" Jack frowned. "Naw, they already know all about Duncan's mom and me. And Todd's dad." The thought of Maddie and Thomas brought a fresh stab of pain and Matt nodded.

"Have you heard from her?"

"Just a text message when they got there. We'll talk eventually. When she's ready. I'm gonna wait this out."

Matt said nothing, continuing his search through a box that said, simply, "Angus" on the side. Eventually, he replaced the lid. "Nothing else in there of interest. You got anything?"

"Nope. There's just that one album there I want to look at." Matt handed Jack the photo album to which he pointed, and Jack began to turn the pages. "Wedding photos. I just want to see if anyone is in the background."

While Jack examined his parents' wedding album, Matt began restacking and neatening the boxes. As he set aside the last carton, his phone chirped and he stepped outside the unit to answer. Jack leaned in close to the pages, scrutinizing the few people who'd attended the small, military-style wedding. No one person stood out. He closed the book with a sigh and slipped it back into the last open carton just as Matt reappeared, pocketing his phone.

"News?"

"Not good news, I'm afraid. The cops just found Frank Danvers. Shot to death in a warehouse in San Pedro."

Horrified, Jack stood up. "What? Really? Jesus. Any sign of Nate?"

"No, but there is blood at the scene that appears to belong to someone other than the vic."

Jack blew out a breath and placed his hand on his forehead. "That's, that's just... "

"Might not be his, Jack. Could be any number of scenarios. The boys are looking for possible witnesses, taking samples, checking for local camera footage. You know. The usual."

By the time the two men had returned to the Hollywood Hills house, Matt had more intel. "The driver of a delivery van reported a suspicious smell coming from the warehouse near where he parked. He reported it and that's how our guys got the tip. Danvers had been dead a couple of days. M.E. says he bled out."

Jack grimaced and pulled two beers from his refrigerator, handing one to Matt. "I need to like, just rewind this week, dude. This is God-awful. How did I get so wrapped up in all this? I'm supposed to start a new job in a couple of days. My wife is, Jesus knows where in France, my step-son is now a loose cannon with a set of car keys. I've adopted an unknown, maybe-dead guy as my maybe-little-brother, and I'm reeling from the possibility that my dad had at least one or two lovers. And I feel so God-damned helpless!" Jack threw his hands into the air in frustration just as the front door opened.

"We're back!" Rebecca called out, preceding Emelie into the room. "Matt. I finally found the perfect desk lamp. This great little shop on Melrose—"

"Bec. Bec. Listen. We have news."

"Oh, no. What?"

Emelie paused, her jacket half-off. "Did they find Nate?"

"No. But they did find Frank Danvers," Jack began.

"Did he say where Nate is?" Emelie demanded, tossing her coat onto the couch. "Is he all right?"

Jack licked his lips, momentarily at a loss. Matt placed a hand on Emelie's shoulder. "Danvers is dead, Miss Marin. Nate was not with him."

Emelie's face went ashen. "Dead? How?"

"He was shot in the stomach at close range. He was already dead when our guys got there."

"Oh." Emelie sank down onto a chair. "So that's it. No

more leads. He is dead and that's it."

No one spoke for a moment. Jack took a long draught of beer and put the bottle on the counter. "Tell her the rest."

Matt frowned. "It might mean nothing."

"Tell her."

"We found other blood at the scene."

"And only one guy left. A dead guy."

"Well, that's actually better than it could be," Matt reminded her. "And it's more than we had to go on before."

"But it seems to me, we still have nothing."

"I'm afraid I'm gonna have to ask you to turn over Nate's belongings. Any papers, notes, Daytimers, photos, etc." Matt responded. "I can drive you back over to your apartment if you'd like."

"So it's real, now, is it? Now they're finally taking notice? Now that someone is dead?"

Jack went to Emelie and took both her hands. "I'll take you over there. And we should get in touch with his family back in Arizona. He has family, right?"

Emelie nodded. "His father, um, grandmother...he has an uncle and a cousin, too." Emelie recalled the night Nate had told her about them. The night of meteors and memories.

"His grandmother. Is it his father's mother?" Jack asked.

"No, I believe she's his mother's mom."

Jack tilted his head. "Wouldn't she know about his mother's...relationships?"

"She's very old. Remember, they are Hopi. They have different customs and values than we do. It might not be okay for him to delve."

"Well, you'd think some things...never mind." *I'm not Hopi; I won't hesitate to ask the old lady if it comes to that.*

Emelie pulled the blankets up to her ear and drew up her knees. Jack's house was chilly. In the darkness, she could hear the muffled sound of Jack and Todd talking quietly in the next room, which she supposed was Todd's.

Recalling the day, Emelie felt better than she had upon wakening that morning. Nate was alive. He was hurting, he was cold, he was scared—but he wasn't dead. She couldn't explain to Jack how she knew, because Jack's skepticism prevented his acceptance and the poor man was already dealing with so much. Too much. But Emelie knew, when she held the backpack against her chest while carrying it to the car from the apartment. The vision wafted into her brain, so strong that she nearly fainted in the parking lot.

"Whoa, there!" Jack had hollered, quickly coming to her aid as her knees buckled. Eyes closed, Emelie let Jack guide her to the car and help her into the passenger seat. Still, the scene remained clear in her mind. Nate was somewhere dark, and very cold. His leg was injured in some way, and he was hungry and weak. He was thinking of her. There were sounds rushing nearby, as if he were sitting in traffic on some freeway; as if he were in the eye of a storm, with wind blowing gales around him.

Why hadn't the backpack conjured for her before? She'd touched it several times, even hauled it into the Starbuck's the day she'd met Jack. Why now?

Emelie reached for the extra pillow on the bed and hugged it to her chest. The fact that Nate was still alive was enough, for now. She could go to sleep knowing that there was still a chance she'd get him back.

Chapter 15

November 10 - Saturday, Late

Matt called a meeting. Nobody seemed to mind, despite the late hour. Rick, Chuck, and Chuck's rookie partner, Will, sat in Matt's office, a near-empty pizza box in the middle of the small conference table.

"Again. We're missing something."

"Okay. This lady says she saw the car, a Ford Taurus—she called it 'old' but couldn't really determine the year—pulled up in the lot next to the Cabrillo Beach Yacht Club. She says Danvers was driving and Sinquah got into the passenger side. That's here," Matt said, his laser pointing to a map displayed by an overhead projector, "on 22nd. This was around 4 P.M. Tuesday. The security cam in the restaurant next door catches a glimpse of this same car with two occupants heading south. Next, we got a UPS driver calling in gunshots from here. Warehouse on Earle Street, Wednesday. After he's seen not two, but three guys go inside."

"Which we didn't follow up on, correct?" Chuck asked.

Matt lifted his chin, looked away. "Apparently there was a lot going on that day. A commemorative celebration or something down by the Iowa."

"Three guys?" Will asked.

"He returns a couple of days later and now he smells the corpse, so he calls again. This time, we get him in here, he identifies photos Danvers and Sinquah, and a third man. You have the composites in front of you. Officers respond and find Danvers, dead. Blood of another guy. Bullet casings, .38 caliber."

"Has Miss Marin seen the composite?" Rick asked.

"No. Not yet. We'll get her back in here tomorrow."

"Can we match the other victim's blood to Sinquah?" Will asked, clearing his throat and moving in his seat.

Rick looked over at the kid, sighed. "Not yet. We're trying to locate his family in Arizona. We don't have a lot to go on. No phone numbers; they're Indians. Most of 'em live on a reservation, if you can believe that."

Matt nodded. "We do have a lead. Emelie called me this evening and said she remembered that Nate worked in a school. There aren't many, we're running them down now. As a school employee, they would have records of family members, references, the like."

"I hate this." Chuck stood up, stared at the projected map. "If there's blood, but no body, it's likely the kid was still alive when he was taken away from the warehouse. If it's Sinquah that's bleeding, of course. If he was dead, the perp would have just left him there with Danvers. So let's say it's about these coins. They abduct Sinquah and demand the coins. He refuses to give them up. There's an argument. Somehow, Danvers is shot. The unsub takes Sinquah, maybe back to the apartment, to get the coins. He gets the coins, so now has no use for Sinquah."

"*Unsub*? Really? You've been watching too much *Criminal Minds*. But look, if Nate was at the apartment, wouldn't there be blood?" Rick tossed his pen down on the desk. "Why drag him around? Why not just finish the job, leave him there?"

"This tells me the *bad* guy—does that work for ya?—doesn't really want to kill. Danvers wasn't shot in such a way as to kill him immediately. If you're gonna kill a guy, shoot him in the head or the heart. Not the spleen." Chuck sat back down, began to doodle with his pen.

Rick shook his head. "I don't know. He left the guy to die."

"Maybe. Maybe not," Matt said. "Maybe he went for help, but Danvers died before he could get back. Plus, he's dragging around a wounded guy at the same time."

"I think you're being too generous. This guy is a killer. Or someone completely willing to kill in order to get a seven million dollar coin he can only sell overseas," Rick said.

"We could be looking at this all wrong," Will spoke up. "What if the blood is not Sinquah's? What if it belongs to the other guy? Sinquah shot Danvers and took off with the other guy, stopped at the apartment to get the coins and left the bleeding guy in the car? Or... Danvers shot Guy #3, and Sinquah shot Danvers. Maybe Guy #3 is Sinquah's pal?"

All eyes were on Will as the others digested his theory. Finally, Rick shook his head. "No. Not going for that. And right now, I'm even wondering if any of them stole those damned coins. Could have been someone else entirely. That could be why Sinquah hasn't been dumped yet."

Matt's eyebrows lifted and he tilted his head. "You could have something there. A good reason why the unsub still has Sinquah—he doesn't have the coins, yet. But what gets me is, no ransom call, no contact with Emmie or, well, I guess there isn't anyone else to contact."

"Did we find the Taurus?" Rick asked.

"Got a BOLO out, no sighting yet. Has to be a second car, too, where they probably met Guy #3." Chuck yawned. "I'm fried, guys. Let's sleep on this, get the little gal back in here tomorrow, and see what's cookin' on the reservation. Maybe something else will pop."

Once, in the fifth grade, Nate had thrown up in the classroom. His mother had tried to keep him home that day, worried that he might become sick at school after having spent the night running back and forth between the bedroom and the bathroom. The kids stared, some of them smiling, some of them pale-faced in sympathy. Nate quietly and quickly cleaned up the mess himself before heading down to what the school generously called the "nurse's office." The nurse, who also ran the cafeteria and supervised the playground, had sent him home.

Now, as he lay on the icy floor in the dark, Nate feared he'd throw up here, unable to get out of his own way. Unable to clean up the vomit from around his face. He lay still, hoping the queasiness would pass. What worried him more was the probable cause of the nausea: the gunshot wound in his leg had stopped bleeding but was swelling and likely infected. Too weak to reach the wound with his hand, Nate could only guess at its condition.

The last forty-eight hours seemed like a week. He thought about Emelie, how worried she'd become when he was late coming home before. By now, she was probably a basket case. He smiled; ah, Emelie. Her concern could only mean one thing—that she cared about him. Maybe not as much as he cared about her, but certainly enough to give him hope. Hope! Her nickname for him. Hope. Stupid. There wasn't much of that going around at the moment; he couldn't get up, couldn't call for help. Frank was likely dead. Frank, the guy he couldn't stand to be around another minute, had taken a bullet for him. Jumped right in the way to push him aside when Wayne Dodge had leveled his .38 at Nate. In his fury over this stark injustice, Nate had charged Dodge and was rewarded with his own slug, buried deep in his thigh.

Nate shook his head at the memory, and the movement enhanced his nausea. He wondered where Dodge was now, if he'd ever come back or if he just expected Nate to die, alone, in this cold and lonely place. Like Frank. Frank had only wanted to get a beer; neither of them had expected to see the big man walk into the bar moments after they were seated. Nate thought it odd, at the time, for Dodge to show up like that, and at first suspected it was a plan between them. When they drove to the warehouse and Dodge demanded the whereabouts of the coins, Nate turned to Frank, who'd merely shrugged. It wasn't until Dodge pulled the trigger and Frank went down that Nate realized it was Dodge all along. He must have followed them to the bar. But how could Dodge have known about the coins?

What did it matter, now? No one knew he was here, no one knew about Frank or the warehouse or all the blood. The memory sparked a fresh wave of delirium.

The blood. Emelie can't see me like this! I have to clean this up. She will be so disappointed in me and the mess I have made. I will clean this up and go down to the nurse.

November 11 — Sunday,

Emelie toyed with the charms hanging from her purse strap. One, a butterfly, was her favorite. The other, a quill pen and ink jar, only stayed on because her father had given it to her. It was supposed to represent her ultimate collegiate success.

"Have you remembered anyone else who might know about the coins?" Rick Cordell was asking, leaning down to peer into her downcast face.

"I don't know who Nate might have told. Together, we took the coins to Abe's shop. He was very interested in the coins. He wanted us to come back and let him buy them. Oh! And he has a son. The son was there, he saw the coins. He came out to the car as we were leaving."

"Why?"

"We dropped the card with the phone number on it."

"Did you ever see this Abe or his son again?"

"No."

"So, no one else."

"No."

"Do you recognize either of these men?"

Emelie stared at the two pictures, one taken from a

California Drivers License and the other an artist's composite.

"No. I never met either of them. Is one of them Frank?"

Rick placed the photos on the table in front of Emelie and pointed at the first one. "Him. Frank Danvers. The other guy is unknown."

Emelie looked again. "Nate didn't like Frank. How is this other guy involved in this?"

"Witnesses put the three together in a San Pedro bar the afternoon Nate went missing. The delivery guy saw him go into the warehouse with Nate and Danvers. We're thinking he might be the shooter. But we're not ruling out Danvers. He might be in with this other guy. We know he has a handgun permit, and he was also in financial trouble."

A chill brought goose bumps to Emelie's skin. *Shooter. Frank Danvers is dead.* The mention of financial trouble also brought to mind someone else, someone who knew about the coins but couldn't possibly have had anything to do with their disappearance. Angela didn't need any more trouble in her life, and Emelie couldn't see the point of involving her. Still...whoever had "tossed" the apartment had known all the right places to look. All the places Angela had suggested she hide the coins. All except one, the place Emelie had kept a secret from everyone.

"Can I go, now, please?" Emelie asked, watching Rick hobble to the file cabinet and back.

"Sure. In just a few. I need your signature on this report." He sat down and handed Emelie his pen. Emelie stared at the report, momentarily distracted by the pen in her hand.

"Is this your pen?" she asked.

"Yeah. Nice, isn't it? The guys got it for me when I, you know, got out of the hospital."

The pen was black and gold, and glossy. It warmed in her hand and she closed her eyes. "Your back is healing,"

Emelie said. "You don't need the surgery. As soon as you can feel it, you need to start exercising."

"What the—? You're mistaken, missy. Doc says it's permanent damage, and the surgery has only a 15% chance of fixing things."

Emelie opened her eyes and smiled. "At least postpone it. Give it time to fix itself. You don't have to believe me, but don't get all cut up just yet."

Rick frowned. "Uh, yeah. Right. Just sign, Miss Marin."

Emelie drove from the precinct to Mystic Moves, which was, of course, now closed. Angela lived upstairs, in the loft, with her sister. Angela looked surprised when she saw Emelie at her door.

"Sure, come on in. I'm just packing to go, you know. You want a soda or something?"

"No. I just wanted to stop by and tell you, well, the coins, they were stolen."

"What? Really? How did that happen?"

Emelie put her purse down on the couch, then sat down beside it. "I don't know. I mean, someone broke in, took them all. I'm just sick about it. Nate's missing, he may have been shot, then I come home and my place has been bugled."

"You mean burgled. Wow. That's awful. No word on Nate, yet?"

"No."

"You think it's the same gig? Nate's disappearance and the theft?"

"Well, it seems likely, don't you think? Except that, if they got the coins, why haven't they sent Nate back to me?" Emelie's eyes began to fill with tears. Angela sat down beside her.

"Aw, hon. He's probably okay. You'll see. Say, maybe he got smacked on the noggin, and now he has amnesia!"

Emelie looked at Angela, wondering if all those blonde

jokes were for real. Clearly, Angela had been watching too many crime dramas.

"I guess that's possible," she said at last.

Angela stood and wandered over to the kitchenette. "So...did they get all five coins?"

"Yes. They are all gone. Even the Double Eagle."

"Did you use the places I told you? The toilet tank and the kitchen light fixture?"

Emelie nodded. "And two in the freezer. They got them all."

"And where was the fifth one, again?" Angela asked.

"Um, it was under the mattress. Maybe I'd better look again, to see if it's really gone. I was so upset, you know, I let the cops look. But on second thought, I didn't really look closely under that mattress. I think I just assumed since the others were all gone, it was gone, too."

"Right." Angela stood in front of Emelie now, stuffing her hands into the pockets of her jeans. "So, what you up to the rest of the day?"

Emelie picked up her bag. "It's hard to do anything until I know Nate is safe. But I have to stop at the market for coffee and eggs. The people are supposed to be fixing my door this afternoon, so maybe I'll kill a few hours somewhere. I don't want to go there too soon. Feels so empty now."

"I completely understand." Angela walked toward the front door as Emelie stood to go. "I'll give you a call before I leave town, to say goodbye."

"That would be good. Thanks, Ang. You've been such a good friend."

Angela looked away, and Emelie thought she heard a brief cough.

Once in her car, Emelie dialed Rick Cordell's cell. "Can you meet me at my apartment? Now?"

Abe and his son Levi weren't thieves. Rick slipped the report on the coin dealer back into the folder. First off, they didn't need the money. Second, both had ironclad alibis. The son was a bit squirrelly, and Rick didn't trust him, but he also felt in his gut that the pair was not involved in the theft of Emelie and Nate's gold coins.

As he made his way down 20th Street, Rick recalled Emelie's prediction about his injury healing. As much as he held such mysticism in contempt, he secretly hoped she was right. The girl did have something about her, and he also hoped her "feeling" that Nate Sinquah was still alive would prove true. He parked the car and labored to get out. She was waiting for him at the bottom of the stairs.

"Sorry we don't have an elevator," she murmured, climbing the steps alongside Rick in case he needed help.

"Hey. I'm cool."

Emelie laughed. "Yup, you're cool, Detective Cordell."

"What's this all about, anyway?"

"I just want you to hide with me for a while."

Once inside the small apartment, Emelie explained her unfortunate suspicions. "Angie is a good friend. But I think something's going on with her, something bad. She's nervous. She asked lots of questions. And she was particularly interested in the fifth coin."

"What about it? You said it was stolen along with the other four."

"No, I didn't. I just said it was missing. It's missing because I hid it. Angela knew where all the other coins were, but not the fifth. If I'm right, and I hope I am not, she or someone else will turn up here very soon to look for that last coin."

"So you lied before when I asked if anyone else knew about the coins."

Emelie shrugged. "I forgot. It didn't seem important, because she is a trusted friend. But she actually helped me find the hiding places. And she also has...financial difficulties."

Rick nodded. "So. Where do we hide?"

"In the bedroom closet. She's going to look under the mattress. If I'm right."

Rick set up a small webcam on the dresser and activated the interface on his phone. Emelie quickly dragged two kitchen chairs into the walk-in closet and they sat.

"You lock the door?"

"Actually, I did not. I don't relish having it repaired again. Hopefully, if they come, they'll just try the knob."

Rick nodded, sighed. "So, uh, that stuff you were saying about my leg. What makes you so sure?"

"Your pen. It showed me what was going on. It's like all these cells are busy, busy, busy, like little workers, all putting things back together." Emelie held up her hand. "I know, before you say, it's crazy. I've been considered certifiably crazy by all kinds of people, all my life. So you are completely allowed to think it, too." She giggled, shook her head. "I once got in a lot of trouble at school, because I sat in my teacher's chair and I discovered he was having an affair with the vice-principal. Couldn't keep a secret, and I told my friend, who told her mom."

"You sat in his chair, and what? You saw something on his desk?"

"No. I saw *him*, with her, in my head. I almost threw up."

"Hmm. That's interesting. So it was true? Why would you get in trouble?"

"They thought I'd been stalking him or spying on him."

"But you can't 'see' where Nate is?"

Emelie shook her head. "My connection with him is very weak, which makes me think he *is* very weak."

They only waited around twenty minutes before they heard muffled voices in the living room, a male and a female. Soon, Angela and a man entered the bedroom and appeared on the tiny iPhone screen. The two lifted the mattress and leaned it against the wall.

"Well, where the hell is it?" the man demanded.

"She said it might be here. She's upset. Her old man's gone rogue and she doesn't know which end is up."

"Damn it, Angela. We need that coin. Keep looking."

Rick drew his service revolver and pushed open the closet door. "Probably not necessary. The coin isn't there."

Angela shrieked and her companion put his hands up, all the while edging toward the bedroom door. "It's okay, officer. We were just trying to help Emelie out. She's distraught, you know, and she told Ang here she needed help to find the coin. We'll just head out."

"I think not," Chuck Beeman said from the doorway. "I also think Miss Marin would say this is a B&E, not a helpful search."

Emelie emerged from the closet. "Detective Beeman?"

"Thought it might be prudent to have a little backup," Rick said, holding his gun steady as Chuck moved into the room.

Emelie turned toward the two who now held their hands over their heads. "Angie, why did you do this to me?"

Her friend and former employer wept as she was being handcuffed. "I'm sorry, Em. Really. I had no choice," she explained, then looked toward the man also being cuffed by Chuck.

"No choice," Rick said. "That's what they all say."

Chapter 16

"Timothy Cole," read the caller I.D. on Jack's phone. With a heavy sigh, Jack answered.

"I'm sorry I've been missing your calls," he said, squeezing his eyes shut over his blatant lie.

"No worries, dude. I'm calling to tell you that Shannon's mother is ill and she's postponed the vid for a month or so. Hope you're not too disappointed."

"Disappointed? Hell, no. That's fine. I mean, I'm sorry about her mom. Truly. But this might work out better for me in the long run."

"Okay, great. You take care, Jack. I'll call you in a couple of weeks."

"Yes." Jack pumped his fist after hanging up. "I need this time," he muttered. He sat down at the kitchen table and rubbed his temples. All this crap had to end, and soon, or he would lose his mind.

He made himself a sandwich and stood to eat it in front of the dining room windows, which offered a view of the Hollywood Hills to the west. He'd opened one of the windows, the weather being unseasonably warm for November. He wondered if Maddie would be home before Thanksgiving. She always roasted a bird and made stuffing, green bean casserole and cranberries. Maybe they would talk on the phone. Maybe he could coax her into telling him the secret about the pills.

Must prioritize. With so much happening, he had to let go of some things while focusing on the most important. Clearly, Nate Sinquah's whereabouts posed the biggest problem, but it was out of Jack's hands. Maddie's impromptu trip to France was done and he couldn't do anything about that, either. The ball was in her court; he could only wait for her to come around. In the meantime, he could see to Emelie's comfort and help where he could. He glanced at the file on his table, a collection of papers and letters he'd brought from the storage unit. Gus's discharge papers, a couple of property deeds, and Gus and Lucille's marriage certificate. The photo was in there, too.

Jack rummaged through a kitchen drawer where he'd seen a small magnifying glass. It wasn't very strong, more like a cereal box toy, but Jack bent over the photo with the lens and scrutinized the people in it. His dad was a handsome soldier, with a wide grin and a trim mustache. The Asian girl had long, black tresses—assumed black, as the photo was a pre-Kodacolor shot—and a demure smile. The other man was definitely an ethnic sort, but with the film grain and poor focus, his features were hazy. Both men wore Garrison caps pulled down onto their foreheads.

Jack shook his head slowly. Who were these bright young men? Most importantly, who was Angus McKenzie? Certainly not only the man who once used his belt on his two mischievous sons. Not the guy who drank himself stupid four out of five nights a week. This happy, friendly looking G.I., the same who once decked a neighbor over a political joke about President Nixon?

"Unreal," Jack muttered, carefully turning the pages over one by one. Here, a record of Gus McKenzie's World War II service to the Army of the United States. The 480th Anti-Aircraft artillery battalion. The words stuck out as if printed in red, which they were not: England, France, Belgium and Germany. And Normandy. A soft whistle escaped Jack's lips. Why did he not know Gus had fought in some of the worst battles of WWII? Growing up in a world where someone else always put their lives on the line for freedom, Jack didn't have a clue about combat and he knew it. Too young for Vietnam, too busy for the Gulf War and

Desert Storm. But Gus had been out there. Crouched in the trenches, hoisting an M1, crawling through frozen mud and praying his helmet would protect him. Wishing he was safe and warm at home. Carrying a talisman, a photograph of someone back there he could focus on during the darkest moments of the war. Who was she? His buddy's girl?

The questions dug at him, burned within like a creeping, acidic, swelling bug. Why did it matter so much? It had started with Nate's mother's letters. Yet Tiponi Honanie was not even close to the Asian girl—not in looks, age, or location. Two completely unrelated women, part of his father's secret life. Not unexpectedly, his own mother's face appeared in his mind. Dear Lucille Ellen McKenzie lay in a soft bed within a sunny, flowery bedroom, smiling at her own secret thoughts, locked away by the unfairest of memory thieves. Gus even mentioned her in one of the letters, something about hiding from her the fact that he was sending money to another woman.

Jack huffed out a breath. All these years, his father had participated in a betrayal. Jack tried to remember Gus's habits, his travels, over the years. Had he received suspicious phone calls? Made unexplained or poorly justified trips? *Hell; I was playing hockey, reading Cliff's Notes and planning my escape. All I saw was a drunken guy on a couch.* Now, Jack wondered if the women, one or the other or both, contributed to that drinking. Had Dad made regrettable mistakes?

Jack slammed the file closed and tossed it into the open kitchen drawer along with the magnifying glass. If he didn't get away from this stuff, he'd end up the drunken guy on the couch himself.

Emelie accepted Jack's invitation to spend another night at his house. After witnessing her friend's betrayal and subsequent arrest, she couldn't imagine being able to sleep there again, at least not tonight. But after tossing for forty-five minutes, Emelie got up and wandered upstairs to the living room where Jack sat, staring at the television.

"You can't sleep either?" she asked, sitting on the edge of the couch.

"Naw. I think I had too much caffeine today. You?"

"Too much of everything. Mind if I join you?"

"'Course not."

Jay Leno entertained them for a while, but when the grunge-revival-band-of-the-month came on, Jack switched the channel. Infomercials permeated the airwaves.

"How are you doing? Any more...visions?"

Emelie shook her head. "But I still believe he's alive."

Jack nodded. He was quiet, hesitant, but Emelie already knew what was on his mind. She waited until he finally found the words.

"That thing you did. With Maddie's keys. Is it for real?"

Emelie smiled. "It's very real, to me. I've been doing it since I was six. It seems to come and go. I can't make it happen, you know."

"What triggers it? Any idea?"

"Emotion, mostly. Strong emotion. The way I see it, objects have lives, sort of. They are made up of atoms and molecules and sometimes cells, just like us. They absorb energy from living things. They absorb things like DNA, which can be proven, right? So Nate carries this backpack with him everywhere, wears it, puts his hands inside it, puts possessions inside it. He shares some of his energy with it. Now, here's where it gets weird, Jack. If that's true, then why can't that energy continue to communicate with his other energy, the part that he still has with him? Like bees all communicate, even when they're apart."

Jack squinted, stared hard at Emelie. She reached across to him and covered his hand with her own. "I don't expect you to believe or accept this. I know it's a lot. When I held

Maddie's key fob, some of her energy was still connected to it. I saw her in my mind. Clear as if I was right there with her. She had her hair in a braid, twisted up. She was upset, angry with herself. I don't know what it's about. The children around her were fuzzy, but I think there were three."

"So, it was her emotion that created the connection? Not yours?"

"Right. That's why it doesn't always work. Nate's backpack started working for me because he...woke up. He is in distress. He is thinking about me." Emelie paused when her voice began to quiver. "But I can't see where he is. I think it is because...he doesn't know where he is."

Now it was Jack's turn to take Emelie's hand, sandwiched between his own. "We *will* find him, Emmie. And I'm sorry if I insulted you before. I think maybe you really do have a gift. I have a question, a favor, really. You don't have to do it if you don't want to."

"Jack, I am already indebted to you for all of your kindness. You didn't have to get involved with all this. My own father turned his back on me. What is it that I can do?"

Jack got up and went to the coat closet. He returned with a brown leather bomber-style jacket. "This belonged to Gus, my dad. I was wondering...does that trick work with dead people? Or past events?"

Emelie smiled. "Remember what I said about energy? One thing I did learn in that stupid school Papa sent me to is that energy never really goes away. It's only converted into some other form of energy. When people die, their bodies, well, they are no longer useful, but the soul—the energy—stays around forever. You want me to try to connect with your father through his coat?"

"It's probably a stupid idea."

"Not stupid at all. But I have one request. That you put on the jacket. I think the energy will flow through you."

Nate stirred, tried to open his eyes but they wouldn't budge. The darkness had come again. He had only moments of clarity, here and there. The rest of the time was spent either unconscious or hallucinating. How long had he been laying there, on his back, the ground cold and hard beneath him? What made the strange sounds around him, the rushing, the horns, the roar? Why couldn't he move his legs?

Maybe he was in the warehouse. Maybe Frank lay nearby, dead and decaying. The sounds of traffic rushing by outside, people not knowing, not caring? Maybe Emelie was out there, too, cruising by, looking for him. Or maybe not. She might have just moved on by now. After all, he'd been gone...how long? Weeks? A month? Nate had no clue. No point of reference, since there was no way he could have kept track of the number of times the rectangles above had glowed yellow.

Nate licked his lips but found no moisture. He tried to call out, but found no sound. Tried to move his head but only succeeded in imagining the movement. Maybe he was already dead. Dead like Frank. Dead like Mom. Dead like Gus McKenzie.

Gus. The thought of the late stranger, the letter writer, tilted his brain. Fog appeared in his mind, puffy, swirling, surreal, with brief glimpses of faces coming into focus and then disappearing. When the fog cleared, Nate took in a surprised gasp. He was sitting in a car, a convertible, in what appeared to be a drive-in restaurant. The kind with car hops and hook-on food trays. He looked over at the driver, a young man beckoning to an approaching waitress. Nate looked around, then down at the dark woolen pants he wore. There was no gunshot wound, not even a smear of tell-tale blood. What was going on? The driver turned to him grinning. Was it...Jack McKenzie? How could that be? He wanted to ask, wanted to reach out and touch the man, or the car, or anything, but could not. Instead, he could only watch from within as his companion flirted with the server. After observing for a few minutes, Nate realized that the man behind the steering wheel was not Jack after all; rather, a much, much younger Angus McKenzie.

Jack squirmed, twitched, jerked. Emelie watched the movement going on behind his closed eyelids. Clearly, the connection had been made. Jack appeared to be sleeping but was seeing someone, somewhere. Hopefully, his father. Emelie kept her eyes closed, and while she felt the energy flow through her, her glimpses of Jack's journey were fleeting and vague. Still, she maintained her gentle grasp of Jack's hand as she sat beside him on the couch. She wished she could be there, live-time, in his mind. Because unbeknownst to Jack, Emelie had slipped Nate's turquoise necklace and one his mother's letters into the pocket of Gus's bomber jacket. Just in case.

Chapter 17

February, 1942 - Los Angeles, California.

Gus McKenzie edged the nose of the '39 Oldsmobile up to the post in front of the drive-in, shifted into park and shut off the engine. He leaned his head back and stared up at the stars.

"Ah. Great night, isn't it?"

"It's February. It's cold. You're crazy to put the top down." Cheveyo Honanie shook his head. "Glad I wore my uniform."

"Wait'll you see this carhop. I think her name is Alice. She'll warm you up with just a look." Gus jabbed at his friend's shoulder.

Cheveyo grinned and looked away, an unshared thought obvious on his face.

"What? You already met her or something?"

"Nope. Nothing like that." Gus frowned, then brightened as a pretty redhead approached his side of the car.

"Need menus, boys?"

"Uh, no. Burgers and fries. That okay with you, Chev?"

"And Pepsi, please."

"Make it two, dollface. Hey, when you gettin' off work?" Gus wrapped his fingers lightly around the waitress's wrist.

"Past your bedtime, soldier. But thanks."

Gus couldn't help the blush that spread across his face as the woman sashayed back to the restaurant. What a looker. Tearing his eyes away from her retreating back, he turned to Cheveyo. "So what's the matter with you? You don't even try."

"I don't need to try."

"What's that supposed to mean. You got girls falling at your feet?"

"Only one."

Now Gus narrowed his eyes. "You holdin' out on me? You got a girl and didn't say nothin'?"

Cheveyo looked down, smiled. "You might say."

"Might say what? Listen, stop playing games. Tell me about her! Where'd you meet her, what does she look like, you know..."

"Okay, but you gotta promise you won't say anything."

"About what?"

"About her. To anyone."

"Ah, secret, huh?"

"Sort of." Cheveyo sighed, took his own look at the sparkling night sky. "She's beautiful. Skin like silk. Long, shining black hair. Dark eyes."

"Well except for the silky skin part, she looks like you, before Uncle Sam lowered your ears."

"Oh, no. She's...she's nothing like me. I mean, she's not Hopi. Not Indian. She's like a porcelain flower."

Gus looked from Cheveyo to the brightly lit restaurant. "Sounds like a real prize. Why the secrecy? You steal her from another guy?"

"Nothing like that. You promise?"

"Sure. Of course. We're buddies, right? Damn. I've known you all my life, Injun. What could be so bad?"

Cheveyo licked his lips, then pushed back an imaginary shock of bangs from his forehead. "Well, she, uh, she's... Japanese."

Gus felt his eyes widen involuntarily as his face began to heat up. "A Jap? Oh, Jesus, Chev. Oh. Crap. You're kidding, right?"

"Would I kid about a thing like that? Gus, she's the most wonderful thing that's ever happened to me. I swear. She's really Japanese-American. They call it nisei. Born here! She says the Pledge and everything. Her mom's dead, she lives with her dad down near San Pedro. He's a doc."

The sounds from the other patrons in the drive-in grew louder in the silence that ensued between them. Gus rubbed a hand over his eyes, then his mouth, before taking a deep breath.

"You know FDR's going to round them all up. Ship them out of Los Angeles. They're building camps—"

"I know about the camps."

A high pitched peel of laughter from the next car sliced the air. Gus ran his fingers around the chrome horn ring inside the steering wheel.

"What's her name?"

"Annie. Anika. Watanabe."

Gus nodded slowly, unable to look his buddy in the face. "How old?"

"Eighteen. Well, almost. Christ, it's cold! Could you please put the top up?"

"Eighteen? Does her pop know she's dating a G.I.?"

"Sure he does. He's a solid citizen, too."

"Any family in Japan?" Gus asked, his voice lowered.

"Maybe, hell, I don't know. What does that matter? I only know that I love her. I love her and I have to find a way to keep her out of the camps!"

"Shh! You want everyone at Simon's to hear you? She'll be gone by morning." Gus started the engine and engaged the automatic convertible roof. "There. Satisfied? Jesus. A Jap."

"Look. You gotta meet her. You'll see. You'll see why."

"How can I do that? We can't be seen with...with...the enemy."

"She's not—"

"You know what I mean. How do you see her?"

Cheveyo paused, picked at a bit of lint on his olive-drab

wool trousers. After what appeared to be careful consideration, he turned back to Gus. "In her neighborhood, people are friendly. But I don't wear my uniform around there, you know."

"Well at least you're doing something smart, you crazy redskin. Okay. Okay. I guess I'd better meet this dame if she's got my best pal on the string."

February 24, 1942

Gus looked around, up and down the quiet residential street while waiting for Cheveyo and Anika to come out of the small stucco house on the corner. The sun was almost down, but he tugged on the bill of his baseball cap self-consciously, imagining that all the neighbors were peeking from behind their dark draperies. Surely the convertible with the nervous-looking Caucasian American kid behind the wheel didn't belong here. He was tempted to honk the horn, but didn't want to draw unwanted attention. Finally, the front door opened and the wood framed screen door swung wide.

A Japanese man emerged first, stepping down from the porch and then turning to watch Cheveyo and a girl Gus assumed was Anika joining him. Gus strained to hear their words from his vantage point across the street.

"Sayounara," the father said, bowing slightly toward Cheveyo, who bowed in return.

"Sayounara, sir."

Anita hugged her father quickly. *"Dewa mata, chichi.* I won't be late. You stay inside."

The father waived his hand as if dismissing his daughter's concerns. He watched from the porch as Anika and Cheveyo crossed the street. Gus quickly got out of the car.

"Nice to meet you, Anika."

"Annie."

"Well, hop in, Annie," Gus said, holding the passenger door open so that Anika could slide into the middle. Cheveyo followed as Gus trotted around the back of the car and quickly got into the driver's seat. "Where to, Chev?"

"Gee, I don't know. How about we get a nice steak?"

Gus watched with amusement as the couple across from him in the booth giggled and stared into each other's' eyes as if they were alone in the restaurant. Any doubts he might have had about Cheveyo's commitment to the little Jap girl evaporated as he found himself charmed by her sweet demeanor. She was every bit as beautiful as his buddy claimed.

The restaurant was fairly empty. The blackout order on Los Angeles had been lifted, but apparently most people chose to stay home. Ever since the news about the Japanese bombardment of Ellwood, on the coast north of Santa Barbara, Californians were a nervous lot; L.A. was sure to be bombed any day now.

A waitress appeared and broke into his thought.

"Jennie's gone on break. My name is Terri and I'll be serving you now. Some dessert?"

"Sorry. None for me. You two want something? A shake? A malted?" Crap. Gus didn't know if Japs ate that kind of stuff. He'd already felt stupid telling Anika how great the rice was when she'd gone on and ordered a baked potato.

"I'd like a chocolate malt," Anika said with a smile. The waitress opened her order pad but did not look at Anika. Instead, she addressed Cheveyo.

"Something sweet for you, hon?"

"Sure. A chocolate malt. Make it two," Cheveyo told the waitress.

"Okay, a chocolate malt. Got it."

"It was two malts," Cheveyo corrected with a smile. "You got her order, right?"

"Whose?"

"Hers. My friend."

Anika giggled softly and Cheveyo put his arm around her. Gus watched with guarded interest as the waitress turned to go.

"I don't serve Japs," she said over her shoulder.

Cheveyo's face contorted from his happy grin into a scowl. "What did you say, ma'am?"

The woman continued to walk toward the kitchen, and Cheveyo got to his feet. "Hey! I'm talking to you!"

Gus stood also and placed a hand on his friend's arm. The waitress spun and sauntered back to the table. Gus gave Cheveyo a look he hoped would tip him off.

"Yeah?" The waitress drawled.

"Uh, look," Gus began. "She's not a Jap. She's Chinese on her mother's side. Her dad's a pilot stationed out at Edwards. You don't want to go insulting the United States Army Air Corps, do you, sweetheart?"

The waitress lifted her eyebrows. "Well, uh, that's different. Sorry, miss. I'll get those malteds right up."

The ice cream went untouched after Anika's first small sip. Cheveyo didn't utter a word until they were back in the car.

"You should'na had to lie," he blurted. "There's no shame in being—"

"No shame, no. But that won't account for much when they're hauling her off to some secret desert prison," Gus asserted. "That broad would have likely called somebody after that little exchange. So just cool it."

Anika touched Gus's arm as he held firm to the steering wheel. "Thank you, Gus. I'm proud, but not so proud to let them take me away. If I need to be Chinese tonight in order to stay with Chevy, so be it."

The gentle feel of her small hand on his forearm made Gus forget the whole scene, forget where he was driving and even that his best friend was in the car. Cheveyo's voice brought him back.

"You're right. Of course. Gus is always the cool head around here."

"No, actually, it's usually you. You're just distracted, that's all," Gus assured. "So where to now?"

"I should get home. My father will be waiting up," Anika said over a sigh. "He worries, you know, about...things."

"It's early! We got the whole night off. Can't you just stay out another hour?" Cheveyo grasped Anika's hand, looked down at their laced fingers.

"Maybe if we stop by and let him know. I don't want to worry him. He's already too burdened."

"You okay with that, Gus? You're the driver."

Gus nodded, kept his eyes on the road. "Why not. We're not that far from there."

"Thanks. Hey, let's get some music on." Cheveyo turned on the radio and began punching buttons, finally settling on a lively Andrews Sisters' boogie. Leaning back against the seat, he started to sing along, humming in the places where he didn't know the words. Gus chimed in; he knew all the lyrics to all the top 40 hits and was clearly proud of his knowledge. Soon, the two men were harmonizing while Anika giggled.

As Gus made the turn onto Anika's street, the sight of a van parked in front of her house made him quickly pull over a block away and turn out the headlights.

"What the—" Cheveyo began, but Gus quickly hushed him.

"Something's going on up there." The three remained quiet and after several minutes, Gus took the key in hand. Before he could turn it, however, the screen door slammed open and three men emerged from the house. In the dim streetlight, they could just make out Doctor Watanabe and two MP's. Anika's father was carrying a suitcase.

"No!" Anika gasped, but Cheveyo pressed his hand over her mouth.

"Shh! They can't see you."

The tears she shed ran over the back of Cheveyo's hand as they waited for the van to drive away. He let her go when it turned at the next corner.

Gus was at a loss. Anger burned within him, anger at the Army, the President, the Japanese and even Cheveyo. This was all such a bad idea. Getting involved with a Japanese girl was stupid in the first place. Now, the father was gone. What would she do?

"I know what you're thinking. If we hadn't taken her, she'd be in the van with her father, heading for God knows where," Cheveyo whispered. He pulled a cotton handkerchief from his pocket and gave it to Anika. "I'm so sorry, Annie. We'll find out where they've taken him. Somehow. But it's not safe for you to go in there right now. They might trap us. They might come back, knowing you would show up eventually. We'll have to find a place to hide."

"Any ideas? We gotta start our shift soon."

"What about your place?"

"My place? Chev, you know I barely have room to turn around in that one-room shack. It's not even a real apartment—it's a pool house!"

"Well I can't take her home. My roommates will turn her in!"

Anika continued to weep softly. "I am sorry. You can just let me out here. I'll take my chances that they won't come back."

"Do you have any neighbors you can trust?" Gus asked, his expression pained.

Cheveyo grimaced. "You can't trust anybody these days, man. Besides, they'll all be taken anyway. They just ordered

1,000 people to be removed from Terminal Island yesterday. C'mon, let's just leave her off at your place, just for tonight. I'll think of something else tomorrow."

"What if my landlady comes by? It's just not a good idea."

The three sat in silence until headlights ahead of them sparked their attention. Gus started the car and made a U-turn in the street. He drove as fast as practical without drawing attention to himself. Finally, as they cruised along South Beacon Street, Gus pulled into the parking lot of the Lighthouse Café.

"We close in a half hour," the counter waiter said. "You might want to try the Clover Club across the street."

"No, this is good enough," Gus muttered, tossing down his keys. "We won't be long. Got any coffee?"

The waiter looked at Anika but didn't say anything. He brought them each a cup of coffee and dropped the tab on the table.

Cheveyo rubbed his eyes. "I been here before but I never realized that this place is the 'Lighthouse' café on 'Beacon' Street." He spun a pack of cigarettes in front of him, then stopped and looked Gus in the eye. "I just gave myself an idea. The lighthouse."

"Yeah, what about it?"

"Angel's Gate. We can take Annie out to the lighthouse for tonight."

"The lighthouse? What about the squids? You can't bring her up with them there."

"She can hide in the horn house until we make sure they're not there."

"Risky," Gus muttered. "You really want to risk that?"

Cheveyo turned to Anika. "She's brave. Those lugs won't have any reason to peek in there before they go off."

"Okay, but what about our shift at the base in the morning?"

"You won't mind covering for me, will you Gus, old buddy, old pal?"

Gus sighed. "Somehow I knew that was coming."

Chapter 18

The three of them picked up the small motorboat at the dock and motored out toward the mouth of Los Angeles Harbor. Gus swore he'd never seen a night so dark. No brightly lit schooners or yachts in the harbor, no beach restaurants with glowing neon window signs. He figured most people were hunkered down after the yellow alert that had been issued earlier in the evening.

"Quiet tonight," he murmured.

"People are scared after that, uh, incident up north yesterday. I don't mind saying it has me looking over my shoulder," Cheveyo called as they approached the breakwater.

Gus tied the boat to the mooring at the rocky base of the lighthouse. Cheveyo helped Anika climb out and silently walked her to the tiny structure that housed the foghorn. He handed her a heavy flashlight.

"Don't use it unless you're desperate," he whispered, then gave her a kiss on the cheek. "I'll be back to get you soon, okay?"

Anika nodded in the darkness. "Is it... are their rats in here?"

"Naw, they can't stand the sound of the horn. But don't worry; it won't be sounding off tonight."

They were in luck. The Navy "squids" had left the lighthouse, probably due to the alert, and Gus was able to unlock the door with the key his buddy Joe Halleran had given him. Gus shook his head, thinking about Joe's blatant disregard for the law and propriety. Of course, his childhood pal had never played by the rules. Now, as an enlisted ensign with the U.S. Coast Guard, Joe pretended to care but clearly didn't. Hence, the key to Angel's Gate Lighthouse, recently commandeered by the U.S. Navy as an occasional command post.

"I'm going back down for Annie," Cheveyo said, clattering down the staircase that clung to the walls of the lighthouse. "It's empty up top."

"Okay," Gus muttered. He didn't like being there, didn't like that they'd brought the young Japanese girl with them. On edge, he ascended the spiraled staircase himself and headed for the radio room.

Once seated before the console, he tuned in to the frequency used by nearby Fort MacArthur. There didn't seem to be much going on, so he turned the volume down and continued on up into the gallery. Soon, Anika and Cheveyo joined him.

"Oh, my..." Anika clasped her hands together beneath her chin. "It's so dark. So... scary. I can hear the waves but I can't see them."

Cheveyo put an arm around her shoulders. "It's okay. We're completely safe up here. If you look out there, well, sometimes, you can see Catalina Island. But they got all the lights turned off now because of the subs."

"Subs? What subs?"

Cheveyo looked to Gus, who shrugged.

"You know, war subs. There's rumors..."

"Japanese submarines, you mean," Anika said softly, looking away from the two men beside her. "Yes. I've heard about that. My father says it's not true. That it's all made up by the military because they want to scare us."

"Aw, who knows? Anyway. Don't let's worry about that tonight, okay?" Cheveyo said, smiling broadly and lifting Anika's chin with his finger. "Tonight we can just sort of forget about all that."

Gus huffed out a short sigh. "Yeah. Tonight. And tomorrow we might get orders to ship out."

"We won't."

"We might. We just might." Gus pulled a half-empty package of Lucky Strikes from his breast pocket and flipped one out. Anika stared as he lit the cigarette, and he held out the pack to her.

"Thanks," she murmured, then carefully withdrew one from the pack with her fingertips. Gus waited, but when Cheveyo didn't offer her a light, Gus flipped opened his lighter for her.

"Anyway, if I get orders, I hope it's for Williams Field in Arizona. Close to home," Cheveyo said.

"You mean Higley?" Gus took a drag off his smoke. Cheveyo stepped between Anika and Gus.

"It's called Williams, now." He turned to Anika. "It's where they train the pilots for the Air Corp. It's what I really want to do." After a pause, Cheveyo leaned close to Gus. "You, uh, think you'd better check the radio again?" Cheveyo raised his eyebrows and nodded toward the open stairway.

Gus frowned. "I just checked."

"I think you should. You know, just in case. Anything could be happening. Right, doll?" Cheveyo ran his fingers down the length of Anika's hair, and Gus nodded.

"Oh. Right. Sure. I'll just be down a level if you, you need me."

What a dolt. He should have realized that the lovebirds wanted to be alone. At the radio, he lifted the heavy earphones and slipped the springed arch over his head. The chatter was distorted and monotone. He sighed.

We shouldn't have come out here. Now, he was stuck in the lighthouse with Chev and his girl. A girl he'd rather be stuck with—alone.

I can't think that way. She's his girl. Not mine.

He listened for a while, listened to reports of sub sighting from earlier in the day. They still talked about the shelling up at Goleta, and something about Brookings, Oregon.

Gus lit another cigarette. He glanced at his watch; it was only one A.M. This was going to be a long night.

Joe Halleran bummed a smoke off of another dancer and leaned in close to his partner to light it off of hers. The booze burned in his belly and he reveled in the feeling. He didn't care anymore, didn't care about the military or the war. Didn't care about his dead mother or his long gone father. Nothing mattered but the music, the liquor, the dame and the fact that tomorrow he was going AWOL. Tomorrow, he'd hop on a ship, or a train, hell, he'd hitchhike out of L.A. for parts unknown. He was sick of his life. The irony of it was that no one would miss him.

The Navy nurse bought him another drink and he kissed her lustily while sliding his hands across her breasts. She giggled and he laughed back, all the while trying to keep up with the band. The din was deafening, with war-weary young adults clinking glasses, singing aloud, desperate to forget and grasping at a sense of normalcy in the midst of near hysteria. That frenzy became real when, just before 2:30 A.M., the lights at Shanghai Red's winked out and the air raid sirens began.

The band members ceased to play in varying degrees, a lone tenor sax the last to fade away. Alarmed patrons stumbled to the doors and windows to look outside, spilling out onto the street where searchlights scanned the skies overhead.

"What's happening?" the girl beside him shrieked. "It's the Japs! They're bombing L.A.!" She flung herself on to Joe and held him tightly around the neck.

Suddenly sobered, Joe shoved the girl aside and pushed his way through the panicky dancers toward the door. Once outside, he peered up at the bright cones of light traversing the night in search of some threat. He started walking, slowly at first, then quickening his pace, eyes never leaving the sky. If Los Angeles was going to be bombed, he didn't want to die on the street outside a dive like Red's.

The sirens screamed. It wasn't like he'd never heard them before; but the previous drills were expected, and he was always with his division. Never in the middle of the night with a head full of booze and dark thoughts. This time, the shrill sounds seemed to be coming at him from all directions, as if he were caught up in some kind of vortex. Over and over they sounded, warning, threatening. Danger, they called. You are about to die.

People came out of their houses. Despite the obvious call for a black out, bedroom lights were on. Cries for help, sobbing, raised voices. Joe walked on, taking it all in. This was his hometown, these were his people. A man stepped out of a small business, a rifle in his hands, and took aim at the sky. Joe shook his head.

"You think you're gonna shoot down a Zero with that thing? Good luck, friend!"

The man snarled back but kept the gun leveled overhead.

Joe laughed. A hearty laugh that bubbled up from deep inside. So maybe the Japs were finally here. He'd always wanted to be a flyer, but didn't make the cut. It was his dream to be soaring off from the U.S.S. Saratoga or the Lady Lex as a B-26 top turret gunner.

"Don't matter now!" he hollered, picking up his pace, laughing as he ran through the streets of San Pedro. Nothing mattered now. Nothing, except—

His thoughts, and his feet, came to a stuttering halt as the first anti-aircraft shells launched from Fort MacArthur, bursting overhead in an intense, fiery display. Wide-eyed and agape, Joe took a timid step backward and to the side, pressing his back against a brick building. He stared, chest heaving with excitement as more bombs flew skyward, adding to the pandemonium of the sirens and the peoples' screams.

This is it. This is the war, come here, to Los Angeles.

Fascination overcame him. It was like he'd never actually believed the war was real. The big war, double-ya double-ya two, was something like a myth, something in the newsreels at the afternoon cinema. Front page stills on the Herald and the Times. FDR on the radio. Guys getting their heads shaved and putting on olive drabs, khakis and white caps. Women crying at the airport, at the train station, at the dock.

Bombs were for places like France, and England. Pearl. Wake. Not L.A. These were his streets! The brilliant explosions in the sky above lit his face with excitement and reflected off of the window glass beside him. The glass rattled with echoed vibrations as each bomb burst. Joe turned to look at the window displaying musical instruments, tools and small appliances. He'd been in the pawn shop before, trading in bartered items. Just yesterday, he'd traded a ukulele for enough cash to keep him in cigarettes for a month. The proprietor made him wait while he examined a coin collection. "Keep your shirt on, Swabbie. I'll be with you in a minute," he said, so Joe wandered around the store looking at bicycles, ermine coats and a very nice slide trombone. In the glass case was jewelry and foreign currency, some of it brought home from the front. He tried not to be too obvious as he looked to see if his mother's wedding ring had sold yet. Nope! There it was, a lonely gold band with a few tiny chip diamonds mounted halfway around. Nobody could afford gold these days; not even the cheap ring of a cleaning lady.

Impatient, Joe moved in behind the current customer and looked over his shoulder, prompting the already irate patron to snap, "Do you mind, buddy? This is private business we're conducting here."

"Sorry." Joe put his hands up and walked backwards, almost upsetting a garish crystal table lamp. But he saw the coins, laid out in a velvet-lined, wooden box with a tiny brass latch. The coin owner and the pawn shop proprietor seemed to be having a disagreement about the value of the coins. Joe flicked his finger at one of the cut-glass crystals hanging from the lampshade, doing his best to listen to the conversation. The crystal dangled and flickered with a prismatic reflection. It mesmerized Joe, and he tapped another and another in quick succession, causing a multitude of sparkly images on the adjacent wall.

"Final offer, Mr. Jarvis. Take it or leave it. I'm a busy man." The pawn owner sniffed, lifted his chin, and Joe almost laughed aloud. Busy? Ha!

The customer grudgingly accepted a payout and left the shop in a hurry. Mr. Pawn, as Joe liked to think of the shop owner, smiled and ran his fingers over the small wooden box, then slipped it onto a shelf beneath the cash register. He turned to Joe and his ukulele.

Tonight, with bombs bursting all across the sky above, Joe saw the uke in the window. He chuckled, then laughed. It was funny, hilarious, that he should find himself in front of the pawn shop on this night. The night when everything would change.

The lights were off on this whole block. Joe looked around, saw no one but a couple down the street, loading the trunk of their car. Escaping! Like he would do, first thing in the morning. He glanced back at the ukulele and wondered how thick the window glass was. He searched the area in front of the shop for a large rock or a brick, but found nothing. Once again, he checked the street, then kicked at the plate glass as hard as he could. The window shattered, sending shards of glass both inside and outside the shop. Joe continued kicking at the jagged edges until there was room enough for him to enter the shop.

The cash register was empty. Joe slammed the cash drawer closed with a curse. All he needed was a hundred bucks to get him out of this god-forsaken town. But of course Mr. Pawn had taken all the money to the bank after closing time. Or maybe the sucker had just taken it home and stuffed it into his pillow case. It didn't matter; what mattered was that Joe needed some cash. Maybe he'd just take back his mother's ring and a few other pieces of jewelry and hit another pawn shop in the morning. As he squatted down to figure out how to open the jewelry display case, another aerial bomb lit the night sky, illuminating—ever so briefly— the small wooden box stashed beneath the register.

"Oh, yeah, baby." Joe couldn't believe his good fortune. Didn't the old man have a safe for such things? His mother's pitiful little ring was one thing; the coin collection was quite another. Leaving it out in the store was just plain stupid. Joe swept the dozen or so coins out of the box and squeezed them in the palm of his hand. They felt good, heavy, valuable. On a whim, he grasped the back door of the display case and ripped it from its hinges, then reached in for his mother's ring. On the same shelf lay a small, burgundy velvet jewelry bag. Joe snagged it, too, and left the store singing a song under his breath.

The shelling continued for another half hour. Each aerial explosion sent a shockwave down to the earth, like a meteor hitting the ground, Joe thought. *Boom! Rumble!* The occasional crash when a piece of shrapnel fell from the sky and struck the street nearby gave him a start. In his near-inebriated state, he stumbled along, the gold booty in his pocket. He needed someplace to hide out until morning; there'd be no getting out of town tonight, not with this circus show going on.

As he walked along the causeway, he tried various warehouse doors and factory entrances, all locked up tight.

Closer to the water, he looked for a boat moored, one he could walk onto and sleep the rest of the night. Sleep off the booze. In the morning, he'd trade one of the coins for passage. But nothing looked vacant, or safe, or accessible. As he neared the end of the pier, several anti-aircraft shells hit the sky at the same time, lighting the waves in various flashes all the way out to the breakwater. There, at the end of that wet, rocky path, guarding the entrance to the harbor sat his salvation: Angel's Gate. A place where he could hole up for the night, get some rest, and plan his future.

Chapter 19

November 12, 2012 - Monday, Morning

"I just had the strangest dream," Jack said, turning to Emelie on the couch.

"Are you sure it was a dream?" she asked, standing up, arms akimbo. "Did you...see your dad?"

"I did. It seemed like a dream. He was young, and he was with the guy and the girl from the photograph. Sheva-yo, or something like that. She—her name is Annie. Man, she was something. He—my dad—he really liked her. Wow. I feel...hung over. I need something to drink."

Emelie already had a soft drink ready for him. "You okay?"

"I think so. Was I gone long?"

"You sort of went into a twilight. For about a half hour. I could see you were quite...involved. After that, I think you just went to sleep."

"Could you see any of it? Did you see Gus? Or these others?"

Emelie shook her head. "Only a few brief images. It was channeling straight to you. It was strong. Was there anything else?"

"Yeah. There was this other guy. I'm not sure what his name was, but he stole a set of gold coins during this big wartime air battle. He wasn't a model of ethical behavior. Could have been that Joe guy."

"Coins? Really? My coins?"

"Well, it stands to reason, doesn't it? But I don't know how or why he is connected to Gus or his friends, or why I got his...story. Maybe that part was just a dream. I don't know."

"Was there nothing that might connect with Nate?"

Jack frowned. "I'm not sure. This guy, *Shevy*, my dad's friend, he looked sort of Native American. Maybe he's a connection, but no way to tell."

"You should tell Detectives Cordell and Beeman about what you saw."

"They'll think I'm crazy."

"But maybe it will help with identifying the head they found. And the owner of the coins."

"You know what? My dad was really cool, Emmie. I feel like I just got to really see him for the first time. I don't know how you do this, or if it's just an imaginary thing I did myself, but I am...so very grateful. Thank you."

Despite her disappointment that Jack had turned up nothing to help find Nate, Emelie smiled and squeezed Jack's hand. "It's all good. Either way. You needed to see another side of Gus and now you did."

Nate opened his eyes. The arched air vent was bright gold, again. Daylight. Above him, he saw his grandmother's face, hovering in the airspace. Her white hair did not hang down, so he figured she was actually lying down somewhere. Her bed, where he saw her last. He always thought Sobo had some kind of mystic power. She'd once been asked to assist the tribe's shaman and she did so, for a year or more when Nate was a child.

Although her lips were not moving, Nate could hear Sobo's voice inside his head. "You must be strong. There is still much work to be done. This is not the end, Na'tanial."

"It might be," Nate whispered.

"You must do this. For her."

"Do what? For who?"

The vision of his grandmother evaporated. Nate turned his head to the side and closed his eyes tightly. He wanted to cry, but even the tears he needed to soothe his dry eyes would not come. Still, a sob grew in his chest and he wept inside.

For her. The words echoed in his head. Who was Sobo talking about? Emelie? Tippi? Someone else? Of course, he would have done anything, anything at all to save his mother. To please her. To give her happiness. Now that he thought about it, he felt much the same way about Emelie. He had so much to give this girl who had fallen so auspiciously into his life.

A bus ride, through the desert. Who meets a girl on a bus? What made her choose the seat next to his, on a bus only half full of riders? He remembered their easy banter, her soft chiding. The offer to look her up in L.A. Oh! Was he ever glad he had. It wasn't just the sofa when he needed it; it was the camaraderie, the companionship, the simple way they'd fallen in together. His Hopi sensibilities, her yoga and zen mentality. They both loved Steve McQueen movies and cilantro.

Nate smiled, despite the pain of his cracked lips. He still wasn't sure what Sobo meant, but he did know now that he must get up and out of this room, for her. *For Emelie.*

Rick hopped between his sink and stove, his crutch stowed against a nearby wall. He broke two eggs into a frying pan and covered them with a lid, then dropped two pieces of bread into the toaster. It felt good to have a day off, a day when he could put everything back into its rightful place. Everything being: all the facts, revelations and clues concerning the Nathanial Sinquah case. Sitting at his work desk down at the precinct was distracting, because half the time, he was dealing with his handicap and learning to do things differently than he'd done for the past decade and a half. At home, no one watched as he knocked over items he couldn't quite reach or stumbled over a throw rug put in his path by invisible gremlins. No one stopped by his desk to say, for the hell-teenth time, how sorry they were and did he have any feeling back yet?

It wasn't as if he wasn't trying. Every day, for thirty minutes or more, he sat on his bed and tried to move his leg. Tried to wiggle his toes. Tried to will his muscles into waking up and getting a move on. This morning, he thought maybe he felt a tiny twinge in his knee. Unsure, he repeated his effort, only to be met with disappointment as the twinge disappeared.

Maybe I imagined it, he thought, flipping the eggs in the pan. He was afraid to think otherwise. The toast popped up and he grabbed it, dropping the slices onto a paper towel he'd already laid out. Hopping a few steps to retrieve the butter, Rick heard his phone ringing from somewhere. Far enough away that he'd never get to it in time. What did it matter? It was his day off. Then he heard the Caller I.D. over the speakerphone.

"Call from...Emelie Marin..."

Crap. Grabbing his crutch, Rick made his way into the living room where his phone lay on the coffee table. He sat down first, then reached for the cell.

"Hi Emelie. Watcha got?"

"I do have something for you. How did you know?"

Rick could hear the sweet smile in her voice. Just a hunch."

"Can I stop by?"

"I'm at home today."

"Oh. Well, that's even better. What's your address?"

Rick wasn't sure he should have told Emelie where he lived. It broke one of his cardinal rules, but somehow, he didn't think it would be a problem. She arrived twenty minutes later as he was rinsing off his plates.

"What have we here?" he asked, giving way for her to walk into his small house. She put down a shopping bag and took off a pair of gloves.

"It's chilly today," she said. "Have you eaten?"

"Um, yeah, I just ate. Sorry, I should have waited and made you some."

"Oh, no! That's not why I asked. I brought you some special soup and a few other things. I'll just put the soup in the fridge and you can heat it up tonight. It's healthy stuff. You need it."

"You think?"

Emelie grinned. "I know. Here, can I move your coffee table?"

"Sure, but—"

"Don't worry, I'll put it back." Emelie went about pushing furniture around while Rick watched, his eyebrows raised. She dug further into the bag and pulled out two rolled up mats, which she unrolled on the floor. Okay. Over here, Detective."

"What? I don't think—"

"Here. Now!"

Rick worked his way onto the mat, with his crutch firmly braced beneath his arm. "Okay, now what?"

"Now, we're going to work a little on your *atman*. We'll start with some simple movements."

"Now wait. I know you believe in all that yoda-stuff, but honestly, I—"

"Honestly, you what? Your leg getting better by itself? Or you want to let that doctor cut you open? Detective Cordell, with all due respect, sir, this won't hurt you to try! I promise you."

Rick stared at the little powerhouse before him, her face pink with emotion, and he stopped talking. He sucked in his upper lip and waited for her to continue.

"Listen. I gotta do something or I'll just fall apart. I can't find Nate, I can't help him, and I can't fix Jack and Maddie. I can't understand why Angela hurt me, and I wish my father was not such a stubborn mole. But you, you are here before me and I can do something, so please, let me! And it's not Yoda, it's *yoga*. Now, you just watch me, and do what I do. Dammit!" Her eyes were bright with unshed tears.

Rick nodded slowly. "Okay, Princess Leia, I'm game. But don't expect too much. After all, I'm pushing forty-five and I've got a bad—"

"Ohhh!" Emelie hissed and wrapped her hand around the middle of Rick's crutch. "Now, I'm going to take this away. Can you balance?"

"I think so."

"I think it's best if I stand beside you. Wrap your arm around my shoulders. Now, we are going to bend, together, slowly, downward..."

Emelie was bone-tired when she left Rick's house and headed home. After her experience with Jack the night before, then the therapy session with the detective, she longed for a hot bath and something else to distract her. She'd told Jack she'd be staying at home tonight, and he reminded her to keep her phone charged and her door locked.

Once inside, she looked around, wary, but nothing seemed out of place. The new doorjamb and deadbolt seemed secure enough. She heated up a portion of the soup she'd made for Rick and found some sourdough bread rolls that weren't too old. On the table was a half-bottle of Merlot she and Nate had been sipping off of for a couple of weeks. He wouldn't mind, she thought, if she had a little tonight.

The hot water would have been too much for her mother, who'd always preferred cooler temperatures. Emelie, however, sunk into the steaming water with relish. "Take it out of me. Cook me," she muttered, eyes closed as she lay back and let the heat rise to her chin. She didn't have to look past the mirrored medicine cabinet to know that the fifth coin, her coin, was still safe in its hiding place. Rick mentioned that the other coins had been retrieved from Angela's apartment, and the infamous Double Eagle would be turned in to the Powers That Be. The remaining three would be held as evidence, for now.

It was okay. Aside from the one they couldn't keep, she'd held onto the second most valuable one. The one that would buy the steak dinner. She also still had the velvet bag.

"Oh, Hopi, where are you? If I could just see, if I could just hear your voice, a clue, anything..." She wanted to cry, hard. But crying wouldn't bring him back. She took a gulp of wine and sniffed. As the water in the tub grew cool, so did her mood grow worse. Why had her life become so miserable? It all started when her father had intervened, cruelly trying to force her into a world in which she did not belong. Yet, had he not shut her down, she would not have boarded the Greyhound; she would not have met Nate. The thought of his dimpled chin tore at her heart. He'd been gone a week.

Emelie got out of the tub, pulled the chain on the plug and then wrapped herself in a terrycloth robe before the mirror. Her reflection revealed sorrow, fatigue, and remorse. She took the near-empty wine bottle to the bedroom. The little cloth jewel bag was in her nightstand and she retrieved it, grasped it to her chest before lying down on the bed. The backpack no longer worked, but maybe the velvet bag would. She closed her eyes, hoping with every fiber that a vision of Nate would come.

Chapter 20

February, 1942

Gus leaned forward and stared hard at the lights in the skies over Los Angeles. His heart quickened. The aerial bombs could only mean one thing: Los Angeles was under attack. Quickly looking all around, he scoured the darkness, looking for any sign of incoming aircraft, but found none.

"Chev! Chev! Something's happening! Need to check the radio!" Gus clattered down the stairs and into the radio room, just as Cheveyo arrived from the floor below, tucking in his shirt and smoothing back his hair.

"What is it? Zeros?"

"Can't tell. Didn't see anything, but the base is sending up all kinds of crap! There seems to be some central point they're focused on. Oh, damn. And we're here! We should be there!"

Cheveyo turned the dial on the radio, this way and that, searching for any voice, any instruction, and news on what was happening.

"Nothing but static. It's blacked out. No radio transmissions. God. Do you...do you think we should go back? Report for duty?"

Gus stared at Cheveyo, eyes wide. He tilted his head subtly toward the doorway where Anika stood, her face even paler than normal.

Cheveyo nodded. "We have to take her some place safe. Somewhere where no one—" Before he could finish his thought, the sound of the entry door slamming shut got their attention. Gus went to the stairs.

"Hello? Who is it?"

No one responded, but they could all hear someone moving about below. Gus took a few steps down the stairway. "Hey! Who's down there?"

Now, a man ascending the stairs answered. "Just me, Angus McDoodle. Just old Jazzed Up Joe. You see that big party goin' on out there? They're shootin' at some big craft. Somebody said it was a Jap reconnaissance plane. What the hell you doin' here?"

Gus met Joe halfway down. "Nothing. Just...killing time, you know. We got a great view of the fireworks. You?"

"Aw, same. Hidin' out. I figure if they can't find me, I can't get called in. Who else is here?"

"Just Chev and me. We, uh, had a couple of beers, you know. We don't report 'til 0700."

"Let's go up to the gallery. I wanna see the sparks from up there."

Gus stepped in front of Joe. "Nothing really to see. It's all moved on down to the south. Somewhere over Palos Verdes, I think."

Joe paused, stared at Gus. "What you hidin', G.I.? You got more booze up there you don't wanna share?"

"Naw, nothing like that. Hey, I think it's all over, anyway. You wanna head on back and get some more beer with me and Chev?"

Joe pushed Gus aside and continued up the stairway. "Nope. I want to go see what's up here."

Gus hurried after him. If Joe saw, *when* Joe saw Anika, there would be hell to pay.

Anika, of course, had no place to hide. Joe looked from Cheveyo, to Gus, and back to Anika. "Well, well. What have we here? You captured a little Jap girl?"

"You could say that," Gus answered, giving Cheveyo a look he hoped conveyed an idea. Cheveyo, however, wasn't amused.

"She's not captured. She's my girl, and you need to just

forget you saw anything here, Halleran."

"Your girl, huh? Are you blind, man? I mean, it's one thing for you to be a crazy Apache or whatever, but this girl's a nip! You can tell by the shape of her nose, she's not a Chinee."

Cheveyo stepped forward, his head tilted upward toward the taller man's face. "She's an American, same as you and me. Now why don't you just take your drunken ass outa here and back to Red's or whatever other hell hole you were watering in."

"Not so fast, Honanie. We may have known each other a while. Maybe you did get me outta that jam with that MP that time. But I don't like you so much as I'd let you harbor a war criminal and not say anything about it. I will take her in and they can do whatever they think's best. Now, step aside."

"War criminal? Are you crazy? She's just a girl, Joe. A nice girl. She hasn't done any harm to anyone, and she won't, either. Now if you won't leave, I'll just take her somewhere else. Please, move aside."

"I'll bet there is some kind of reward for finding these slanties and bringing them in. And I could certainly use some kind of reward about now. I might even get a medal for arresting a Jap who's planning a bombing. Maybe she's a spy! That's it—she's getting classified stuff from idiots like you and feeding it back to Hirohito."

Gus stepped forward. "Joe, look. We can take her in. Tomorrow. Tonight, with all that's gone on, well, it isn't a good time. We'll take her in. In the morning, when we report."

"No dice, McKenzie. She could get away by then." Joe took another step closer to Anika, who shrunk back. Cheveyo moved closer. "You can forget about that. Forget you ever saw her. Forget everything. Just get outta here."

Joe's smile drooped and he held up a fist. "You wanna fight me on this, Geronimo? Sure, let's go. C'mon. Let me have your best shot."

"No reason to fight," Gus began, but his words were lost as Cheveyo launched his fist at Joe's cheek. Joe responded in kind and soon the two were locked onto each other in hand-to-hand combat. Anika shrieked at them to stop, but Gus gently pulled her to the side. "I knew this was a bad idea," he muttered. Halleran, of all people. A died-in-the-wool Jap-hater.

Joe may not have qualified for flight training, but Cheveyo was no match for Joe's fighting skills. Again and again Joe punched Cheveyo in the face; the blood ran freely from his nose and his torn ear. Anika continued to call out, beseeching the two soldiers to stop. Gus's efforts to intervene only gained him a sock to the jaw. When it looked as though the much larger Joe would finish off Cheveyo with kicks to his midsection, Anika crossed the small room and grabbed her purse from the desk beside the radio. Gus again tried to pull Joe off of his friend, this time earning him an elbow to the ribs. Gus doubled over, gasped for breath, and Joe returned to the moaning soldier on the floor.

"You've always thought you were pretty hot stuff, Honanie. Just because you're a heathen, a damned redskin savage. You shoulda stayed out on the reservation! You know what's gonna happen when the Army finds out what a fucking Jap-lover you are? They're gonna ship you off with all the rest of the slanty-eyes and dump you out in the desert."

Gus straightened and moved to stand beside Anika, who looked ready to bolt. Cheveyo tried to get up, but Joe held him down with his boot.

Cheveyo gritted his teeth and stared up at Joe, his face a mass of blood and hatred. "You can burn in hell, Halleran. And you will, too!"

Newly incensed, Joe uttered a curse and a groan. Just as he raised his boot to slam it down on Cheveyo's neck, a shot rang out and Joe grasped his chest before falling across Cheveyo. A small, double-barreled, pearl-handled Derringer hit the floor beside him.

Stunned, Gus turned to Anika, and their eyes met for only a moment before she dropped her gaze and rushed to Cheveyo's side. "Help me," she called to Gus. "Get him off!"

Gus rolled Joe's lifeless body off of Cheveyo, who looked up at them in awe. "What just happened?" he asked, groaning as he tried to sit up.

"Never mind that. Are you okay?" Anika asked. "So much blood. He almost killed you."

Cheveyo looked up at Gus. "Did you shoot him?"

Gus merely stared back, then lowered his eyes. "He would have killed you, Chev."

Cheveyo returned his attention to Anika. "Are you okay?"

After cleaning up Cheveyo's bruised and battered face and hands, Anika sat with him and Gus as the three of them tried to avoid looking at Joe. Gus finally spoke. "We have to get rid of the body. No one can know about this, about tonight. You understand? No one. If anyone finds out either of you were involved, you'll be hanged without so much as a kangaroo court."

"What can we do with him? We can't leave him here. Should we take him back to the port?"

Cheveyo pondered, then shook his head. "No, too likely someone will see us. Bad enough if we're seen at all, but worse if he's in the boat. I do have an idea."

"Dump him in the water," Anika said suddenly. "We can just toss him out like the trash he is."

Cheveyo looked up. "Yeah, that's what I was gonna say. We'll have to weigh him down some, so he doesn't float back up anytime soon. He just won't turn up tomorrow for roll call. They'll call him AWOL, especially after all that happened tonight. He got scared, they'll say, and ran off."

Gus licked his lips. "I don't know. I don't like this much."

"Oh, so you want to swing for saving my life? Or Annie? For ridding the world of this piece of scum?"

"He might have a family. They should at least know?"

"Sorry, pal. Not this one. Not this time. Annie's right. We'll just throw him over. Man overboard!"

Unable to argue against the possibility that Anika would be arrested, Gus agreed to assist. "What about his wallet?" he asked.

Cheveyo paused. "Let's take it. That way, if they do find the jackass, it will look like a robbery."

Gus set his jaw and dug into the dead man's pocket for his wallet, then stuck it into his own jacket.

"We better get this done quickly and get out of here. The squids could show up at any time."

Gus nodded and reached down to grasp Joe's ankles while Cheveyo took his shoulders. They lugged the body down the stairs and outside. Gus helped Cheveyo stuff Joe's pockets with rocks from the breakwater.

They carried the body to the lowest part of the exposed breakwater, their shoes getting wet from the spray and rising tide. "Jesus! He weighs a ton!" Gus complained, setting down his end of their heavy cargo.

"It's the rocks, my friend. Remember?"

"I know, but still...You think he's heavy enough to sink?"

"Hope so. Can't worry about it. If we are careful, it won't matter if he bobs back up later, 'cause we'll be long gone by then. We have to swing him, get some momentum going! The breakwater widens beneath the surface," Cheveyo called over the din of the surf.

Gus nodded, and they swung the body back and forth as

Cheveyo counted, "One...two...three!" upon which they tossed Joe Halleran's remains as far as they could into the water and watched as it disappeared into the surf.

Back inside, Anika was busy cleaning up the blood from the floor. She worked in a methodical, matter-of-fact way that surprised Gus. *She's very cool. She knows what she's doing, and she's not upset.*

Both he and Cheveyo stood by, silent, watching her work. Soon, she stood. "The sun will be up soon. We should go. May I stay at your house, Gus? Until I find someplace else to stay?"

Dumbfounded, all he could do was nod.

The blackout ended at 7:21 A.M. Both Gus and Cheveyo stood at attention while their C.O. described for their battalion the details of the night before.

"As you all are aware, our anti-aircraft batteries were put on Green Alert this morning at 02:15 after the 14th Interceptor Command's radar tracked an unidentified craft approximately 120 miles west of Los Angeles. Various conflicting reports were received about what the hell it was up there, but shortly thereafter, gunners of the 65th Coast Artillery Regiment in Inglewood and the 205th Anti-Aircraft Regiment in Santa Monica began firing on it. I've also heard that the 37th Coast Guard Artillery joined in while the target was hanging over Culver City. And I do mean hanging; this thing just floated along.

"In light of the events of the past few months, weeks and days, it could not be ruled out that the Japanese had sent either bombers or reconnaissance aircraft across the Los Angeles basin. The shelling lasted approximately twenty minutes, during which time over 1,400 shells were fired. To the best of our knowledge, no bombs were dropped and no planes were shot down, despite several reports of same. There were a few civilian casualties, traffic accidents and heart attacks."

Gus groaned inwardly. There was another casualty last night, one that would go unnoticed for some time. He hazarded a glance at Cheveyo, who stared straight ahead.

"Now, Secretary of the Navy Frank Knox has attributed the whole thing to what he calls 'Jittery nerves.' Clearly, Commander Knox was not here. That's all I've got to say about that. We dropped a lot of shrapnel this morning, so be aware. We will have patrols out picking most of it up.

"Okay. Now if there are no more questions, I need to see PFC Simpson, PFC Lamont, and PFC Honanie in my office. The rest of you are dismissed to your morning duties."

Honanie. Gus caught up with Cheveyo as he walked quickly behind the Commanding Officer. "What's up, you think?"

"What do you think? I'm getting orders. I'll meet you later."

March 1, 1942 — California-Arizona border

"Do you have any family in Japan?" Gus asked.

"Yes." Anika paused, twisted her long, single braid. Gus tried to keep his eyes on the road.

"He never did anything wrong. My father was—*is*—a good man. He raised me after my mother died."

"I will help you find him. So far, I've only been able to find out that he's being held somewhere in San Gabriel, and word is they are setting up a temporary detention center at Santa Anita Race Track. From there, who knows? Good news is, being a doctor, he'll be needed. We'll do our best to find him."

"He bought me the gun. He wanted me to be safe, after Pearl Harbor. He wanted to send me to Japan. Can you imagine that?"

Gus chuckled. "No."

"I would never have met Cheveyo. Or...you."

Gus stole a glance at his passenger and saw Anika's warm blush. *Stay the course, Gus. She's still his girl.* "He really, you know, cares about you."

"I know. He wants us to get married, after the war."

"Do you...want to?"

"A lot can happen."

"Sure." Gus nodded slowly, eyeing the straight, empty highway ahead. They rode in silence as the moon rose from the east. Finally, Gus spoke again. "Are you okay with what happened at Angel's Gate?"

"You mean, about Joe? Yes, I think I am. I suppose we didn't have to kill him. But all I could think was, he is killing Chevy. We had to stop him. I didn't think about aiming, it was enough to just pull the trigger."

Gus detected a tremor in Anika's voice. Maybe she was not as solid with it as he thought. He reached over and squeezed her hand. "It's okay. We did the right thing. And no one will ever know, except for the three of us."

"What about Chevy's family? What will they think of me? I know nothing about the Indians. I mean, I know I look foreign, but I'm American. I went to American schools and I love Judy Garland and Perry Como and Spike Jones. I eat hot dogs. I salute the American flag. And yet, I'm pointed at and accused of being a spy. I know little about Japan, I've never met my aunts and uncles and cousins there. They would hate me, anyway."

"No one could hate you."

"You're too sweet, Angus. But these Hopi Indians—I know nothing about their ways. They might hate me, too."

"Nonsense. Chev contacted them before he shipped off. You know that. His family is anxious to meet you and keep you safe until he gets back."

"I wish...I wish I could just stay in Los Angeles. With

you."

Now Gus felt his own face heat up. How many times had he wished the same thing? He swallowed the lump in his throat. "Naw, you don't want that. You'd be hiding, every day. My place isn't even big enough to open my closet and your suitcase at the same time, and my landlady is a crazy, nosy old bitch. Don't get me wrong, it wasn't bad having you there the past few days, but it wouldn't work out in the long run." Gus sighed quietly, adding, "For many reasons," under his breath.

"I know you're right. I'm sorry."

"No, don't be."

"It's getting so dark. How much farther?"

"We got a late start. Wish I could have gotten out of maneuvers. It's another two hours to Flagstaff. Then, I'm not sure, maybe another hour or two to the reservation. Chev wasn't very clear about that part."

"It will be late. We should stop in Flagstaff for the night, refresh, and go there in the morning."

"You think so?"

"I have money. I will pay for the rooms."

"That's not necessary. I have money, too. But I'm a little concerned about the clerk seeing you. I hate to say it, but it might be smarter for us to just sleep in the car."

Anika sighed. "Why don't we just get one room. You can tell them I'm your wife, I'm not feeling well, and they don't even have to see my hateful face."

"Share a room? Um, I'm not sure—"

"No one needs to know. It's just so we can rest and be our best tomorrow. We can figure something out. I can sleep on the floor."

"Nonsense. If anyone is sleeping on the floor, it's me."

"Okay then? We can get a room?"

Gus felt something in his gut knot up. "I guess so. If that's what you want."

"I really think it's best."
"Okay."

Chapter 21

November 13, 2012 – Tuesday

The phone on Rick's desk rang again. At this rate, he'd never get anything done. But this call got his immediate attention.

"My name is Sam. Samuel Sinquah. I got a message that you called. Is this about my son?"

Rick cleared his throat. "Thanks for calling back, Mr. Sinquah. I'm afraid I have some unsettling news." As Rick relayed the story about Nate's disappearance, Sam Sinquah remained silent. "Sir? Are you there?"

"Yes. I'm...I'm just wondering how something like this could happen. He's a very, very careful person. He doesn't get involved with...those types."

"Well, we don't think he was involved with anything, you know, shady. We think he was just an innocent victim of a greedy person or persons. As I said, we'd like to either confirm or rule out that the forensic evidence from the scene belongs to Nate."

"You want his blood type. We don't normally need to know that kind of stuff, but I think it's possible that the school might have taken a sample of his blood when he went to work there. It's First Morning Elementary School."

Rick made notes as Nate's father read him the phone number of the school.

"Should I come out there? I could be there by tomorrow."

"Honestly, Mr. Sinquah, I see no reason for you to make that trip at this time. I promise you, now that I have a contact number for you, I will keep you informed of each development. Emelie is working very closely with us on this, too."

"Emelie? Who is this person?"

Rick drew in a breath, shook his head. "Just a friend of Nate's, who's very concerned for him."

"Please, do call me. Nate's all I've got now."

Rick wasted no time in contacting First Morning Elementary. But while Nate Sinquah did receive immunizations, he did not give a blood sample. A dead end. Rick hung up the phone and ran his hand across his face, rubbed his eyes. The photograph of Nate Sinquah etched upon his brain, so clear and all-encompassing that he couldn't get the young man out of his mind. What was it about this guy, this case, that had him by the short hairs? He hadn't been this personally connected to a victim since his rookie days. He didn't know Sinquah, never met him, had no reason to care more about his fate than any number of other missing persons.

It was part Emelie, he realized. The girl had a way of getting under your skin. She was so clearly devoted, so trusting, so very intuitive. The night she'd come to his house with the soup, and the determination that he should exercise, had changed him somehow. She was, in fact, the only one who really made an effort to help him. Sure, his ex had called, sent him a funny card. The guys at the precinct brought him a burger now and then. Chuck had driven him around in the weeks after the hospital gig. But Emelie had jammed her skinny shoulder beneath his arm, pushed him to stretch, insisted he could fix his own stupid body just by trying. Trying harder. Rick smiled in surprise. Yeah, it was Emelie's passion and perseverance that pushed him to search for her beloved man.

His smile faded. Young Sinquah had been missing—and possibly wounded—for eight days. At this point, every passing hour diminished the possibility that he'd be found alive. Despite Emelie's assertion that Nate was still alive, Rick sensed her connection also grew weaker as the days passed. Something had to break soon, even if it was the discovery of a corpse.

"I'm not doing anyone any good today," Rick mumbled, reaching for his crutch and then pulling himself to stand up. He looked down at his desk, the neatly stacked file folders, the desk phone, the calendar. *What else can I do?* "Aw, shit. There's nothing I can do. A missing person in L.A. is worse than a proverbial needle in a haystack."

"I might have a clue to that needle," Chuck said, striding into the room. "We got a break. Not sure if it will help us find Nate, but it's something."

Rick felt his pulse quicken. "What'ya get?"

"We got a new witness who gave us a description of the car that took Danvers and Sinquah away from the restaurant. A waitress who was out for a smoke. She's been on vacation and just got back today. We got a new BOLO out on a 2011 Ford Explorer with a dent in the right front fender."

"No plate number?"

"No, unfortunately. We're just hoping the damage is spotted. She also confirmed the composite as the driver."

"Good. Good. That's something. You know it's been over a week."

"Yeah," Chuck muttered. "I'm not real hopeful on this one. We don't know if the guy's gotten any medical care from the unsub. I've got BOLOs out at all the area hospitals. But...nothing."

Rick sighed, felt his spirits fall. "My bet is the perp and Sinquah are holed up somewhere. Look, I gotta get out of here. I'm going home. You call me if—"

Chuck was already nodding when Rick's desk phone cut him off. Bracing himself, Rick reached for the receiver. "Cordell."

Emelie was close to hysterical. "A man—he called—he

wants the coins. He says, he says he's got Nate!"

"Calm down, Em. Take a breath. Chuck's here, I'm gonna put you on speaker."

There was a pause while Emelie tried to compose herself. "I was just sitting here, looking online for places we could maybe look for Nate, and the phone rang, and I answered, and he said he knew I still had the coins and if I give them to him, he will tell me where to find Nate. And I asked to talk to Nate but he wouldn't let me."

Chuck grimaced and shook his head. "Did he give you any specific demands? Like where to meet, or where to drop off the coins?"

"He said to bring them to the shipyard. He gave me directions. He said to come alone, of course, just like they always do on TV."

Rick licked his lips. "When?"

"Tomorrow night at nine o'clock."

"Did you tell him you didn't have the coins?"

"No! If he knew that, he wouldn't tell me where Nate is!"

"Okay, okay, it's all right. We'll figure this out," Rick consoled. "You just sit tight. I'm coming over there."

Chuck nodded and pointed to himself.

"*We're* coming over there," Rick continued. "Chuck will be with me. We'll make a plan, okay? Do you have any more of that great soup?"

Chuck drove. "Thoughts?"

"Dunno. Maybe we substitute fakes?"

"Risky. If this guy knows anything about the coins, he'll spot counterfeits."

"So, we get the coins out of evidence and give them back to Em?"

"We'll have to," Chuck said. "First, we have to come up with a plan to pull this off."

"His dad called, you know. Sounded like a straight up guy. Worried."

Chuck huffed out a breath. "This whole thing just stinks."

"Yeah, well, at least the perp has come out of hiding. We have a chance, now." Rick drummed his fingers on the arm rest. "You think the kid is still alive?"

"I'm concerned that he refused to put Sinquah on the phone."

"Me, too."

"If he's dead, it's gonna tear that girl apart."

Jack wandered. He started by wandering in his car, driving through the Hollywood Hills, down Sunset and onto Beverly Drive. Then Coldwater Canyon, which took him into the San Fernando Valley. While he managed to negotiate traffic fine, he wasn't really seeing the other cars on the street. His thoughts ran a myriad of pictures, most of them involving Gus. He needed a day off from all the anguish, the worry over Nate Sinquah, the questions about his father.

He drove east for miles, passing his old apartment in Studio City, eventually turning from Alameda Avenue to Bob Hope Drive. Without thinking much about it, he parked the car and turned off the engine.

The Johnny Carson Park buzzed with activity. People, kids, dogs, balls, fancy built-in exercise stations. Jack got out of the car and continued to wander, now seeking a park bench nearby. A specific bench, one laden with memories of a past on which he hadn't reflected in several years. He sat down, ran his fingers over the semi-smooth concrete. They'd replaced the former wooden version, the one with all the words and initials and symbols carved into it. He'd never actually cut into that bench, but had always considered it his and Maddie's property. It was here that they had met.

Sure, he'd known Madelyn Cross in high school. She

was a couple of years younger, pretty, quiet, giggly. He was athletic, shy, and devoid of the confidence he'd later gain. It wasn't until the chance encounter, years later at this very site that he and Maddie had truly connected. He almost hadn't recognized her; after all, it had been, what—twenty years since graduation? She was married, had a son, seemed happy enough. He was hopeful that things would work out in his own life, with his infant son and domestic partner; they were already fighting at that point, and Maddie arrived on the scene at just the right—or wrong—moment.

What he hadn't known was that Maddie wasn't actually happy at all. Her loveless marriage to Ray Tyler was anything but joyful, and she had a deep and carefully guarded secret about her past that was never too far from her mind. After giving her his best shot, all of his charm, every bit of his loving heart, Jack had almost lost her to that secret. But Maddie had come around, melted into him and they'd made a beautiful life together. She'd fought beside him for custody of Duncan, and had conceived two more incredible children with him. Now, she was back in the realm of that dark time, back with those who'd tried to take her away from him.

He toyed with the idea of getting on a jet. Traipsing to the south of France, driving one of those crazy rental cars until he found her. He'd get to the bottom of this...this problem. The notion of Maddie taking drugs more than rattled him; he'd never even seen her drunk. That she had taken his children, too, troubled him. Had she been planning this trip for months? He recalled with a start how she'd suggested all the children get passports after school let out in June. "Just in case," she'd said. In case what? In case she suddenly wanted to leave Jack?

Maybe it was all wrong. Emelie's "vision" couldn't be true. Maddie was just pissed off about the job he'd taken, and overwrought with family issues. She was simply cooling off somewhere in the beautiful French countryside and would be ready to come home soon. That had to be it.

She needed to be reassured. Needed to know he loved her. That's what it had taken last time, right? His sincerity, his passion? They were soul mates, dammit. They belonged together, not a half a world apart.

Jack dug into his coat pocket for his phone, and before his mind could make another U-turn, he dialed. Maddie's phone rang several times before a woman answered. A French woman with a lilting, mellow voice.

"Bonjour, Jack. How are you, my friend?"

"Monique? May I speak to Maddie?"

Chapter 22

November 14, 2012 - San Pedro, CA

Emelie sat in her car, two blocks away from where she was to meet the man who would trade Nate for the gold coins on the seat beside her. She turned on the vanity light and pulled down the visor to open the mirror, then applied her lipstick. Had anyone, even Rick and Chuck, who were at the moment parked two car lengths behind her, asked why she wanted to wear red lipstick tonight, she couldn't have explained. It was something about who she was, a display of power and choice and independence. She never wore lipstick.

Looking down at her hands, she examined the red nail polish, probably applied for the same reasons. She ran her fingers through her hair fluffing it up just a little.

"Emelie...what are you doing, babe?" Chuck's voice came from somewhere deep within her ear, a bud so tiny she worried it would fall into her brain somehow.

"Nothing. I am ready."

"Good because it's almost time. Do you need to go over it again?"

"No. I am good. I will give him the coins when he brings Nate to me."

"Don't do or say anything that will give him reason to attack you. We assume he's armed. We will be there, Em. In the shadows. And don't worry about the coins, or the guy. You get Nate back to the car, let us worry about everything else."

"Ten Forty," Emelie said, then pulled back out into traffic. Two slow blocks down, she pulled into another parking space at the curb and willed herself not to look in her rearview mirror. She had to forget about the detectives, forget about everything but getting Nate back.

She quivered inside as she approached the darkened dock, and she slowed her pace, looking from side to side. He was here, somewhere, watching. She kept her hands, one of them clutching the velvet bag, deep within the pockets of her woolen trench coat.

"Hello?" she finally called out, not as strong as she'd like; she cleared her throat. "Hello?" she repeated, louder this time.

A voice came from the darkness behind a storage container. "Over here." Now Emelie did glance behind her, unable to not wonder if Rick and Chuck were behind her somewhere.

Focus on Nate, she reminded herself and walked into the dark space behind the shipping container. A man stood facing her in the shadows. "You got the coins?"

"Yes. But first, where is Nate?"

"He's fine. He'll live, if you get to him soon."

"What? You didn't bring him?"

"He's not far away. Now, hand over the coins and then I'll tell you where he is."

Emelie went cold and hot at the same time. Disappointment overwhelmed her. Nate wasn't here! She squeezed the coins in her hidden fist. If she handed them over, there was no guarantee the man would even tell her where Nate was. She couldn't see his face, and with Nate left to die, no one would be able to identify his killer. The man who also killed Frank.

"How do I know you'll tell me?"

"Well, I guess you're just going to have to trust me on that. Now, hand them over. You're wasting time."

Emelie stood up straight, lifted her chin. "No."

"No? Are you kidding me? Look, I hate to tell you this,

maybe you're not as smart as you look, but I have a gun here, see? And as the saying goes, I'm not afraid to use it. Now, make this easy on yourself and your boyfriend, because frankly, if you don't get him some help soon, he ain't gonna make it. And I'm sorry about that, I truly am. I like the kid. I do. But business is business, chickie."

"No. You tell me where he is first."

"Now why would I do that? That's my leverage, kiddo. You truly don't know how to play this game, do you? The coins. Now!"

Emelie shook her head. She heard the gun cock. Then Rick's voice was in her head. "Give him the coins, Em. Go ahead, take them out of your pocket and toss them down on the ground and then back away."

"No," she repeated. "You can't get away with this. You killed Frank Danvers and you shot Nate."

The man issued a growl and stepped from the shadows in front of Emelie. He grasped her by both shoulders and shook her. "Where are they? You even have them?"

Emelie struggled and tried to pull away. Her assailant slapped her hard across the face and then tried to rip her hands from her pockets. "No!" she screamed again, keeping the coins firmly encased in her fist. "Tell...me...where...he...is!!"

At this point, the man pushed her against the side of the steel container and shoved the gun against her cheek. "This could have gone another way. You could have saved your pal. Now, you'll be dead, he'll be dead, and I'll still get the coins." He began to frisk her with his free hand.

"L.A.P.D.! Turn slowly around and drop the gun!" Chuck called out from behind them. Emelie's attacker did turn, but as he did, he maintained his grip on her neck and kept the gun pressed to her temple.

"So you brought some friends," he said. "Figures. You don't even have the coins, do you?"

Emelie didn't respond. Her heart was pounding so loud she could barely hear him. She closed her eyes and prayed that it would be over soon. It had to be a nightmare, right? A nightmare that began the very day Nate brought home the coins. She would wake soon, and it will have never happened. But the barrel of the gun was hurting her skin, digging into her face so hard and she knew at any moment it would go off, sending a red hot slug into her brain.

Oh, Nate. We could have had a wonderful life together. I love you, Hope. I truly love you. Her eyes were still closed when a scene began to appear in her mind. It was Nate, and he was lying very still. The rushing sounds around him were softer this time, and there was another sound, a new one. A "fwap-fwap-fwap" noise that repeated quickly, from somewhere overhead. Emelie struggled with every available brain cell to recognize the sound, one she'd heard before. The noise made by blades hitting air. The blades of a helicopter.

"You don't want to do this. Put the gun down and let her go," Rick called out this time, shining a high powered flashlight into the killer's face. "No sense in adding to your list."

"No sense in not," he called back. "You back off. Come any closer and I don't know what I might do." He pressed harder with the pistol and Emelie screamed. She began to flail about, swinging her arms around in an attempt to hit him with her fists.

"I have to get to Nate! Let me go!" Lifting her leg, she bent her knee and delivered a backward kick to the attacker's shin. It was enough to cause him to loosen his hold and she wrestled free of his grasp, but his arm shot out and he grabbed a fistful of her hair. Enraged, Emelie spun, swung at him and connected with his jaw.

"You little bitch," he yelled, bringing the gun down level with her chest. Two shots rang out in quick succession, and

Emelie was pushed to the ground just before the gunman fell beside her, his face inches from hers. She stared into his lifeless dark eyes as realization dawned. The kidnapper was dead, and gone with him was the location of Nate's prison. As she tried to get to her feet, she realized that someone kept her from moving.

"Is he down?" Rick called out from above her.

"He's down," Chuck answered, leaning over the dead man with his fingers pressed to the gunman's neck. "Permanently."

Rick released Emelie, who quickly stood and stared on in awe. She looked around and saw the aluminum crutch some four yards away on the ground. She went to retrieve it, and when she returned, Rick was carefully putting weight on his bad leg and rising to stand. Emelie's lips parted in surprise. "Look at you! Look! You're standing up!"

Rick smiled in the dim light. "Yeah, how about that?"

"I knew it. I told you, didn't I? How did you do that?"

"When I saw him aim that piece at you, I didn't think about it, I just went. Like something just lit up inside me, a current, a wire or something, you know?" Rick's amazement warmed Emelie, but she was unable to fully appreciate the miracle.

"Did you shoot him?" she asked.

"No. Chucko over there." Rick gestured to his ex-partner, now on the phone calling in the incident. "When this sick bastard pulled the trigger, I moved in and Chuck shot him."

"He..." she Emelie began, pointing at the dead man, "he shot at me? The first shot was his?"

"Yep. So, we had no choice. You'd be dead."

"Wow," Emelie whispered. She reached up to touch the bruise on her face. "Detectives?"

Rick looked up just as Chuck joined them.

"I heard something. There's a helicopter flying over

Nate. Wherever he is, there is a helicopter."

His muscles were weak, but Rick was able to walk. Emelie had been right all along. Why didn't he feel better? He saw her sitting in the waiting room, a Styrofoam cup in her hand. She was hunched over, a picture of despair, and he knew why. Because all the gold coins in the world meant nothing without the one you loved.

He stood up, still amazed at being able to get around on his own, and went to her. He sat down beside her, took a moment to compose his thoughts. "I'm sorry, Em. You know the plan was not to kill the guy. It was you or him, and we had to do what we had to do. Don't blame Chuck, okay?"

Emelie mustered a weak smile. "I know. I really am thankful. I just wish..."

Approaching voices got their attention and Rick looked up to see Jack McKenzie and Matt Farralone entering the precinct. They both rushed to up to Emelie.

"Just got the word," Matt explained.

"You okay?" Jack asked, squatting down to look Emelie in the face.

"Yes, I am okay. The detectives saved my life." She reached out and took Jack's hand. "Thank you. Thank you all. I think I should go home now."

"I can take you home," Jack said.

After assurances all around that she would survive the night, Emelie left with Jack.

"You sure you don't want to crash at my place?"

"Do you know where most helicopters fly around here?"

"Huh?" Jack stole a glance at his passenger. "It's four a.m. I'd feel better if you stayed with me."

"He was close by. I could feel it. There was a helicopter flying overhead, fairly low."

Jack shook his head and got onto the 405 freeway north.

"Um, hospitals, police, rescue, coast guard, news copters, tours, training, traffic..."

"Ugh. No, that's too many." Emelie's small voice broke Jack's heart.

"I'm sorry." He didn't know what else to say, but then remembered something. "His name was Wayne Dodge. He was Nate and Frank's boss."

Emelie snapped to attention. "Really? Oh my God. Nate liked his boss!"

"Matt says they found his car a block from where you, uh, met him. Their CSI-type people are going over it for clues."

"Yes? Yes. That is good. Good! Maybe there is something. I saw this show once where they found some sticky stuff on the tires of a car that led them to this place where there was only that sticky stuff on the ground."

Jack smiled. Such innocence. Such faith. "Let's hope for sticky stuff, then," he said softly.

"Yes. Let's."

She was quiet for a while and when Jack looked over he saw the tears. He turned into the steep driveway of Matt's house and into the garage. He got out and opened the door for her, offered his hand. "Come on. Let's go inside."

Matt kept a fully stocked bar in the home, and Jack picked through the many expensive bottles before selecting a port wine. He poured them each a glass just as Todd walked in from downstairs, rubbing his eyes.

"It's almost morning," he moaned. "You guys okay?"

"Go back to bed, TJ. Everything's fine. We'll talk later."

Todd left the room and Jack sat down on the couch. Emelie sat on the floor behind the coffee table.

"I was looking for you tonight. I didn't know about the stake out," Jack began.

"Detective Chuck thought it was best not to tell anyone."

"You were pretty damned brave to do what you did."

"I was scared. But that didn't matter. I had to do it. Why were you looking for me?"

Jack took a sip of port, then swirled the glass before him. "I talked to Maddie today."

Emelie brightened. "And?"

"She's...okay. We talked for a long time. Big phone bill. But she's coming home."

"What? Really? Oh, Jack!" Emelie put down her glass, leapt up and rushed over to Jack with a spontaneous hug that almost had him spilling the wine. "I am so happy for you. I cannot wait to meet this wonderful woman who stole your heart."

Jack chuckled and kissed Emelie on the forehead. "Thanks, Em. It's all because of you. Your...vision, or whatever, helped me to see her differently. You helped me to remember why I loved her so much. She was scared, too. She felt like we'd become...disconnected. And you know what? It was good that she went to see Monique. She has a calming effect."

"That is wonderful." Emelie sat down beside Jack and took a gulp of wine. "Now if only my dream will come true, too."

"Yup. That would ice this cake, all right." Jack nodded, turned to face her. "How old are you, anyway?"

"Twenty-three. How old are you?"

"Old enough to know better," Jack said with a laugh. "Old enough to be your father. Old enough to be Nate's father. I'm forty-three, Em. That's why it's hard for me to imagine that when I was your age, my father was fooling around with Nate's mother. When I was in my early twenties, Dad was already retired, and he and Mom were taking cruises and doing charity work. Always on a second honeymoon. It just doesn't fit."

"Do you think we'll ever find out, Jack?"

Jack drew in a deep breath, sighed. He wrapped an arm around Emelie and gave her a brief squeeze. "I hope so, little sis. I surely hope so."

Chapter 23

March 2, 1942 - Kingman, Arizona

Gus sat on the bumper of the Olds and lit a cigarette. The sun hadn't quite appeared above the eastern horizon yet, and the saguaros around him were just waking, stretching their thorny arms skyward. A lizard skittered past his foot. His fingers trembled slightly as he brought the cigarette to his lips again. His brain was on fire.

He glanced back at the motel and the white door marked "12," where, inside, Anika was probably repacking her bag. The thought of her stirred the smoldering ashes of last night's blaze, both arousing and sickening him. He'd known all along, though. Hadn't he? Hadn't he coveted his best friend's girl from day one? What he hadn't expected was Anika's own obsession with him.

Any moment now she would emerge from the room. Would she be happy, embarrassed, angry with him? They hadn't spoken yet today because Gus left the room while she slept, the memory of their illicit, carnal lust robbing him of any kind of restful sleep. Chev could never know about what had transpired between them. But just how many secrets could Gus keep? The question churned up his stomach.

Gus rubbed his forehead, wishing the trip was over and he was back in L.A. Wishing he was deployed, and taking aim at the enemy. With bombs falling around him, maybe he could forget, for a time, the enormous betrayal of which he was so guilty. Sleeping with Anika was the worst, a true testament to his character—or lack thereof. Worse, even, than his involvement in Joe Halleran's death.

He wanted a cup of coffee but was afraid he'd just toss it

back up. Dropping the burning butt into the dirt, he stubbed it out with his shoe and reached into his pocket for another, just as the door to number 12 opened. Gus held up on lighting the smoke, his eyes riveted onto the beautiful girl stepping out, illuminated by the first rays of the Arizona sun. All the guilt in the world couldn't dim the immense rush of desire he felt upon seeing her again. She hadn't caught sight of him yet and turned her head slowly, perusing the parking lot. When her eyes at last found him, she smiled. A warm greeting, at once knowing and sympathetic. She clearly perceived his suffering.

Gus lifted his chin in a brief nod, then turned to open the trunk. Anika dropped in her small bag and Gus lifted her heavier one.

"Ready?" he asked.

"No." Still smiling, she reached up to caress his cheek. "Please don't try to make yourself believe that it didn't happen. Maybe it shouldn't have, but it did, and it was all that I ever wanted, all that I will ever need. I don't know what I am going into, but at least I will always have this. And don't worry, I will never bring it back upon you. Never."

Speechless, Gus looked away. He wasn't prepared for this kind of talk. Anika spoke more like a worldly woman of thirty than an innocent girl of eighteen. And right now, he felt more like a gangly kid of thirteen. He tried to swallow the lump that had grown in his throat and nodded, stumbling a little as he walked around to open the car door for her.

Mid-May, 1942 - Burma

"If the bugs don't get us, malaria will. If malaria don't get us, the Japs will," Cheveyo huffed, pausing to re-hoist his heavy pack onto his shoulder.

"Look at it this way: with the Japs, it'll be fast," Gus responded over his shoulder. He slowed his pace so that

Cheveyo could catch up.

"Only if they don't take us as POW's."

Gus nodded. Neither of the young Americans were prepared for the biting ants, bloodthirsty bugs and leaches, the thirst and hunger, the innate fear that came with being chased across Burma by the Japanese. His own legs were a mass of scratches and abrasions, bruises, bites and some nasty, unidentifiable rash. His body ached like never before.

"How much farther you reckon?" he asked. "We've been walking for a week already."

Cheveyo shrugged. "You wanna ask the general?"

"Vinegar Joe? Whoa-oh, not me boyo. I like my body parts where they are, thank you very much." Gus altered his path to go around a tree. The path, or what they loosely called a path, was steep and so heavy with brush they could not walk side by side. Thus far, they'd crossed immense gorges, down one side to where wide, fast-flowing rivers at the bottom were made up of 'ice melt' water from the mountains. The climb out was back up another 2,000 feet. When they got to the top of each gorge, they would look back to see the other side. A half a mile in distance would take several days.

Gus found it hard to sleep at night; even the slightest insect sound put him on edge. The Japs were known to be stealthy and silent upon approach. At any moment he could wake to find the bayonet of a Type 44 carbine pointed at his nose.

As they approached the village of Saingkyu at the army regulation rate of 105 steps per minute, the general marched them right down the middle of the shallow Chaunggyi River because the heavy vegetation on the riverbanks would have made overland travel difficult. The midday heat was oppressive and Gus felt light-headed. Just when he thought he would pass out, he heard a splash and turned around to see Cheveyo face down in the water. Quickly regaining his wits, Gus pulled his friend from the river and dragged him to the bank. He beckoned for a medical officer, who eventually revived Cheveyo with ammonia crystals.

Cheveyo was not the same in the days that followed. He tired easily and complained of dizziness and fever. Other times, he shook violently with chills. Still, the platoon forged ahead, ever mindful that they had to reach India before the monsoons and, more importantly, before the Japanese caught up with them. Gus did his best to help Cheveyo along, at one point commandeering an inflatable mattress on which to tow his friend down the river.

The rains began on May 11th. Once, the troops received food drops of tea, porridge, rice and corned beef. Transportation down the tropical Burmese rivers on rafts constructed by local tribesmen was a periodic godsend. When the monsoon began in earnest, the men were told they were only a few days' travel from Imphal, their destination. *A few more days.* Gus dumped most of his gear and threw Cheveyo over his shoulder as he slogged through ankle deep mud, unable to see two feet in front of him through the heavy raindrops. Travel speed slowed to little more than a mile an hour, and the men wondered if their goal was really within thirty-six hours' sight.

Gus knew Cheveyo had lost consciousness when his weight grew heavier. He set his jaw and plunged onward, angry, scared, hopeless. He was glad for the rain on his face, rain that hid his unstoppable and silent tears. The last couple of days demanded every ounce of strength he had left as the climb to 7,500 feet brought altitude sickness on top of his other challenges. Fortunately, a British relief expedition met the ragged troops and provided ponies, limited food and a doctor. Cheveyo was strapped onto one of the ponies. Upon reaching the Indian town of Litan, motor vehicles arrived to transport the group on to their final destination.

As General Joseph Stilwell led his exhausted and ailing

column into Imphal, India, on May 20, 1942, more than half of the 114 went for immediate medical treatment. So worried for his best friend, Gus hadn't noticed the wound in his own shoulder, festering and infected. The medic that took Cheveyo from his arms told him to wait.

Gus was able to bum a cigarette from another G.I. and sat down. It was strong and sent him into a coughing fit that lasted several minutes. The doctor returned. "Your friend has malaria. It's not good. He been sick a while?"

Gus nodded. "I think so. Hard to know. We've been walking for over two weeks."

"Let me see that shoulder."

Gus removed his rotting shirt and tossed it to the ground. Looking down, he was astounded by the sight of his ribs showing on either side of his trunk. The doctor, however, was more concerned with his shoulder. "What happened here?"

"Sharp branch stabbed me. I fell, slid, in the mud near Magyigan. I didn't notice it much. It doesn't really hurt."

"Hmm." The doctor grunted. "It's bad. I'll give you penicillin. You should be sent home for a while. It'll only get worse in this climate. You and your friend both; I will recommend medical leave."

Gus nodded and reached down for his now poor excuse for a shirt.

On the morning of May 22nd, Gus was told he would not return to the States just yet. Every man was needed, even the injured—if they were not dying. "Dammit," he muttered, anxious to get Cheveyo back home. He rushed through the pouring rain to the hospital tent, his apprehension building. "Chev? Chev?" he called, searching among the many cots filling the tent. "Doc! Where's Chevy? Cheveyo Honanie? He was in the corner yesterday. He's going home today! Where is he?"

The doctor on duty turned a tired face toward Gus, his

expression nearly devoid of emotion. "Who are you looking for?"

"Private First Class Cheveyo Honanie, sir. He has malaria. He was just over there..." Gus stopped when he glimpsed two soldiers transporting a cot out the back door of the tent. His gut cinched. The man on the cot was covered.

"Wait! Wait!" Gus called, walking quickly away from the doctor and weaving his way through the maze of patients. The two carrying the cot stopped in the doorway, and Gus motioned for them to put the cot down. His throat swelled, but he leaned down and carefully peeled back the sheet. Gus slowly sank to his knees. "Oh, Lord, no. No. Why? Oh, God, so this is my punishment?" He clamped his left hand over his mouth to stifle his sobs and reached out to touch Cheveyo's chest. "I'm sorry," he whispered against his fingers. "I'm so damned sorry."

Chapter 24

November 15, 2012

Todd typed more words into Google, then clicked the mouse before taking up a spoonful of cereal. He crunched, swallowed, scrolled down. "Here. Here's a good number."

Jack poured himself a cup of coffee and carried it to the kitchen table. "Whatcha got?"

"A number for San Pedro Air Traffic. A division of the Port Authority. They would know what helicopters fly around the harbor area."

Jack reached for the phone and dialed. He wanted to have something, anything, before Emelie woke up.

The information officer was helpful. She talked about the same uses he'd already thought of, but narrowed the list down some. He wrote on a tablet as she talked. "Thank you. This is great. Oh, are any of these more prevalent at night? I see. Okay. Thanks again." Jack circled some of the words on his pad.

"Anything interesting?" Todd asked, still scrolling and clicking.

"She mentioned Starlight Tours. They have a new, nighttime tour of the two harbors that leaves out of Long Beach."

"What are you looking for?"

"I don't even know, Teej. She, Emelie, said that she thinks Nate's somewhere where copters fly overhead. She had the vision last night, when Dodge was accosting her. She thinks it's because Dodge had manhandled Nate and put him in this place."

Todd nodded slowly, chewing another mouthful of

cereal. His fingers flew over the keyboard. "Starlight Tours. 310-555-STAR."

Jack frowned. "So if I call them, what do I say?"

"I dunno. Get their flight paths."

"Yeah, but what good does that really do me? Unless the guy is lying out in plain sight, which I doubt, but even if he was, do I tell them to watch the ground for a wounded guy as they're flying around? I mean, how stupid does that sound?"

"How stupid is what?" Emelie said, emerging from the stairway.

"Oh, nothing. I'm rambling, as usual. Coffee?"

"Sure."

The three sat at the table, the only sound that of Todd's occasional keyboard entries. Jack finally decided to tell Emelie what he'd learned.

"It's not much, but I thought if you want to, we'll check out the tour."

"It's better than doing nothing," she agreed, and Jack again picked up the phone to make reservations. While he talked, Emelie's cell phone rang. She stared at the number on the screen in disbelief.

"Hi Emelie."

"Mom?"

"Are you all right? I've been worried sick about you! When I saw your name in the news this morning, I was horrified. Why didn't you call?"

"I was in the news?"

"You're telling me you don't know you were in the news? Oh, Emelie. Is this about that man you were living with?"

"Mother, don't run off on some tangier. They made a big deal for nothing," she lied. "I am fine. Don't worry about me, okay?"

"But you called your father for help. He should have

come to you. Now you're involved in something terrible. A man is dead! Is he the one? Where are you? I went to your apartment this morning, and you're not there."

"I am staying with a friend."

"Is she one of your school mates, I hope?"

"No."

"Come home, darling. Please. I need to see you. See that you are all right. Daddy promises to be nice."

"Don't treat me like a child, Mom. I don't need Daddy to be 'nice' if he doesn't want to be."

Her mother stopped talking for a moment, then Emelie heard her sigh. "Will you promise me this? Will you call me sometime, let me know if things are okay?"

"I will call you, Mom. But I don't want to talk to him. He's a self-centered and egotistical dictator. He doesn't listen to anyone but himself."

After Emelie hung up the phone, she caught Jack staring at her. "What? You don't like the way I talked to my mother?"

Jack tilted his head. "It's not that. You can talk to her however you want. I was just thinking about my dad, and what an ogre I thought he was most of my life. I had no idea what he'd been through."

"Trying to make me feel bad?"

"Not at all. Just reflecting."

Todd spoke without taking his eyes off the laptop screen. "I thought *my* father was dead," he stated. "But he turned out to be an international spy. He's French, you know."

"Not a good time to bring up Thomas."

Emelie turned to Jack. "This is *the* Thomas, the one Maddie went to see in prison? He is Todd's father?"

Jack nodded. "Yup."

"I thought he was just a family friend."

"I wouldn't call him any friend of mine."

203

Nate woke up crying. The dream was incredibly sad, but he didn't remember who was in it or what it was about. He remembered rain, lots of rain. He remembered that someone was saying goodbye. Someone that died.

Death was all around him. The death of his mother had triggered it all. She was the reason he'd come to Los Angeles. Arrived in time for the funeral. Death. Now, as he lay in the near darkness, he recalled that Frank Danvers was also dead. Perhaps it was Frank in his dream?

"No, it was not." A voice came from above him. "Death will come again unless you rise above it. Get up, Nathanial. Get up and let the spirits help you. Show them you are willing to try."

Nate looked all around but saw no one. The walls seemed to be moving closer, folding in at the bottom, cloistering him. The hallucination was too real, yet oddly cartoon-like, replete with dark shadows and odd angles as the room groaned and creaked and changed shape. The floor began to rise behind Nate, helping him into a sitting position. Dizziness filled his head, but the pain in his leg wasn't unbearable. Now, for the first time, he recognized his surroundings. The door was right in front of him. All this time! The door to the outside, to the sunlight, to freedom.

He tried to get up, but his legs would not cooperate, so he rolled to his side and then front, using his arms to pull himself along. He dragged his body toward the door, propped on his arms, his one good leg helping to propel him forward. When he reached the door, he strained upward to reach the door knob. "Please don't be locked," he said aloud, and the echo of his own raspy voice startled him. The knob turned easily. And why shouldn't it, he thought? *It's brand new. I installed it myself.*

Nate flung the door open wide and stared out at the brilliant blue November sky. Gulls flew overhead, screaming at one another as they soared over the surf. The salt spray reached his nose and he breathed it in, delirious with joy. Still unable to stand, he struggled to pull himself outside and onto the concrete pad, where he collapsed, tired but happy. Ahead lay the mile long breakwater. He rolled over onto his back and stared up at the beautiful, white, octagonal building before him. It was her voice that had saved him. Her walls that had lifted him up, helped by the spirits of his people. Now he knew why they called her Angel's Gate.

Chapter 25

May 22, 1942

Gus pressed the field telephone to his ear, straining to hear a voice. Patched through a local circuit, the connection was still poor, worse, probably, because the destination phone was also weak. "No, I said *Anika*... Annie. Yes. The Honanie family. Could—could you please—oh, hell." He had to wait again, and he only had a few minutes before his time ran out. Finally, a miracle; Anika said hello.

"Annie? It's Gus. I can't talk but a minute. Look, I don't know how to tell you this, I'm sorry, I just have to say it." Gus swallowed hard, willed his eyes not to flood again. "It's Chev. He's—he's gone. Malaria." The line was filled with static and he wasn't sure if he lost her. "Anika? Are you there?"

"Yes, Gus. I am here. *Kami wa kare no tamashī o yasumaseru.* God rest his soul. I pray he did not suffer. Are you okay? Are you hurt?"

"Naw, I'm fine. Annie, they are burying him here. Today. I asked about sending him back, but it's just not possible. It would take a month, anyway, by ship, and, you know, that would be pretty awful. You need to talk to his parents about this. Tell them I will see that his customs are honored, okay?"

"I will. They will want you to wash his hair. Find symbols of nature to go with him..."

"I'll try. He once told me about it. Jeez—I'm sorry you have to do this. It should be me. But they won't let me, uh, let me come home..." Gus looked up as one of his buddies gave him the cut-throat symbol.

"It's okay. I understand. I can do this," Anika said, her voice weak despite her strong words. "When will you get to come home?"

"Well, I really just got here, you know? It'll be a while. I'll write you, okay? I gotta run. You take care. And thank you, thank you for, you know, talking to his people."

"Keep yourself safe, Angus."

Anika put down the telephone at the post office and thanked the clerk. She walked outside and wandered, her mind in a haze and her heart in pain. Cheveyo, dead? It wasn't like she'd never considered it; the lists of the fallen grew longer every day that the war continued. But the realization was stark. He wouldn't be coming home, and she was living with his parents and brother. What would happen now, now that she was completely alone?

Her father was at Manzanar, a camp in California, but going there was out of the question. At least on the reservation she had some sense of freedom and caring. Some little bit of security in a world filled with uncertainties. As she entered the small house with the thick walls and wooden plank floor, she met Makya just leaving. A year older and a little taller than Cheveyo, his brother was handsome, if quiet. He was also single.

"Makya. I need to talk to you. It's about Cheveyo." Suddenly weak, Anika felt her knees begin to buckle. Makya caught her just as she collapsed. He helped her to the tattered couch.

"What it is, Annie?"

"He's...dead. He caught malaria. His friend called me. They are burying his body in India."

Makya paled, looked away.

"We need to talk to your mother and father."

"He will be buried here, with his people. Why lay him beside those whose stupid war caused his death?" Makya turned and stormed out of the house. Anika watched him go, then clutched at her stomach and burst into tears.

That night, Anika listened quietly while Cheveyo's family debated. A female cousin sat beside her, explaining the discussion, which was largely carried out in the Hopi language.

"Auntie says she is proud of Cheveyo for his service to the United States. Uncle says he is saddened that his son has died for the senseless fighting in another land," the girl whispered. Makya remained quiet, but it was clear that he sided with his father. Another, older woman waited patiently for the words to die back before she spoke. The cousin translated.

"It is unfortunate that Cheveyo has passed on in such a faraway place," she began. "It is Hopi tradition that the deceased is buried as soon as possible, at least within four days, so that his path to the Lower World is not affected by the delay. She wants to know..." The girl waited for the old woman to continue. "When the body of Cousin Cheveyo will arrive. She seems to assume he will be buried here, even though Auntie feels the special cemetery in India is better."

Anika shook her head. "They don't understand. He's been buried, within the four days. They can't ship him back. Who is that poor old woman?"

"She is Cheveyo's grandmother."

"Ah. I understand."

It seemed like everyone started talking at once, and Anika's translator shrugged. Finally, Makya stood up and spoke in clear English. "I will go to this India place and bring Cheveyo back here. We will begin the four days when he arrives. Right now he is waiting, his spirit is asleep until it can move freely."

The father nodded, the mother grunted, the cousin smiled. Anika sighed, her own fate still undecided. She got up and followed Makya outside, where he leaned against the out building.

"Makya. Listen to me. Cheveyo can't come home. The Army will not ship him home. We could pay for them to do it, but it would be a month, on a ship, and those ships are in constant danger from the Japanese. His body would be...violated by exposure. The way it is, at least he has been buried. Gus told me he washed his hair and made him a burial mask. He put in feathers of local birds. He did his best. Chevy will have no trouble reaching the afterlife, I promise you." Her words made assumptions, not lies. She touched Makya on the sleeve, and he turned to face her.

"What will happen now, to you? Will you stay?"

"I doubt I will be welcome. I will return to Los Angeles."

Makya grasped Anika gently by the shoulders. "No. You should stay here. In California, they will capture you and send you away. Here, you will be safe among Cheveyo's people. You are welcome to stay."

"Easy for you to say," she murmured, walking a few steps away. "Your family, they are very nice people. They have been so generous with me. But now that Chevy is not coming back to support me, it wouldn't be right for me to stay. Especially since...I am going to have a baby."

Makya stared at Anika so long she felt her face flush with embarrassment. Finally, he spoke. "Then there is no question. You must stay here. Chev's child must be born into the family, as he would want. And he must be born with honor. If you will agree, I will marry you and give you and the baby a home. A Honanie home."

Anika's jaw opened and her eyes widened. She was later to consider that she'd never been more shocked in her life.

Gus knelt on his best friend's grave. Cheveyo didn't deserve this. He deserved to go home a hero, with a hero's welcome, with people smiling, clapping and throwing confetti and flowers. He deserved the love and devotion of the woman he left behind.

Gus wondered how it went with Cheveyo's family. He'd only met them once, the day he took Anika to live with them after Cheveyo shipped off. They were kind, courteous, peaceful people. Cheveyo's father was a farmer, and his mother sewed garments and helped process the corn crop. He had a brother, too, a tall, brooding man who nonetheless doted on the younger Cheveyo. Now that Cheveyo was gone, what would Anika do? He hoped she could stay on the reservation until the war ended. It wouldn't be too long, he believed. And then, maybe, he'd ask her to come back to L.A. with him. With Chev gone, maybe she'd consider... He pulled his wallet from his pocket and peered at the lone photo he now carried, a picture of Anika he'd recently removed from Cheveyo's own wallet.

Gus squeezed his eyes shut. Here he was, hanging over his dead buddy's grave, already thinking about marrying Cheveyo's fiancée. He hated himself in that moment and knew that whatever grief his life placed upon him was well earned.

Chapter 26

November 15, 2012

"Three tickets. Please." Jack handed the woman behind the counter a VISA card. Behind him, Emelie paced the lobby of Starlight Tours while Todd sat fiddling with his iPhone. "Let's go," Jack said, and the two followed him out the door.

"What? We can go now?"

"Amazing what a little tip can get you these days," Jack answered, dipping his head as he motioned for Emelie and Todd to go ahead and board the helicopter, already warming up on the helipad. Once seated, he shook the pilot's hand.

"The usual tour?" the man asked.

"Yep. Show us the sights. But stay as low as you can."

"What are we looking for?"

Jack paused, a brief smile passing over his face. "A man. Possibly wounded. On the ground somewhere."

"Somewhere?"

Jack wagged his head left and right, feeling silly. "Just...let's go."

"Roger that," the pilot said, and after seeing to his passengers' seat belts, lifted the copter up alongside the Queen Mary. Each wore headphones to listen to the pilot's tour script.

Todd suddenly became animated. "Wow! Look at that!"

"As you can see, they're getting ready to begin the refurbishment project on the Korean Bell of Friendship, just down to your right. Then, a little to the west, you'll see Point Fermin Lighthouse, which is open for tours. Check their website before going as hours do change. Next we'll take a spin out to sea, and make a pass over—"

"Nate worked at a lighthouse," Emelie said.

"Not this one," Jack told her. "It was—"

"Angel's Gate Lighthouse. Also known as Los Angeles Harbor Light. This unique structure was built in 1913 and recently underwent a massive restoration."

"That's right," Emelie said. "That's where he met Frank Danvers and...Wayne Dodge." She craned her neck to see the small building that acted as the terminus to the mile and a half long breakwater. "I always wondered what it looked like."

"It's a beauty," the pilot said.

Jack frowned. "Hey, can you take us down closer? Make a turn around that lighthouse?"

"My pleasure."

The helicopter dipped and banked, tilting its occupants so that they looked almost straight down out the side of the craft. Jack squinted, held his hand up to shield the bright afternoon sun. "There's something down there."

Emelie leaned across Jack and made her own perusal. Todd, too, made a closer look.

"How low can you go?" Jack asked.

"This ain't a limbo game, bud, but I can get pretty close." The pilot made one more small turn and lowered the aircraft as if to land on the breakwater. Hovering, it made a slow approach toward Angel's Gate.

"Oh my God! It's him! It's Nate!" Emelie squealed. "Is he okay? Jack, is he okay?"

"I don't know, Em. Can you land here?"

"No. Not enough room. I can radio for help."

"Let me out!" Emelie yelled. "I can jump! Please, let me out!" She began wrestling with her seatbelt.

"I'm sorry, ma'am. You'll have to sit still and quiet down so I can get help. Can you do that?" the pilot asked.

Chest heaving with emotion, Emelie sat back and

crossed her arms. Jack closed his eyes and prayed. He couldn't remember the last time he asked God for anything, but right now he could think of nothing else. *Please let him be alive.*

Within minutes, a fast Coast Guard cutter could be seen speeding toward the lighthouse as the helicopter kept watch overhead. Jack watched as Emelie clasped her hands so tightly in her lap that her knuckles went white. Paramedics rushed over the rocky base and reached the young man who was spread out on his back, eyes closed.

No one inside the helicopter made a sound as the medics examined Nate below. After a preliminary look, the EMT turned toward the helicopter and gave it the thumbs up. Emelie began to laugh and cry. The pilot found out that they would transport Nate to Providence Little Company of Mary Medical Center.

"If we head back now, you should be able to get there within an hour. Depending on traffic."

"I'll bet they have a helipad there," Todd said.

"Good thinking. Let me see if I can get permission to set down."

They landed just a few minutes ahead of the ambulance. Emelie stood beside the Emergency Room entrance, chewing on her thumbnail. Jack fed quarters into a coffee machine while Todd took possession of a couch in the waiting room. The eerie scream of a siren ramped everything up as the ambulance approached, then backed into the ER bay. The emergency techs wasted no time getting Nate out of the back. They burst through the double doors with their patient on a gurney. Hospital personnel met them as they rushed him inside.

"Patient is a white male, approximately 28 years of age, BP is 80 over 55, respirations are fifteen, temp 103; patient exhibits signs of hypovolaemic shock, a rapid and weak radial pulse, cool and moist extremities; the patient is unconscious; presenting with a gunshot wound to the left thigh, appears septic..."

Emelie hurried to keep up with them but was halted when they came to the interior doors leading to the hospital's trauma center.

"I'm sorry, miss. You'll have to stay out here. Someone will be back out momentarily to give you an update."

"But...I'm his wife!" Emelie called, but the doors had slammed shut.

Behind her, Jack tilted his head. "Come on, Em. Let's sit down. We got him. He's in the best hands. Nothing we can do now but wait."

"He wasn't awake. He looked so bad, Jack. So bad! What if he dies?"

Jack pulled Emelie against him and held her close. Across the room, Todd peeked over the top of his iPad. "I don't think he's going to die. He has too much to live for, right?"

"But he doesn't know," Emelie whimpered against Jack's chest. "He doesn't know that I love him."

"I got a suspicion that he knows. Come. Sit down. We have to let Detective Cordell know we found him, and we have to call Nate's father."

Emelie awoke with a start. Stiff from sitting up all night in the waiting room chair, she got to a wobbly stand and stretched her back. Across from her, Todd slept prone on a couch and Jack sat reading a magazine beside him. "What time is it? Has there been any news?"

"It's one-thirty. I didn't want to wake you. Nate's out of surgery, he's doing fine."

"They got the bullet out?"

"Yeah. And they've been rehydrating him and getting him some nourishment. Knocking down the infection with antibiotics. They said he's doing remarkably well, and we might get to see him in the morning."

Emelie hugged herself and almost leaped into the air but thought better of it. "Did Rick or Chuck come?"

"They both came. And Matt."

"I'm sorry I missed them."

"You, my dear, were exhausted. You hungry?"

Emelie considered. "Well, yeah, I guess I am. But you said it's like one in the morning. Where could we eat?"

"Cafeteria is open 'til two. If we go now we can grab something."

"What about Todd?"

Jack shrugged. "He's a big boy."

They sat across from each other over hot soup and crackers. Jack rubbed his eyes. "I wonder if anyone called his dad."

"Nate's father?"

"He's gotta be worried sick. They should let him know his son has been found."

"*His* son. Maybe."

Jack shook his head. "Emmie, don't even go there right now, okay? My brain is like a medicine ball. So much is packed in there I can barely keep my head up. We can deal with that particular mystery later, okay doll?"

Emelie pushed out her lower lip, but recovered almost immediately. "I can't wait to see him. I have so much to tell him. He doesn't know about anything that's happened! Rick says we might get to keep the coins, except for the evil one, and then maybe Nate and I will find jobs, and we won't have to move. And just maybe Nate won't sleep on the couch anymore."

Jack slapped a hand across his eyes. "This is more than I need to know."

Emelie giggled. "I am sorry, Jack McKenzie. I am just so filled with happiness right now I can't stop."

She sat beside Nate's bed most of the next day. He remained still, unconscious, but she liked to think of him as just sleeping. Sometimes she talked to him. When no one was around, she sang, but not too loud—she considered her own voice atrocious. Still, it calmed her to sing. Mid-afternoon she got a call from Matt.

"I just thought you needed to be aware. My office is compelled to determine the rightful ownership of the remaining coins. The Double Eagle has already been turned in to the Treasury Department. It will go into the Smithsonian. But the other coins, well, they were technically owned by a pawn shop. Halleran stole them, and hid them in the lighthouse."

"And Nate found them. Should be, finders, keepers, don't you think?"

Matt laughed. "Well, for your sake, yeah, I think. But in reality, it's our duty to get the coins to the owner or heirs of the owner. We're looking into that now."

"Great. Just our luck. Okay, Mr. Farralone, sir, whatever."

"But I still only have three. Do you know where the fourth coin is?"

"What fourth coin? I thought you had them all."

"You originally told us there were five coins in the bag."

"Did I? Oh, well...with all the stress about Nate, you know, I might have said something wrong. I don't remember now. There might have been four altogether."

"Uh huh. Okay. We'll talk about that later. How's Nate?"

"Still sleeping. But he'll wake up anytime now."

"Let me know, okay? And Rebecca says hi."

Emelie hung up, her stomach newly knotted. Not only was there really a fifth coin, she knew exactly where it was hidden. No one could say precisely how many coins Joe Halleran had stolen, and she'd heard the detectives mention that some coins were found in the ocean with the Halleran's skull. She shuddered. The thought of his body—or at least a part of it—being there all these years made her skin crawl. She wasn't good around death, and the visions she had upon touching the bad coin had left her badly shaken. She now knew the identity of the man whose last moments she shared. Joseph Halleran was murdered, and he knew it.

"Em?"

So distracted by her thoughts, Emelie hadn't noticed the slight movement of Nate's head. His whispered word now had her full attention.

Chapter 27

Emelie couldn't speak at first, so great was the swelling in her throat. She leaned over Nate and embraced him with all her might.

"What's happening?" Nate asked, his lips against her ear.

Emelie pulled back, let her eyes roam all over his face. "You are alive. You are here. In the hospital. Do you want to sit up?"

Confusion passed through his expression as Emelie pressed the button to incline the bed. "We need to call the nurse, but I just want a minute with you alone. First. Oh, Hope, you don't know what we've been through!"

Nate frowned. "Frank is dead."

"I know. But so is Wayne Dodge. Chuck killed him. He was a bad man, Nate."

"Who's Chuck?"

"He is Rick's partner. Ex-partner, only I think that will change now that Rick's back is better."

"Who's Rick?"

"The detectives, silly. They were helping me and Jack to find you. Oh, Nate. I'm so glad you're okay..." She pressed her hands against his cheeks, wanting to kiss him, wanting to tell him how she felt.

"Who's Jack? Can I have some water?"

"Sure. I'll get you some. Jack is Jack. You know, McKenzie."

Nate's eyes widened. He stared as Emelie poured him a cup of water. "McKenzie? You met him? How did that...whoa. I am so dizzy."

Emelie grabbed the call button and pressed it. "We'll get

you fixed up right away. You're going to be fine. And I can't wait for you to meet him. He is the nicest man ever. And his wife is coming home, soon, and they are patching things up."

"His wife? She's been gone? How long have I been...out?"

"Ten days." Emelie sobered, caressed the back of Nate's hand. "The worst ten days of my life."

Nate reached over and covered her hand, sandwiching it between his own. "I'm so sorry."

Emelie was just about to chastise him for apologizing when the nurse came in. "He's awake! See? But he's dizzy. Please help him. Tell the doctor."

The nurse ignored Emelie and went straight to Nate. "So how are you feeling, young man? Any pain?"

Nate considered, his eyes moving left to right as he tried to determine if anything hurt. He adjusted his legs and winced. "Yeah, my leg is not feeling real great. I think I have a headache. I'm really hungry, too."

The nurse took his vitals and made notes. "The doctor will be in to see you in a bit. When he gives the all clear, we'll get you some lunch."

"Thank you," Nate said, his voice still hoarse. "So, what happened with Jack? Did you find out anything about, you know, his dad?"

Emelie smiled. "Not really. We were too preoccupied with finding you. We did, you know. We found you. At the lighthouse. We flew over and saw you down there. Thank God you were outside!"

Nate watched Emelie as she flitted about, smoothing his sheets, untangling his tubes, moving the table closer. She'd never looked prettier, never appeared more charming.

Ten days. And so much of that ten days was spent in darkness, hallucinating, he barely knew what was real and what was imagined. So Frank Danvers was truly dead, and his ex-boss, the one who'd shot Nate in the thigh, was also dead. Emelie had managed to connect with Jack McKenzie.

He'd had wild dreams. Dreams about soldiers and war, about a beautiful Japanese girl. About murder and gold coins.

The coins! Wayne Dodge had demanded them. Nate refused to get them. The ensuing argument had gotten him shot. Then, Dodge had threatened to go after Emelie. Nate had been helpless to—

"Nate? Are you listening?" Emelie asked. "This is Jack."

Nate turned his head to see the man that had eluded him for so long. Jack smiled and held out his hand. Nate lifted his, albeit weakly, and received Jack's warm handshake.

"So, finally. We have a lot to talk about, dude. Not now, of course, but when you're well. All in good time."

Nate nodded. "I'm...I'm so glad to meet you. It sounds like you went out of your way to help Emmie while I was...away."

"How could a guy not succumb to her charm?" Jack said, smiling at Emelie. "She's the reason you're still alive. It was her tenacity, her will."

"I had visions, Hope. I saw you. I just wasn't sure where you were until you went outside."

"I had them, too. The spirits..." Nate looked down. "Sounds crazy, now. But I heard things, saw things. Things I don't understand. But in the end, it was the voice that saved me."

None spoke for a time as the image Nate described hung in the air. Eventually, he smiled. "So when can I break out of this place?"

"Soon, I hope. Chuck and Rick are going to want to talk to you," Emelie said.

"And who are they, again?"

"Homicide detectives. They're the best."

"Can't wait."

It took thirty-six more hours for the doctor to spring Nate. Emelie pulled her small car up to the curb as they wheeled Nate out, a bag of patient care items in his lap. Emelie chattered along the way home, and while he didn't listen too closely, he delighted in the sound of her voice nonetheless.

"I did the shopping late last night, so we have plenty of groceries," she said.

"Hate to ask, but what are we living on?"

Emelie grinned. "We are living on everyone else's good graces, so to speak. Jack, Matt, and I almost hate to admit it, but my mother sent a check just yesterday. Everyone has been so generous. I guess I looked pretty bad on television."

"Ha! Well, if that's what it takes," Nate quipped as Emelie parked the car in the carport beneath the apartment. She quickly ran around to open his door.

"I can do this," he assured her, holding up his hand as if to prevent her interference. "I need to keep myself moving, the doc said."

Emelie backed away but clasped her hands. Although he struggled, Nate was able to get out of the car and then slam the door shut. "See? I'm a superhero at this stuff."

She did help him up the stairs and inside. He marveled at the new wooden door jamb and locks.

"Nice, huh?"

"Actually, it just pisses me off. I still can't believe Dodge pulled that." Nate sat down on the couch, clearly winded.

"Well, it wasn't all him. Remember, Angela and her asshat boyfriend really stole the coins. That hurt me. But I think he pretty much forced her to do it."

Nate shook his head. "There are a lot of bad people in the world, Em. Makes it so much harder for the good guys."

"Like us?"

"Like us. What time is Jack coming over?"

"Six-thirty.

"Good. We have a lot to talk about."

Jack showed up with Chinese food and sparkling water. After distributing the Kung Pao Chicken and the Moo Shu Pork, Jack sighed. "I don't know about you, but I'm so relieved we finally get to talk."

"I saw you in the lighthouse."

"I saw you at Best Buy."

Nate grinned. "Fair enough. So, Em tells me she shared the letters with you."

"I hope you don't mind. I was amazed."

"Yeah, I was pretty surprised, too. What do you think? I mean, they obviously knew each other. You authenticated them, right?"

Jack nodded. "I did. It's his writing. I admit to not understanding it at all. My dad was a bastard sometimes, but he loved my mother."

"My mom and dad were inseparable. It doesn't make sense."

"Have you asked your father about it?"

Nate looked down, pushed the food around on his plate. "No. It didn't seem right. I mean, to expose something, my mother's secrets, and it could be hurtful to him. He's a good person."

"So is my mother. But I couldn't ask her now if I wanted to."

"His mother has memory problems," Emelie explained.

"I'm sorry to hear that. Is there anyone else around who knew your father?"

"Just my older brother, and he's just as perplexed as I am. How about you? Anyone back home your mom might have confided in? A sister or a girlfriend?" Jack asked.

"Not really. She has a brother, my uncle, but they weren't very close. My Aunt Crystal, my Uncle Bob's wife, was friends with her. I just couldn't get up the nerve to ask her."

"Maybe you should."

Emelie stood up. "I think we should all go to the mesa. Nate's father is very anxious to see him after what's happened. Maybe we can come up with some answers if we go there. I can talk to Aunt Crystal, if you don't want to."

Nate nodded, but remained non-committal. "Let me think about it, okay?"

"Absolutely. I mean, it's not going to change anything when we do find out, right? Other than our personal feelings. We've both lived all our lives without knowing." Jack pondered. "I keep asking myself, is this really important? Will it change how I feel about my father?"

"I've asked myself similar questions. But I just couldn't stop thinking about it. So I did the research, went online, I found your father through some veteran's group he belonged to. One of the letters came from an Army base, so I went that direction."

Jack pushed his plate away and sat back in his chair. "I wonder. What were you planning to say to him if he'd been alive when you got here?"

Nate shrugged, smiled. "I don't know. I guess I was just going to shove one of the letters into his hands and ask him if he wrote it. Hoping that would lead to some grand confession."

"*Nate. I am your father,*" Emelie said, using her best Darth Vader voice. The others laughed.

Jack shook his head slowly, still chuckling. "I've only read a couple of the letters. It's hard to imagine they aren't as intimate as they seem. I mean, if he wasn't my dad, I'd totally, immediately believe the worst. That my dad had some mid-life affair with a much younger woman, a woman who lives on an Indian reservation in another state. And if it's true, that means, well, we're brothers."

Nate got to his feet while fending off Emelie's attempt

to help him. "If it's true, then I'd have to say that despite all the unpleasantness that comes with affairs, I'd still be honored to be your brother."

"Same here, Nate." Jack stood also and stuck out his hand, which Nate took and held for several moments before turning to hobble over to the kitchen counter.

Presently, he turned around. "You know, yeah. Let's go to Winslow, and I'll take you all around to meet the family. I need to see my dad and my grandmother anyway, and maybe we can all use a little vacation from what's happened here."

Despite the annoyance of Emelie's flitting about, Nate truly enjoyed her attention. Jack left just after eight, and Nate helped Emelie to clean up the dishes. They worked in quiet contentment, each keeping their own thoughts private for the time being.

"You go sit down. I have a surprise," Emelie said when the last dish went into the dishwasher.

"Oh, yeah? I'm game."

Emelie happily reached into the cabinet for a bottle of champagne. "Look. For us. To celebrate."

"And what are we celebrating?"

"Bunches of things," Emelie responded, handing him the bottle. "You can open it. These things scare me." While Nate unwound the wire around the stopper, Emelie brought wine glasses and placed them on the coffee table. She ducked when the cork popped and flew across the room. Nate poured.

"To?"

"To...us," Emelie said. "You and me."

"For surviving all this crap?"

"Yes. For that and more. In the future."

Nate clinked his glass against hers and took a sip. "And what do you see in our future, Miss Marin? Something better than more crap, I hope?"

Emelie didn't answer verbally. She took Nate's glass and her own and set them back onto the table. Nate tilted his head, wondering what she had in mind as she leaned close to him and finally slipped her arms around his neck. "I have something important to tell you."

Nate turned more toward her on the couch and tentatively grasped her waist. "I have something important, too. Can I go first?"

Emelie nodded, her gaze never leaving his.

"While I was gone, while I was laying in that lighthouse all those days, my worst fear, my very worst thought, was that I might not see you again before I died. Nothing else seemed to matter. I knew you were looking for me. The thought of being able to be with you again was the only thing that kept me alive."

Emelie sighed. "I felt it, Hope. I knew when you were thinking about me. It kept me going, kept me searching, made me my most annoying self with the police. I could see you, feel you in my head. I knew what you were feeling, thinking, and oh, I was so afraid that you would die and that would be it. My life would be over."

"Your life? Why do you say that?"

"Because you are my life. And you know me and the silly things I say and how I can never say just one thing in a sentence, but honestly, Nate, I love you. With all my heart—"

"—and soul and I never want to be away from you, ever again," Nate finished for her. "And I'm not saying that because I'm psychic, but because it's true. I've never known anyone like you, Em. Never. And I know it's trite and stupid sounding but you complete me like a jigsaw puzzle piece. You are the one Sobo said I have been waiting for. I love you, I love your eyes and your forehead and your crazy talk. I love how you can be a human pretzel and how you're not afraid to stare life in the eyes. You are everything I want, everything I need, everything I am not. And if I don't get the chance to show you that love soon, you know I'm just going to—"

"—burst. Yes, I do know that, because so will I. I will be your human pretzel anytime you want, and I don't care if we ever get another penny to spend, I will be happy to be with you..."

"Stop talking," Nate mumbled, just before pressing his lips to hers for the kiss he'd imagined a hundred times. A thousand times. The kiss didn't disappoint, and evolved into several more kisses, interrupted only by the occasional need to take a breath. Eventually, he dragged his lips away from her mouth and found her ear. "Tonight we retire the couch-as-bed," he whispered. "If you agree."

"I thought you'd never ask," Emelie whispered back, sending hot shivers down his back. "And we might as well go to bed early. We can have pie later if we want, and watch Downton Abbey in bed."

"You got it. Although I don't have a clue what that is," Nate murmured against the corner of her mouth as he tried to regain her lips.

"It doesn't matter," she moaned. "Let's go."

They were both shy, at first. But Nate had never been one to hold back his feelings, once released. "It's been a while for me," he murmured, noticing how Emelie held the covers up to her chin.

"Good. Me, too."

"I mean, I've been around and all. It's just that, well, I've never done this with anyone I, you know, really cared about. That much."

Emelie giggled and pinched his cheek. "Me, either. I mean, once I thought I did, but it was a humungous no-go. I thought it was going to be fun, but then, all I could think about was how to get rid of him." Emelie closed her eyes.

"And now I've just said too much."

"No, I get it. And I'm glad. Because this does feel different, doesn't it? It does, to me. So let's just, you know, see what happens."

Emelie giggled again. "I think I know what's going to happen, Hope." She reached out for him, slowly sliding her body closer and he met her halfway. He kissed her forehead, her cheek, then dragged his lips onto hers.

"Then let's make it happen." He took it slow, at first. For as much as he thought he knew Emelie, their relationship had moved into a new dimension. They were naked, and vulnerable, and both just a little scared. He wished he knew more about lovemaking, about pleasuring a woman. What if this vibrant, sassy, intoxicating girl found him boring, lacking in sexual prowess?

Nate slid his hands around her waist and pulled her against him. As their bodies touched, melded together from chest to knee, something completely unexpected occurred.

"Whoa," he whispered. "Do you feel that?"

"Yes!" Emelie pressed her cheek against his, her lips close to his ear. "We are like magnets. We are magic, Nate. It's because we are absolutely meant to be together. It's the cosmos. It's nature. It's God. It's the Hopi spirits and the alignment of the planets, and--"

"Stop talking," Nate repeated, rolling her onto her back. "Let the spirits do their magic."

Chapter 28

November 26, 2012

Henry Stavros died intestate; he had no heirs, no survivors, and no one bought his pawn shop from him before he died of lung cancer in 1965. With Matt's well-placed influence, the District Attorney's office determined that the finder could, indeed, be the keeper, deeming it too expensive to pursue any alternative legalities. Their own appraisal of the remaining coins exceeded that of Abe's by more than a thousand dollars. Nate took their assessment back to the coin shop and gave the collector the first opportunity to buy the Liberty Heads.

"You took care of that Double Eagle?"

"Yep. It's winging its way to D.C. even as we speak. Now. What's your best offer on these three?"

Abe lifted his eyebrows and again employed his loupe. He went to the calculator and ran some numbers before returning to Nate. "The best one is missing, you know. What happened to that one?"

"Forget about that one. What are these three worth?"

"Well, I quoted you six grand for the four. These three aren't as good, so I'll say thirty-five hundred."

Nate picked up the coins. "Thank you very much." He turned to go.

"Wait. Don't leave. What did the feds tell you?"

"They said they're worth five thousand. They gave me the name of another dealer, so I'll check with him. I just promised to see you first and now I have. But thanks."

"Here here here. Five?"

"You want to see the appraisal?"

"No, no, not necessary. I'll give you five. But if you find that fourth coin, the prime one, I want first look. Okay?"

Nate grinned. "Of course. No problem."

Five thousand dollars. Nate couldn't stop smiling as he drove Emelie's car back to the apartment. Eight days had passed since his release from the hospital and his leg was nearly healed. He wouldn't win any swimsuit contests, but he knew how lucky he was to have survived at all. Now, he was healthy, had confessed his love to Emelie, and they had shared their first Thanksgiving dinner just nights ago. With cash in the bank and in his pocket, he practically trotted up the stairs when he arrived.

Emelie was packing their bags. "Did you get it?" she asked, rushing him with a hug.

"He offered thirty-five."

Emelie's smile faded. "But..."

"But he gave us five!"

"Whoo! Wow! Fabuloso!"

Nate took the opportunity to kiss her, something he swore he'd never grow tired of. "Are we almost packed?"

"Yes. This is when it's a good thing we don't have much," she quipped. "Jack called, and he'll pick us up at around ten tomorrow."

"Good. My dad is looking forward to meeting you, you know."

Emelie blushed. "Does he know what an earhead I am?"

"You," Nate began, tapping her on the nose, "are an airhead, not an earhead."

"Ah. Right. Okay, good."

Nate sat down on the bed and pulled her down beside him. "I have to ask you a question. Abe asked me about the fourth Liberty Quarter Eagle. The one he thought was the best. Do you know where it is?"

Emelie paused, kissed him on the mouth. He kissed her

back, and she rolled onto him in one fluid motion.

"Distraction? Honestly?" he asked with a smile. "Did you lose it?"

"No. I put it in a very safe place."

"Do you remember where?"

"Oh, yes. I remember where. But," she paused, closing her eyes and taking a breath. "I can't get it out."

Nate chuckled in surprise. "You can't get it out? Where, pray tell, is it, my love?"

"In the bathroom."

"In the bathroom. You got more?"

Without another word, Emelie got up and led him to the single bathroom in the hall. She opened up the medicine cabinet and pointed. Confused, Nate started moving bottles around, removing the aspirin and cough syrup, deodorant and toothpaste tube. "I don't see it."

She pointed again, this time touching the back wall of the cabinet and drawing her finger downward toward a two-inch slot cut into the metal." I dropped it in this hole."

"The razor blade slot? Really?" Nate grinned. "Genius. Pure genius."

"Yeah but so genius I can't figure out how to get it back out."

"That will be easy, Emelia Airhead. I can just take the cabinet out and voila; there it will be, probably on top of a pile of rusty blades from decades past."

"Down inside the wall."

"Yep. Down inside the wall. Let's do it."

It took Nate less than fifteen minutes to remove the small cabinet, then reach down into the recess of the wall and snag the shining coin.

"What are you going to do with it?" Emelie asked later, after the coin had been retrieved and gently wiped off. "Should we sell it, too?"

"I have a plan for it, unless you are hell-bent on selling

it."

"They are really your coins, Hope. I'm just so thrilled to have some of the money from the others."

Nate rode in the front seat of Maddie's SUV as Jack drove; Emelie opted to sit with Todd in the back. The trip was light-hearted, as Jack entertained them with tales about his many professions.

"I love this," he said, turning to smile at Nate and Emelie. "A new audience. You guys don't know anything about my past. If Maddie were here, she'd roll her eyes at my stories, she's heard them so many times."

"No, no, I like hearing them," Nate assured. "You've done so much. What did you do after you were a forest ranger?"

"Let's see; is that when I was a male stripper?"

"Chippendale's?" Emelie asked from behind him.

"What's Chippendale's?" Nate asked.

"It's this place where chicks go all schizoid over dudes that dance almost naked. They put money in their g-strings," Todd explained.

Jack turned the steering wheel back and forth, pretending to be shocked by his stepson's words. "How do you know about these things?" he wondered aloud. "And for the record, I was joking. I've never done that. Although I once did pose with my shirt off when I was a lifeguard at Zuma Beach."

Emelie giggled, absently straightening Gus McKenzie's bomber jacket draped across her lap. The men kept the car cold despite the November chill outside.

After consulting a map, they decided to stop in Kingman, Arizona, for the night. Jack pulled the Suburban into the Las Brisas Motel at six-thirty.

"Why here?" Todd asked while pulling his duffel from the back of the car. He eyed the hand painted mural of the desert in bloom and the neon lighted tower with disdain. "It's kinda funky. Why can't we stay at that Hampton Inn we passed back there?"

"This place has history, TJ. It's classic. One of the original way stations along Route 66. And for the record, I think the murals are *über* cool."

"So do I," Nate agreed.

After checking in, the foursome walked to the nearby coffee shop for a meal, then returned to Jack and Todd's room to discuss the following day's plan. The room was icy cold, so Jack cranked up the thermostat. Emelie slipped her arms into Gus's jacket and sat down on the couch.

"So tomorrow we'll drive on through Flagstaff, then Winslow. We'll stop at my apartment and from there, we'll make phone calls and set up visits with my family," Nate told them.

"Sounds good," Jack agreed. "Where is the school where you worked?"

"It's in Polacca. Not far from Winslow. My friend Johnny lives in Flagstaff. My parents... my father, he lives in Bacavi, a village in the Third Mesa. Sobo lives there, too. Some parts are little rough. Dad will come down to Winslow, but my grandmother doesn't ever leave the mesa. She's pretty old school Hopi."

Emelie wrapped her hands around Nate's arm. "I'm so excited to meet your family."

"I know they will love you," he told her.

"Too much mush. I'm gonna hit the sack." Jack stood up and stretched.

"You should let me drive some tomorrow. Especially since I know the way," Nate suggested.

"Good idea. You, uh, Injuns know how to drive?"

Nate threw a faux punch at Jack, who laughed and pinched Nate's cheek. "Don't get tough with me, little brother. I'll kick your butt."

"Think you can take me, old man?"

Nate and Emelie left Jack still laughing as they went to their room, a couple of doors down. Emelie went straight to the heater and turned it on. "I am freezing! And I forgot to give Jack's dad's coat back."

"He isn't gonna need it tonight. Hey, I'm gonna take a shower if that's okay with you."

"No problem. I am going to take a hot bath when you're done, though."

Nate started for the bathroom but spun around and returned to Emelie. He bent down and kissed her cheek. "Did I tell you I love you today?"

Emelie curled up on the couch and clicked on the television. Still chilled, she pulled the jacket closer around her neck. As she surfed the channels, her eyelids became heavy and she closed them, leaning back to relax her neck. The leather warmed her, and she let herself become drowsy.

The vision crept in, coming only in brief glimpses. Flashes. A young man, a young woman. His eyes were hazel and his hair cropped short. She was a dark eyed, black haired beauty. They were in the throes of heated passion, tossing on a bed. As the image became clearer, Emelie realized that the room was the same as the one she was in. The door, the window, the bathroom—all in the same places. As she "looked" around that room, she noticed an open suitcase. A comb and brush made of silver and ivory. A pair of dainty silk slippers.

She could barely look back at the couple on the bed, so erotic a vision that she felt embarrassed. Even her own nights of excited lovemaking with Nate couldn't hold a candle to this carnal frenzy. The woman was on top, riding, rhythmically moving as the man matched pace with her, both of them groaning with lust. Emelie felt she had to swallow as her mouth filled with saliva. Who were these people and why had she conjured them?

The woman cried out. The man held her. She began to sob and he stroked her back. They murmured, but Emelie couldn't understand their words. What she did understand was that they were guilty. Shamed. Unhappy. But very much in love.

Emelie felt her own eyes fill with tears. Such profound sadness had no place in her life now; she would finally be happy, now with Nate as her lifetime soul mate. Still, the grief permeated her.

"Em? Emelie? Wake up. You're dreaming, babe. Wake up, it's me, Nate."

"What?" Emelie opened her eyes to see Nate leaning over her, his naked body still dripping from the shower. "Oh, Hope."

"You dreaming, or was it a vision? You're so upset."

"And you're buck naked."

"Life's too short to be modest." Nate smiled, wrapped a towel around his hips and then sat beside her. "You're flushed. It's like ninety degrees in here. Let me take that jacket off."

Emelie started to shrug out of the coat, and then she froze. "It's the jacket. It was him. Gus. He's the man in the vision. He was naked, too."

"What are you talking about?"

Emelie pressed her fingers to her lips and slowly shook her head. "Something happened in this room. Something important. Jack's father and a woman. They were here, and they were...making love. Here. Crazy love. Madness."

Nate's eyebrows lifted. "You...saw them having sex?"

She nodded. "Like a porn film! Not that I've ever watched one," she qualified. "But they were really going at it. Maybe that's why Jack chose this place. It wasn't the murals."

"This is pretty hocus-pocus. Even for me," Nate said, walking back to the bathroom to dry his hair.

"Maybe so," Emelie muttered. She couldn't get the picture out of her head. The woman was so young, younger than herself, and beautifully formed. And something else. She was Asian.

Chapter 29

November 28 – Winslow, AZ

"How is it you still have this place?" Emelie asked when Nate let them into his apartment the next day.

"My uncle owns the building."

"Lucky. Maybe we should just move here."

"You think it's hard to get work in L.A.?"

Emelie smiled, ran her hand along the back of the old brown couch in Nate's living room. "Yeah, but...free rent? We wouldn't have to work."

"I never said it was free." Nate turned to Jack and shook his head. "This girl lives in a fantasy world half the time."

"I know that. Sometimes I'd like to join her."

Nate looked upon Emelie, her whimsical smile and mischievous eyes challenging him to play. Today was not the day. "Dad should be here in a few minutes. We'll talk to him and then we'll all drive out to the mesa together to meet Sobo. You cool with that?"

"Absolutely." Jack sat down at Nate's small kitchen table and flipped through screens on his cell phone. "Todd. Your mom's coming home in a few days."

"About time," the teen muttered.

Nate went into the bedroom and returned with a laptop computer. "Hey Todd, I was wondering if you could do anything with this. It's loaded with all kinds of stuff I don't need, so it runs really slow. You seem good with these things."

Todd put down his phone and took the laptop. "You got the cord?"

"Yeah. It's over there at the end of the couch."

239

Happy to have something to do, Todd took the computer and plugged it in. Jack mouthed the words, "thank you" to Nate, who was now pulling open a drawer in his desk. "I thought you might like to see these," he said, lifting a few photographs out of the drawer. "This is my mother and father, when they got married. A long time before she got sick. She was really pretty."

Both Jack and Emelie gathered around him to look at the snapshots.

"She was pretty," Emelie said softly. "Her eyes are really unusual."

"Her skin tone is a lot lighter than your dad's," Jack observed.

"There are a lot of different colors in the Hopi palette," Nate said, nodding. "Here's one I really like. That's me in the papoose," he added proudly. "And yes, we have papooses. Cradleboards. It was a ceremonial thing, we didn't use it all the time. She also carried me around in a blue corduroy snuggly thing."

Emelie giggled. "You cutie pie, you."

"This is my mom with my Uncle Bob. He and Aunt Crystal make Kachina dolls. These are given to young Hopi girls to teach them about various Kachina roles and responsibilities. Kachinas are like...um...spiritual beings as opposed to physical. In Hopi culture, all things have both. During our ceremonies, men dress up like the spirits, and they connect with the spirit they represent. It's a cycle; it begins in late December."

"They are beautiful. Wow." Emelie stared hard at the pictures of the dolls. "What's this one?"

"I don't know them all—there are so many. But I think that one is Ka-e Kachina—Corn Dancer. As you know, corn is very important to the tribe."

"I'm impressed," Jack said. "I always thought they were just tourist curios."

"I'm afraid they've become just that to some of my people. I mean, I appreciate that they have to live, and selling the dolls is all some of them have to make money. But the meaning gets lost along the way."

"Well, I'd like to buy a couple for Maddie and Claire."

Nate grinned. "I'm sure I can hook you up, bro."

It wasn't long until a knock at the door produced Nate's father. Sam Sinquah was tall, thin, with a narrow face and long, gray hair that he wore tied into a ponytail down his back. His eyes curved down in the outer corners, but the lines around his mouth spoke of a lifetime of smiles. He embraced his son long and hard, his actions speaking where no words were necessary.

"Glad to meet you," he told each of his son's friends in succession. Jack was impressed with his gentle demeanor and politeness. While Todd worked on the laptop at the desk, the others sat around Nate's table. Nate held one of the letters in his hand.

"Dad. The reason my friends are here...well, here's the thing. After Mom passed, I was putting away some of her stuff, you know, the boxes you gave me to go through? And I found some letters." Nate swallowed, cleared his throat. "They were written a long time ago, sent by an American soldier from Los Angeles. He seemed very familiar with her. Some, but not all, of the letters are dated before she and you were married." Sam remained still, unblinking, unresponsive. Nate continued. "The man's name was Gus—Angus—McKenzie. He was Jack's father. Do you know anything about him?'

Sam drew in a slow breath and exhaled easily. "Your mother and I had a most solid relationship. Built on trust, respect. She was every bit the strong Hopi woman. If she had secrets, they were hers to keep. I never doubted her one time from the moment we met until the moment she departed for the Lower World."

Jack looked from Sam to Nate, wondering what Nate would say next. Nate struggled, but nodded. "I know that, Dad. Truly. I just couldn't help but wonder, you know, what this man meant to her. He was...quite fond of her. He says things, uses words of affection in the letters."

His father didn't waiver. Jack felt his own chest swell with something he couldn't identify. Yet he knew it was something he wanted for himself. That kind of solidarity. Completeness. The capacity to love fully, to never doubt, never allow even the tiniest suspicion to cloud that love.

But the letters remained. Could Sam have been completely naïve? Or did he refuse to see?

"Nathaniel, I know you are waiting for an answer. I don't have one for you. If there was a man in your mother's life that loved her, then I'm quite certain she deserved that love. But I can tell you that I never suffered for it, if it existed. Tiponi was everything to me, and she never stumbled once. Never disappointed me or anyone else."

Nate's eyes fixed upon his father's for several moments. When he finally broke his gaze, he sighed. "Okay. That's enough for me."

Sam's eyes twinkled and he smiled. He reached across the table and took his son's hand. "No, I don't believe it is. I think what you need to do is go talk to Sobo."

The room grew silent. Even Todd stopped tapping the keys on the laptop. Jack glanced at Emelie, who was rapt. Nate nodded. "Is she well enough for a visit? I would like her to meet Emmie."

"She is well enough. She is anxious to meet your young lady. As was I."

Emelie blushed. Sam took her hand and joined it with Nate's. "This is good," he said, nodding.

"Do you mind if I stay here?" Todd asked. "This machine is loaded with malware and crap. It's going to take me a while to clean it up."

"If it's all right with your dad," Nate said, to which Jack shrugged. Sam accepted an invitation to ride along, and the four of them left for Bacavi.

"My grandmother lives in kind of an old place," Nate began as he drove. "It's all built of adobe and stone and mud and stuff. It's dark inside. She likes it that way. I'll do the talking, okay? She's a little muddled, sometimes. I'll gauge how coherent she is today before we ask her anything."

It took close to an hour to get to the small village on the Third Mesa of the Hopi Reservation. Nate and his father entered the house first, and Nate returned immediately for Emelie and Jack. Once inside, Nate led them through the small front room to the only bedroom beyond. There, in a narrow bed, lay his beloved grandmother.

"She's almost 88," Nate said softly, and the others nodded. Jack stayed back while Emelie moved forward for an introduction. "Would you like to sit up? Let me get your pillows." Nate adjusted the bedding so that the old woman could converse comfortably. "This is Emelie, Sobo. She's my...girlfriend."

Sobo reached out with a hand that only trembled slightly, and Emelie took it in both of hers. "I'm so glad to meet you, Mrs. Sobo."

Nate didn't bother to correct her. "We have a few questions to ask about Mom. Do you feel like talking?"

"Of course. I always like talking to you."

Nate pulled up a couple of wooden chairs. Again, the nervous cough. He repeated the words he'd earlier spoken to his father. Sobo, however, seemed not to hear.

"I was afraid of this," Nate whispered to Emelie.

"You. Come here," Sobo directed, lifting her thin, wrinkled hand and pointing at Jack, who stood in the shadows. Jack looked around comically, and Sam touched him on the shoulder for encouragement. The elderly woman smiled, her hand still outstretched. "Sit." Jack sat on the edge of the bed and took the woman's hand. "Such a handsome man. Just like your father."

Chapter 30

September, 1945 — Bacavi, Arizona

Anika paused. The corn grits had built up under her fingernails, making it painful to work. Worse, the toddler was crying again. "Tiponi! *Naite teishi shimasu*! Must you cry all the time?" Anika stood from her stool, bent and lifted the little girl from the basket in which she sat. "You are getting too big for your basket. Almost three! Such a big girl," Anika kissed the girl's forehead, already sorry for her bad temper. Tippi was hot, tired, and bored. "Maybe we'll take a little break, okay?"

Anika shifted the young girl onto her hip and threw back one of her long, heavy braids. She started walking toward the path leading to the house, taking her time. The corn wasn't going anywhere, and she needed a respite. She wasn't far when she saw a man walking down the road in the distance, almost to the place where it adjoined the path. She paused. Something about the man's gait, his height, his coloring— and the fact that he was wearing an Army uniform— unnerved her. It had to be Gus McKenzie.

When he caught sight of her he quickened his step, stopping just a few feet in front of her.

"Annie. Oh, God. I've been walking for miles. Is it really you?"

"Yes, it's me. I can't believe you're here. The war is over, isn't it?"

"Yeah...gosh, you look swell. But...you've been working, hard, haven't you? Oh, never mind that. It doesn't matter! The war is over and I'm here and I'm taking you back with me, back to Los Angeles."

Anika had to quickly shift Tiponi to her other side. The child had just grown heavier. "It's nice to see you, Gus. Really. But I can't go with you."

Gus frowned and looked at the child for the first time. "Is...she...yours?"

"Yes. Yes, and I am married now. To Cheveyo's brother. I am committed, Gus. I can't go anywhere with you. I'm sorry."

Gus stared at Anika, horrified. He looked to the little girl's face, then back to Anika. "Is she mine? Look at that hair. Is she mine?"

Anika looked toward the house. Makya could come out at any time. "No. Of course not. She is Chevy's. Her hair is lighter, true, but that happens sometimes. My auntie Keiko had light hair."

"I don't believe you."

"Believe what you want. I can't go. You need to leave, now. My husband is the jealous type. He won't like me talking to you."

"Anika. Listen to me. You don't need to live like that! Look, I am going to walk back to Polacca, where I can get a bus to Kingman. There is a base near there. I'll borrow a Jeep and I'll come for you. Tomorrow night. Be out at the road, near that big tree out there. You don't need to bring anything except...what is this angel's name?"

"Tiponi Ann Honanie. And Gus, don't come. I won't be there. Please. There's so much you don't know. I made some mistakes. A long time ago, back in San Pedro. With my father. Makya found out about those mistakes. If I go, he'll tell, and I'll be taken away."

"But the war is over! Don't you see, it doesn't matter what you did or didn't do, or where your sympathies were. It's over. They're sending all the Japanese home from the camps. All is forgiven."

"Not this. My father was a spy, Gus. A spy for Hirohito.

And I worked for him! Yes, me. It was true. Chev didn't know. No one knew. When they took my father that night, they were looking for me, too. I didn't want to pull you two into it. Did you never wonder why I had the gun? Why I was able to pull the trigger so easily on Joe Halleran? It was because my father trained me not to hesitate. He bought me the Derringer, to protect myself in case I was ever captured!" Her chest heaved with emotion. Gus's face paled at her confession. "So, see? If the American government finds out what I did, I'll be arrested. Possibly hanged."

Gus looked around, then back to Anika. "How...how did he find out? This... Makya. How?"

"I tried to escape him. When I found out my father was at Manzanar, I took Tippi and hitchhiked to Flagstaff. He caught up with me and I told him the whole story, thinking he might be sympathetic. Instead, he turned on me, threatened to turn me in. He is...nothing like Chev. I was devastated. Not long after that, I got a letter. My father was dead."

"I can't believe this. All this time, all these years of fighting, of tramping all across Europe, I thought...I thought you'd be here, waiting for me. You never told me about the baby. You never told me you'd married. All you had to do was write..."

"I'm not a good person. I'm a bad person, Gus. I'm somehow flawed. How else could I have carried messages for Japanese spies? Betrayed the country I loved, the only country I'd ever known? I loved my father. He was my whole world. I did as he asked. My character was weak."

"I don't care about all that. We can get you out of here, I promise. You can't live this way, afraid of a man you live with. I can take him out if need be."

"No! No. You don't know Makya. He'll kill you. He's a trained warrior. Please, Gus, if you ever cared about me, you'll go now. Leave, before he sees us together. Go back to

California and marry a nice girl. A good, honest, American girl. Have children who will love and honor you and make you proud."

The sadness in Gus's face sent pain through Anika's heart. But she couldn't waiver. Could not back down. She knew, and knew well, the power of Makya's anger. Gus's lips formed a hard, straight line. He looked once more into Tiponi's face, as if memorizing it. Then he turned and walked away. Anika willed herself not to fall to the ground and cry.

Her remorse grew in the days that followed. Maybe she should have gone. Perhaps Gus could have helped her and Tippi disappear in the big city. New names, new home, a different life. Would Makya even look for her? He had no money to speak of. But it was too late; she'd broken Gus's heart and he was gone.

Anika never figured out how he knew where to send them, but soon, letters began to arrive addressed to Tippi. The postal worker stopped her on the street and gave Anika the first two. "If any more come, save them, please. I will pick them up," Anika told the delivery woman.

She read them when Makya was working in the corn field. She cried, sometimes so hard she needed to ice her eyelids before he came home.

Gus cried too, in the privacy of his room back in L.A. Regret seeped from every pore in his body; recriminations filled his brain. *I should have just picked her up and carried her and the girl. Carried them all the way to the train station. Anything but leave her there with an abusive, unloving husband.*

The girl was his, he was sure. Her light brown hair, hazel eyes, narrow nose. This sweet child would grow up with savages, thinking she was one of them, never understanding why she looked different. Never knowing the love his parents had shared on one lonely, crazy night. Thinking the heathen Makya was her father. What if he struck her?

I need to go back. I need to rescue them.

Need? No, what Gus needed was a night out, to get away from the solitude that exacerbated his grief. There was another victory party going on in Hollywood. A nightclub where Glenn Miller once played. Gus was invited by some of his buddies, but had declined. Now, he thought better of it and went to shower and shave.

The guys were happy to see him and called him over to the table where they sat drinking, laughing and celebrating. "Hey! The war's over, Gus, so let's see some cheer! We squashed the Nazis and the Japs. No more jungle rot for us!"

Gus forced a smile and ordered a Manhattan, then squeezed into the booth with his pals. The cocktail went down easy, and he began to relax. This was the real world. That dry, hot, desert-y place was far away, and his imagined life with Anika, a fantasy. She'd made her choice. She could have waited for him, but she didn't. It was time to move on.

"Y'all need cigarettes? Cigars?" a girl asked, and Gus turned to answer. He was out of smokes. "Yeah, gimme a pack of Luckies."

"You got it, soldier." She handed over the cigarettes and stashed Gus's money in her box. They exchanged smiles as Gus pulled the cellophane strip from the pack, and then she adjusted the neck strap holding the box in front of her. "Say, what battalion were you in?"

"490th. Why?"

"Aw, my brother was in the 141st Infantry. He was killed in Germany. Just wondered, ya know."

"Sorry to hear it, doll. That was the Texas National Guard, right?"

"Yes, siree. Best in the west. Here's your change."

She was pretty, in an open, friendly, girl-next-door way.

"What's your name?

"Lucille. Lucille Sway."

"Well, Miss Sway, when can you put down that cigarette box and dance with me?"

"Well, just about any ol' time you want, sugar."

Chapter 31

November 28, 2012 — Third Mesa, Hopi Reservation

"He continued to write to us after he married Lucille. He sent pictures of you and your brother, Jack. I kept them." Anika turned to her grandson. "You are probably a little...shocked, Koguma za. It's funny, much of my Japanese comes back to me now, at this late time in my life. Do you remember me calling you Koguma za?"

Nate swallowed. "Yes. I do, now. What does it mean?"

"Little bear."

"*Hoonaw-hoya*," Nate said. "In Hopi. Now that I think of it, I always assumed you spoke only Hopi. I suppose 'Sobo' is Japanese?"

"For grandmother. Yes."

Jack shook his head, a smile on his closed lips. "I don't know what to say. What...what an extraordinary story. I'm sorry for...for your sadness."

Anika squeezed Jack's hand. "It was okay. After a little while, things began to settle. Once I let go of the thought of leaving, I made sure I was a good wife. Makya calmed down. He was a good father. We had Robert, our little wolf cub, and when Makya passed on, I was sad."

Nate's eyes were wide. "Makya was always good to me. He was funny. He worked hard. Did...did my mother know that Makya was not her father?"

Anika's eyes glistened. Her long, white hair still shimmered when she shook her head. "There was no reason to tell anyone. My mother-in-law knew, because Tiponi was born early. But it wasn't the way. Not to be discussed."

All were quiet until at last Emelie spoke up. "Sobo?"

251

"Yes, little one. You are wondering about my daughter's real father."

"Was it Cheveyo?"

Nate gave Emelie a quick glance. Hadn't his grandmother already made that clear? But Anika smiled, then turned her eyes on Jack. "Do you also wish to know?"

"Me? Well, yeah. I do. I need to know if this...young Turk here is actually related to me."

"Would it really make a difference?" Anika asked.

Jack pondered, looked over at Nate. Reaching out, he squeezed Nate's shoulder. "No," he said at last. "I'd come to accept that he was my brother. Whether or not he is actually my nephew or just some smartass kid doesn't matter."

Anika twisted slightly in her bed and gestured to her nightstand where the loan electric light burned. Beside the lamp stood a picture frame, and she asked Nate to hand it to her. She stared lovingly at the black and white photo of the young woman posing before the house in which they now met. She turned the frame around so that Jack could see.

"This is Tiponi. Your sister."

Emelie gasped and clapped her hands over her mouth, prompting Nate to wrap his arm around her. Beside the door, Sam stood shaking his head, chuckling to himself. The laugh infected them all with humor and Emelie giggled. Jack stood and went to Sam, holding out his hand. Sam shook Jack's hand, lowered his head. "I am honored to be your brother by marriage."

"Same here, my man. A true honor. I wish I could have known your wife, my sister."

"Didn't my mother wonder about the cards, the letters? The money Gus sent?" Nate asked.

Anika waved her hand gently. "I told her he was a friend of her Uncle Cheveyo, and that he just wanted to help out the family of his best friend. She had no reason to question it."

Nate stood. "Uh, would you all mind if I had a minute

alone with Sobo?"

"Of course not. We can wait out here," Jack said, as Emelie and Sam joined him in the living room.

Nate sat at his grandmother's bedside. "I don't know what to say. It's going to take a while to absorb all this."

"He was there when you got that mark on your face."

"This scar?" Nate pushed back his hair to reveal the jagged remnant of some long ago accident.

"He was visiting the Mesa. You were only three, I believe. You tripped, running just outside there. He picked you up and brought you inside to your mother. It was the only time he ever came here."

Clearly astonished, Nate looked around the room, trying to envision the scene as it might have been. "And Mom just thought he was this friend of her dead brother-in-law?"

"Angus was a good man. But he was also a haunted man. I'm afraid what we did never left his mind. Neither of us could ever be truly free of our sins."

Nate shook his head. "That must have been difficult for you to admit after all this time," Nate said. "All that stuff about helping the Japanese, and then killing Halleran, losing Cheveyo. Losing your father, then losing Gus. How did you survive it all?"

Anika turned her tired eyes upon Nate. She reached for his hand, massaged it with her bony fingers. "Some things happen in life and we make the wrong choices. Other things, we have no choices, and we have to learn to accept what life gives us. Once I learned to accept, life got easier. I accepted the joy in what I had. My beautiful daughter, my good-hearted son. My grandsons; you and Jacob gave me more happiness than I thought possible. Sam, a good man for my daughter. The Hopi themselves, for saving my life in a time when I might have been hanged."

"You are a brave woman. I hope I can be even half the person you are."

"You have a much better start. You are honest and strong of character. You have a loving family growing around you. Emelie will make you a good wife, with many children to come. Your mother will be so proud, as will I."

"I heard a voice. When I was at my end, in my darkest hour, the voice lifted me. Made me strong."

"She has never left your side." Anika closed her eyes, exhaled. "It is almost time for me to return to the Lower World. And you will not grieve, for I will also still be with you."

Nate nodded, then leaned down to kiss his grandmother's cheek.

Chapter 32

December 24, 2012 — Grogan's Head, CA

Jack stood in the kitchen doorway and leaned against the jamb. Maddie hadn't seen him yet as she carefully lowered a stuffing casserole into the oven while softly singing the chorus to "White Christmas." Still oblivious to his presence, she went to the freezer and withdrew two bags of frozen cranberries.

"May your days... be... merry... where did I put the sugar? Dang. Jack?" she called loudly over her shoulder, then started as her husband embraced her from behind. "Dammit! You scared the bejesus out of me!"

He kissed her neck and she turned to face him in his arms. "You didn't need that bejesus anyway. You've got me."

Maddie chuckled and pressed her lips against his, fully involving him in a passionate kiss. "And I'm so glad I still do."

"There was never any chance you wouldn't."

"Are you really okay with...everything?"

"More than okay. While you were away, I was on a tightrope with no net. I could barely think clearly, I couldn't sleep..."

Maddie leaned in close and whispered in his ear. "I didn't really leave you, you know."

"I know. And I understand. You had a pretty damned good reason to flip out. But next time, I might have to—"

"There won't be a next time," Maddie responded, pulling away to answer the front doorbell.

Maddie opened the front door and stepped back. "Merry

Christmas! Come in!" Nate and Emelie rushed in, carrying a heap of brightly wrapped gifts. They were immediately surrounded by Davey, Duncan and Claire, who were anxious to help put the packages under the tree. Maddie took Emelie's coat.

"Did it take you long? I heard there was a tree down on the highway."

"Traffic was a mess. We weren't the only last-minute shoppers in town," Nate confirmed. "Is everyone here?"

Nate and Emelie made the rounds to greet Matt and Rebecca, Case and Amy.

"Jack tells us you two are staying here for a while," Rebecca said.

"Yeah, we're thinking of moving up here. I'm going to be helping Jack with the video he's shooting. It's been moved to Crescent City, so that's all cool," Nate explained. "I'll be helping to build the sets. We kind of wanted to get away from L.A. for a while anyway."

Emelie watched Maddie, fascinated with her easy manner and love for her friends. How this charming woman ever experienced her earlier problems, Emelie couldn't fathom. She was the perfect hostess, the doting mother, the romantic wife. Jack clearly adored her. Easy to see, now, why he'd become so upset. Madelyn McKenzie was not the type to indulge in substance abuse.

Dinner was a sumptuous and hearty affair. Turkey, ham, all the fixings. Rebecca had baked fresh bread, and Amy, two fruit pies. Everyone was well-sated by eight o'clock, and they moved back to the living room to exchange gifts. Of course, the children were the center of attention. Emelie couldn't stop smiling as Claire turned circles for her extended family, showing off her fairy wings and tutu. The boys set up a long, plastic drag strip for a series of small race cars. Todd couldn't wait to load up the latest PS3 game.

When Jack broke out a couple of bottles of after-dinner

wine, Maddie went to the kitchen to finish up the dishes. Emelie followed her.

"Need some help?"

"I'd love the company."

Emelie washed down the counters as Maddie dried the hand-washed crystal water glasses. "These belonged to my grandmother. They're really out of place up here in the forest, but I kind of like having them here."

Emelie agreed. "They're beautiful. I think it's great to mix things up like that. Too much order is boring."

Maddie smiled. "Jack is so fond of you, and I can see why. He never had a sister, you know, and you fit the bill."

"I like that." Emelie picked up the towel Maddie had just used and folded it. "You know, I met Jack during a time when he was in a lot of dissolution. He was so unhappy and worried."

"You mean desolation? Yeah, it was all because of me. I was freaking out. Everything was going wrong for me; things were happening that I didn't understand. I just sort of lost control. Jack was very focused on his career, and I needed to go somewhere where I could think things through."

"I know. I—" Emelie paused. The towel in her hands changed texture; it felt like Velcro, stuck to her fingers. She knew what would come next. But before the vision manifested, Maddie had grasped her arm.

"Are you okay? You look like you're having a petit mal. Sit down."

Emelie complied and sat down, and Maddie continued to hold onto her. "Do you want some water?"

"No, I'm fine, really." The vision came anyway and was stronger now that she was actually touching Maddie. "Just feeling a little faint."

Maddie leaned close, looked her in the eye. "You aren't pregnant, are you?"

Surprised, Emelie smiled and shook her head. "No. But...you are, aren't you?" Before Maddie could answer, Emelie pulled away and stood up. "I'm sorry. That was rude of me. Forget I asked."

"Oh my God. You really are psychic, aren't you? Unless Jack told?"

"No one told. I just saw it in my head." Emelie grinned. "And now I just realized, that was the problem all along, wasn't it? You didn't want to tell Jack that you were pregnant."

Maddie sighed. "We already have four kids. This was a...a slip up? I'm past forty. I thought...well, it doesn't matter what I thought. It happened. I got scared, then depressed. My hormones did a number on me. I had to wait for an amnio, then wait for the results. Jack was all tied up with his work in L.A. I had to sneak my pre-natals so that Todd wouldn't suspect."

"They were vitamins? Holy crap! Vitamins! All along. Sheesh."

"Yes, and for some reason, Jack thought they were drugs. Can you imagine? Me? I don't take anything."

"Yeah, imagine." Emelie shook her head, feeling remorse for her part in the misunderstanding. "But everything's all right now, isn't it? Jack is okay with it?"

"Jack is ecstatic. And we're going to tell everyone tonight. But I was wondering; Jack told me you are a certified yoga instructor. Are you really into healthy stuff?"

"Yes on the yoga, hit-and-miss on the healthy stuff. Nate and I like a good hot dog now and then. Why do you ask?"

"I could really use some help. This pregnancy won't be the easiest one on me, my doctor warned that I'll have to take it a little slow. With the kids, it will be tough. I thought maybe I could hire you as their nanny, and also help me out with a little yoga now and then?"

Emelie rushed her with a hug. "That would be the most

perfectest thing ever! I was already worrying about what I'd do while Nate is working, and I'm not one to sit on my patootie and not help out."

When they joined the others, Emelie sat close beside Nate and threaded her arm through his, snuggling up close on the couch. Everyone was laughing, enjoying the blazing fireplace and the Christmas jazz coming from Jack's sound system. Nate suddenly got up and tugged Emelie up also. "Come with me," he whispered, and led her down the hall to the room where they'd stayed since arriving two days before. "I want to give you your gift."

Emelie didn't say anything as Nate rummaged in his familiar backpack and pulled out a small box. He handed it to her. "Open it. Go on!" Emelie giggled and tilted open the lid, revealing a delicate gold chain from which hung a coin. An exquisite, gold, 1878 Coronet Type Liberty Head Quarter Eagle. "For luck," Nate murmured. "Unless you think..."

"I think it's incredible. I love it. Thank you, Hope. This was the only one of them that didn't feel wrong."

"It should always be a reminder of our love." He fastened the necklace around her neck before they returned to the others, where Jack was just standing up.

"There you are. Sit down. We have a little tradition. We go around the room and everyone says something, like something good about this year or plans for next year, or good news, you know. And I'm gonna start."

"Here, here," Matt called out. "Give us the news."

"Well...come spring, we'll be adding a new...bedroom to the back of the house."

"That's it? You're adding on? BOR-ING...." Matt yawned.

Jack looked surprised. "Not good enough? Oh, did I forget to mention that the room is for our second daughter, due in June?"

Both Rebecca and Amy shrieked and jumped up,

anxious to hug the new mother-to-be. "I'm so jealous," Rebecca said. "That's great news!"

"Congratulations," Amy said. "I'm happy for you."

"Okay, now, Nate," Jack prompted when everyone had settled back down. "Your good word?"

Nate stood, cleared his throat. "Well, some of you might already know because I didn't know about the game, but Em and I are moving to Grogan's Head next month. I'll be working with Uncle Jack on the video, and Case has also offered me a job at the Institute. We are really excited."

"That's *Uncle* Case, to you, young man," Case said. Applause went around the room.

"We couldn't be happier about that, either." Jack said. "And you are welcome to stay with us, too. Until June, of course! Now, *Uncle* Case, what's the plan?"

Case sighed, got slowly to his feet. He looked around the room, his blue eyes solemn and yet warm. Turning back to Amy, he bent down on one knee, took her hand. "Amy? Not to put you on the spot or anything, but I just couldn't manage to do this on my own. You know you are my whole world, girl. Our life up here has been one miracle after another. Can you just make one more wish come true for me?" Case lifted a diamond ring out of his shirt breast pocket and held it out to her. "Amy Winslow, will you marry me?"

A collective gasp emanated from all the women in the room, and Amy's mouth dropped open. "I—I—You—are you kidding, Case McKenna? I was beginning to think I'd never see this day! Of course I'll marry you!" Tears streamed down her cheeks as Case slipped the ring onto her finger and leaned in for a kiss.

Jack apparently felt compelled to refill all the glasses. "That's the best news I've heard in a long time. And what took you so long, dude? Didn't I tell you?"

Case shook his head and sat back down. He offered Amy his shirt sleeve to dry her tears.

"Okay, I'll cut you some slack. Next up is Todd, I think?"

"Me? Uh, well..."

"Go ahead, babe, tell everyone what you got in the mail," Maddie said.

"I, uh, got accepted at U.C. Berkeley. Computer Science."

Matt reached over and clapped Todd on the back. "Way to go, sport. Big liberal school! Ha! Your dad will like that one. Until he gets the bill."

Jack uttered a mock groan amidst the congratulatory responses to Todd. "What about you, Mr. Ex-Assistant D.A.? And didn't I call that one, too? Knew you couldn't be tethered for long."

"Yeah, yeah, you were right, old son." Matt took a sip of wine. "Well, Bec and I have started up our own investigating firm. We'll be based out of L.A. Yeah, I know, sorry. Anyway, we've already taken on a big case. You guys won't believe this one. I swear, I am not making this up." Rebecca nodded her head in support of her husband's claim.

"It seems my grandfather owned quite a portfolio of real estate, some that even I didn't know about. There's a mountaintop lodge that was supposedly torn down back in the 90's, and records show the land was later sold to a developer. So this builder guy let it sit for a while; he didn't have the money to start his project. But now it turns out, the hotel was not demolished, and has been sitting there empty all these years. I haven't been there, but the builder went up there and says the place looks like it's brand new. The lights come on at night, go off in the morning. The grounds are kept. Yet there isn't a car or any other sign of life. Something fishy going on there."

Case chuckled. "Obviously someone else is squatting on the land. Figured they could get away with faking the demo while raking in some money during the high season."

"I don't know. Sounds more like 'The Shining' to me," Jack said.

"Please. No. Anyway, I've found invoices that show the place was razed, but the photos this guy sent me are clearly of the same hotel owned by Jordan Kent, except it looks just like it did in 1958. So Bec and I are off just after New Year's to check it out."

"Did he try to get inside?" Amy asked.

"Apparently, he tried every door and reachable window. Bolted up tight. He thought he heard voices, but no one answered," Matt said.

Rebecca shuddered. "Tell him the rest, Matt."

"Well, I think the guy's a little cuckoo. He says he saw a man watching him from the widow's walk on the top of the main building. He waved, but the man just stood there staring down. When our pal reached into the car to get his iPhone to take a picture, the guy vanished."

The others exchanged looks as Jack's living room fell into a dead silence.

THE END

Meet Anne Carter

"Everyone needs a little romance in their lives," Anne Carter will assure you. "Some need more than others." She should know. A storyteller since 7th grade, Anne and her younger sister would dream up a new chapter to a romantic saga each night before going to bed. Soon, writing became an obsession. Raised in Southern California where she, her husband and three children make their home, Anne interrupts her passion occasionally to run her bookkeeping business and possibly put dinner on the table.

Angel's Gate is the third book from the Beacon Point Romance series. Anne asks: "What ties these stories of romance and intrigue together? Lighthouses - and mysteries brought upon a group of friends who solve them - while falling in love, of course!"

Ever & Always, the series prequel, details Jack & Maddie's history and courtship. Jack McKenzie goes on to appear as a supporting character in Point Surrender and Cape Seduction. Finally, Jack gets his own romantic suspense in Angel's Gate.

If you enjoyed this book, please consider leaving a review on Amazon or your favorite review site. Thank you!

Visit Anne at http://www.anne-carter.com.

Also by Anne Carter:

Paulie & Kate's Story:
Unmasking Paulie Bingham
For the Love of Katrina Bingham

StarCrossed Romances (Series):
StarCrossed Hearts
A Hero's Promise
The Gypsy in Me (Fall, 2014)

Beacon Point Romances (Series):
Ever & Always (Prequel)
Point Surrender
Cape Seduction
Angel's Gate

Alternative Romance Novella:
Starfire